Peril and Payback

SPOONWORLD BOOK II

Peril and Payback

The Attack on the Guardian

A Contemporary Fantasy

By

Chuck Marsters

To order additional copies of this book, contact:
Xlibris Corporation
1-888-795-4274
www.Xlibris.com
Orders@Xlibris.com
87652

Acknowledgements

As with **The Guardian and the FarCaller**, I couldn't have written and published this book without the help of friends and relatives. Their help varied from a two-minute discussion about the title to hours spent reading the draft(s) and preparing comments for my consideration. I can't begin to mention all of the people who helped, but the standouts include my late wife, Jeanie, Bonita Schulz: a good friend, Colleen Levin: my sister, Tami Levin: her daughter, and Nancy Morales, my daughter.

Also helping, but in an entirely different way: the many people who read **The Guardian and the FarCaller** and kept pestering me about when I would publish the sequel. Well, we're there! I hope all of you enjoy returning to the life of Lee Kaaler and learn how his attempts to protect the Kaaler secrets not only failed, but placed his family and friends in immediate peril.

PROLOG

The balding man still remembered the day that unseen and unheard power filled him with panic whenever he heard someone tell him never to try to get that spoon again. Moreover, how, from that moment on, whenever he even thought about the spoon or the Guardian, or heard a name sounding like "Kaaler," those awful memories returned to haunt him. The pain was so bad, and the terror so deep, that he blanked every thought of it from his mind and gave up the quest, literally fearing for his life. Now Etta, from out of nowhere, calls and reminds him of that search, the search that resulted in such an all-consuming pain. Before he could stop her, Etta continued.

"A couple of my guys saw four of the men you sent up here after that Kaaler guy. They seemed confident about something they were going to do, and how much money they were going to get."

His chest tightened. It took so much energy to breathe that he couldn't speak enough to tell her to stop talking about Kaaler, or anything regarding that chase.

"After a couple of beers, the guys mentioned a 'plan,' and how they were going to finish the job you and Jeff sent them on. To get the Kaaler guy. Then one of 'em told the others to shut up.

"Now they've disappeared, Ben honey, so I checked up on your Mister Kaaler. He seems OK, but his wife hasn't been seen in a couple of days. She's over eight months pregnant, and word is that her husband's frantic. Surprisingly, the police aren't involved, at least not yet. You didn't intentionally try to hide this from me, did you, Ben honey?"

Her alto voice was soothing, but each of Etta's words brought stabs of agony. By the time she stopped talking, Ben Gerit lay on the floor of his bedroom, unable to speak, crawl, or even breathe deeply. Suddenly his chest seemed to explode, and everything disappeared into a kaleidoscopic display of blues, purples, and black.

CHAPTER 1

The Germ

A Small Bar in Rural Fresno County, California, June 2006

"I'm tired a waitin'!" It usually took three beers to start Barnaby Snoyl ranting about his latest pet peeve, but on this torrid Saturday afternoon, it only took two. "Them Gerits cut us off!" he shouted, pounding the tabletop with his gnarled left fist, emphasizing his point to the two others at the table. "We did ever'thin' they asked. Had that Kaaler guy cornered up there 'n Oregon—then we was called off. Right when we cudda got it!" He took a long slurp, emptying the beer bottle, then slammed it down on the rickety wooden table, both to prove his point and to signal Jerrilee, the bartender/waitress, that he wanted another.

It didn't take much to get Jerrilee's ear this particular afternoon: Barnaby, Doug, and Billy were her only customers. Her dad started the small bar in an abandoned travel trailer twenty years earlier. serving beer to migrant farm workers employed in the fields west of Fresno. Inside the screened walls were six rickety tables, each enclosed by four well-used folding chairs. Barnaby and his buddies sat at their regular table: nearest the bar, at the back. This afternoon, however, was different. Doug and Billy weren't given the chance to start their usual discussion about how the local high school football teams would fare, or how Cal State Fresno would do, or whether the Giants or Angels were going to finish highest. Today Barnaby began by cursing Jeff Gerit, their former employer and head of a team formed to locate the Kaaler Guardian and obtain the thing that gave the Guardian some undescribed special powers. After thirty minutes of uninterrupted invectives, Barnaby gave no sign he was going to slow down. "We been waitin' 'most a year now, and nuthin's happ'nin'."

Barnaby then stopped his raving, quickly looked at his friends, then held his hand up, palm out: they were to say nothing.

His eyes flitted around the bar, not seeing the bug screens on three sides, not noticing the holes which admitted the ever-present insects. After an entire minute in which no one even moved, Barnaby lowered his hand, then looked at both his friends. "Know what?" he asked. "We can do it without 'em!"

Before either could react, Barnaby tapped his right pointer finger loudly against the dusty tabletop. "We know who that Guardian guy is 'n where he lives—what else do we need?"

Doug and Billy quickly exchanged glances and simultaneously said, "Money."

CHAPTER 2

Let's Do It

"No," Barnaby countered, "we're OK on money."

Both men started to argue, but again Barnaby's "police" gesture stopped them.

"One thing 'bout them Gerits," he continued, "they usually keep their promises." Now he looked at his two friends. "You been gettin' your checks from Gerit?"

His friends again looked at each other for support, then both nodded.

"So you got y'ur reg'lur jobs, plus the cash Gerit's givin' you ever' month. Right?"

Two "Yeps".

"A thousand extra ever' month, right?"

Two more "Yeps," but their eyes betrayed nervousness about where Barnaby was leading them.

"And d'ya 'member what we did 'round there when Gerit tol' us?" He leaned forth conspiratorially. "All them *illegal* things?"

He looked at Doug and Billy; both merely nodded their heads.

"'N to keep us workin' we jes used the credit card he gave us fer our food 'n rooms 'n fun. 'Member?"

Two simultaneous "Yeps."

"Well," Barnaby continued, ignoring the lack of enthusiastic support he got from the others, "why don't we jes do the same thing now? Why don't we jes get plane tickets on his credit card 'n go to Oregon 'n do what we hafta? Who's gonna stop us?"

Billy now spoke up, a bit tired of doing all the listening. "The Gerits'll sic someone on us when he finds out. *That's* what's gonna happen, Barnaby. He'll have someone on us like flies on cow pies."

Doug nodded, clearly agreeing and clearly concerned.

"Don't think so," Barnaby countered. "Fer one thing, he don't seem to care 'bout us no more. Second, he di'n't give us the card hisself, so I don't think he even knows we got it. 'N third," he said, again pounding the tabletop with his right pointer finger, "by the time he finds out we've used it—if he ever does, it'll be a month *after* we used it, so it'll be too late fer him ta stop anythin'." He smiled again, clearly confident and pleased with his own planning.

"I think we can do jus' 'bout what we want. 'N all we'll be doin' is carryin' out what he told us to do at the beginnin' of all this stuff. We'll get that Kaaler Guardian guy 'n' whatever he's guardin'. That'll give us more money than we know how t' spend, and we'll be doin' the Gerits a big favor."

Barnaby looked up, caught Jerrilee's eye and gestured for her to bring three more beers. Then he leaned forward conspiratorially.

"We gotta figger exactly what we wanta do and how we're gonna do it. Then we jus' fly to Oregon and make it happen. "But the first thing we gotta do is figger out what happened to them Gerits."

Again Doug and Billy exchanged glances, but this time not for mutual support. For the first time since they arrived at the bar, they had to think creatively, and the beer didn't help the process. "Wha' d'ya mean, Barn?" Billy asked. "Somethin' happen to th' Gerits?"

Temper flashed in Barnaby's eyes and his voice dropped almost below the level of hearing. "Billy," he began, "if somethin' di'n't happen to 'em, tell me why they called off th' hunt for th' Guardian so fast? How much brains does it take to figger out somethin' happened to 'em? Ya ain't that stupid!" He peered intently into his cousin's face. "Or are ya?"

Billy's first reaction was anger at the way Barnaby talked to him. He quickly chalked it up to the beer, calmed himself, then, sounding very tolerant, said, "Barnaby, I ain't stupid 'n' you know it. But you've been doin' all this talkin' about how easy everythin's gonna be, then suddenly change and talk about all these things we know nuthin' 'bout and gotta learn. Sounded to me like you jes figgered out maybe *you* weren't as smart as *you* thought."

Before Barnaby could say anything, Billy used the same "police" gesture to stop the man before he could make a sound. "Now, Barn, talkin' nice, start from the beginnin'."

For a few seconds the older man glared at his friend, then smiled. "Yer right, Billy," he said. "I misspoke m'self. Ya ain't stupid." He said up straight and changed his tenor to "nice." "I think the Gerit's been got to by someone or somethin'. Somethin' powerful."

He leaned forward, suddenly become the conspirator again. "What I think is that the Guardian's got some really bad guys workin' for him, and they scared Gerit real bad. Or, the Guardian's got a neat weapon that he used ta make the

Gerits lay off 'im. I'm bettin' on some kind a weapon. Somethin' powerful 'nuff to scare 'em to stop chasin' 'im. Can you 'magine what we could do with somethin' like that? How much money we'd make?" He lowered his voice even more, forcing Billy and Doug to lean forward just to hear his words. "How 'bout we do like the Gerits would? How 'bout we do somethin' to someone the Guardian likes, 'n' tell him we'll do a lotta pain to 'em if he don't come across. How 'bout we do just like we were before Gerit stopped, only fer ourse'fs instead of them Gerits?"

Chapter 3

So *slow!*

"I'm tired of waiting!"

Lee slid next to Verry in their king-sized bed, put his left arm around her, and gently pulled her close. Planting a tender kiss on top of her head, he said, "Every woman I ever heard talk about being pregnant said the last month or six weeks were the worst." He carefully put his right hand on her swollen belly, felt his babies pushing and kicking and twisting around inside. "You're carrying twins, so you've got even more of a burden than most women. But," he said as he leaned down and kissed her cheek, "I'm so proud of you and love you so much I can't begin to tell you."

Verry looked up at him, tears starting to fill her eyes. "I'm sorry I'm complaining," she began. "It's just that it's really different to have these two babies squirming around inside me all the time, each acting like he or she wants more room. And I can hardly walk any more I'm so top heavy."

She wiped her eyes on his pajama tops, then added, 'I'm glad we're starting our family now, though. I'm just really uncomfortable."

"Anything I can do for you—besides carrying our kids?"

They both smiled at the image of a pregnant man, even though they'd heard it most of their adult lives. Here and now, with two little bodies wrestling inside Verry, it took on a completely new meaning.

"Yes," she said, trying to cuddle closer but having trouble moving her belly enough to let her get close to her husband, "you can tell me about your project. I've been so involved in my own problems I haven't even thought about it for a week or so."

"Well," he began, turning onto his back a bit to get more comfortable, "It's coming together." He glanced up at the ceiling, mouth pursed, eyes rapidly

14

blinking—lost in thought. Then he returned his attention to Verry. "Really, any success I've had, besides meeting FarCaller and then reading grandma's letters and solving that puzzle she designed, has been because one of my Guardian ancestors invented our Challenge. It opened several doors for me. Of course, meeting you was one of them." He gave her a loving smile which she immediately returned.

Lee had no typical employment. He wasn't destitute, because his grandmother willed him a hefty sum that, with help from FarCaller, he'd parlayed into several millions of dollars. So instead of working for a living, he worked at something he felt needed to be done—secret philanthropy and compiling a Kaaler family tree. He already knew his next project: writing a family history.

"One thing our troubles with the Gerits did was make me want to know where I could find friends. Through the Challenge, I learned my best friend in college, Thommy K. Pajaro, was a Kaaler, and he helped me get to Des Moines to marry you a couple of years ago."

Verry nodded slowly and solemnly. She vividly remembered how T. K. and her sister, Drella, spirited her out of the hospital in Des Moines into a place safe from people working for the Gerits. That was right after she was injured in an automobile accident arranged by the Gerits, an accident that killed her best friend. The Gerits then tried to kidnap Verry and use her as a lever to force Lee to give them the Kaaler spoon. T.K.'s assistance foiled that plot, which let Lee use the spoon to maintain contact with FarCaller, to exchange visions of the futures that might have been and, ultimately, to escape the Gerits' clutches.

The best part: Lee and Verry got married, and Lee learned how to use the golden plate and spoon: a weapon only Kaaler Guardians could use. It let Lee instill so much terror in the Gerits' minds that they completely stopped harassing him for the silver spoon they'd heard had huge powers, even though they had long searched for that spoon, hoping it would make them rich and powerful. They never knew that they'd need two more things to gain the power and money they wanted: the talent to use the silver spoon—which they lacked, and the cooperation of a FarCaller—the Guardian's counterpart in Spoonworld—whatever or wherever it was. They'd never get FarCaller's cooperation in anything Lee didn't want.

"I've identified four branches of Kaalers and traced the Guardianship back five generations," Lee said, continuing. "Right now I'm trying to compile the names of the Kaalers in areas that have the greatest concentration. That seems to be in Central California and the New York/New Jersey area. But it's really time-consuming, because I have to Challenge every Kaaler I talk to in order for them to trust me enough to talk to me."

Lee stopped a moment, looked unseeing at the mahogany dresser on the wall facing their bed. "One thing's for certain: Kaalers *really* keep their identities secret if it isn't their name. Some of them are three or four generations from ancestors who actually carried the Kaaler name, but the Kaaler traditions have been carefully nurtured."

He could feel Verry relax and start to nod off. He decided to let her sleep, but only after completing his thought. "Even your dad was a Kaaler, three generations removed. No one would expect to find someone named Willards to be a key part of the Kaaler family."

Lee gently kissed Verry's cheek, and then helped her lie down on her left side, her back towards him, her belly and its treasures lying against the mattress. Leaning forward, he whispered in her ear, "Love you, Verry." She squeezed his hand in response, then he turned off the light.

CHAPTER 4

8 months, 3 weeks, 2 days, 9 hours, and 6 minutes

The next morning, Verry had her weekly OB appointment for what she called a "poke and prod". It involved only a few questions, a check of the babies' heartbeats, and then scheduling an appointment for the next week.

She enjoyed driving the new van Lee bought her. It was high enough that she could see all around the traffic and low enough that she could easily get in and out. Plus the seat was comfortable even in her advanced stage of pregnancy. However, with less than one week until her due date, she reluctantly accepted that this might be the last time she'd drive herself. She was getting too big, and the stress of driving was growing every day. Nevertheless, today she'd enjoy the drive and the view.

The road from their house to the main road slithered between sagebrush patches and junipers, letting the magnificent landscape west of Bend slip in and out of view until she reached the paved county road. The suspense of that drive made the beauty of the mountains even more magnificent. From their living room she could see the Cascades from Mount Jefferson in the north southward to Mount Washington, the Three Sisters, and Mount Bachelor.

It was the middle of summer, the morning was already getting into the 80s, and Verry didn't want to be away from her air conditioned home for very long. She decided to drive just a bit faster than usual, cutting down the transit time in both directions, and getting home for lunch.

About a mile south of their road she came upon a flagman wearing the usual orange reflective vest, holding the reversible sign which he could turn to make the traffic either slow or come to a complete stop. As she approached, he casually turned the Stop sign to face her.

So much for making better time to the doctor's office!

As was usual for this road, there was little traffic, so hers was the only car stopped. Shortly after she halted her car, the flagman walked over, obviously wanting to talk. As he neared, she rolled down her window.

"Mornin', Ma'am."

"Good morning."

"We'll be done in just a few minutes ma'am, then you c'n get on yer way."

"Thank you," Verry said as the man slowly turned back to face the equipment and men repairing the highway shoulders.

It was then that she noticed there wasn't any dump truck with the gravel or aggregate they'd use to repair the shoulder. Something was wrong. She couldn't quite put her finger on it when the flagman turned around and returned to her car.

"You're Missus Kaaler, aren't you, ma'am?"

How'd he know my name? I've never seen him before.

Just then a dark, late-model Ford van pulled up behind her car, and the driver and two men got out and approached her vehicle.

Suddenly panicking, she frantically tried to close her window, but the flagman quickly reached inside the car, grabbed her arm, and pulled it away from the door. With his other hand he released the door lock and opened the door.

"If you'll jes come with us, ma'am."

CHAPTER 5

Where's Mrs. Kaaler?

Lee absent-mindedly reached for the telephone perched on the oak desk in his private office. It was just off the hallway leading from the living room to the guest bedrooms and a second bathroom. He wore his usual summer outfit: a pair of gray shorts and a tee shirt emblazoned with a photo of Mount Jefferson. His feet were bare: he didn't need anything that would make his feet perspire.

"Mister Kaaler?" The caller was female, spoke English with a slight Hispanic accent, and was obviously not part of a junk telephone call.

"Yes, ma'am."

"This is Donnella, in Doctor Capetti's office, sir. Missus Kaaler didn't keep her appointment this morning and he asked me to find out if she's still OK." A slight pause. "Is she, sir?"

Lee saw Verry leave, remembered the gate closing behind her blue van on the way out. His eyes flitted back and forth across the room, as if expecting she'd appear any moment. "I don't understand. She left in plenty of time."

"Mister Kaaler," the woman continued, "when she comes back, will you ask her to reschedule her appointment? It's getting close to her time, you know."

Chapter 6

Terror

A domino mask covered Verry's eyes, its eye holes taped over. Her hands were strapped together with duct tape, and then strapped onto her thighs. Almost worse, her bladder was about to explode: she was terrified! All she really knew was that she was in a dark green van with four men she'd never seen before. They seemed to know where they were going because the vehicle was under careful control, but they didn't talk much.

Lee, help me! she screamed in her mind, knowing he'd be worried sick when she didn't return from her appointment. In the midst of those thoughts, her babies began kicking and turning, as if they, too, were afraid.

"Gotta go to the toilet, lady?"

The sudden words startled Verry. It was the man sitting behind her, two seats behind the driver. After what seemed like hours of silence, it was both a relief and a reason for further fear. But the question was both logical and caring.

Might as well tell the truth. The alternative is to sit here and wet my pants. She thought a few seconds, then a conclusion snapped into her mind. *This guy has kids of his own! He knows what his wife experienced. But if he's so considerate, why did he kidnap me?*

She nodded twice.

Once again the voice broke into her thoughts. "We're comin' to a truck stop. Can't trust you to go by yourse'f 'n come back to us, so we' got a little RV toilet thing for ya ta use after we git goin' agin. Ya prob'ly don't like the idea of peeing with guys around, but its gonna be a long ride and ya better get used to it."

She felt hands checking her seat belt, pulling on the buckle to make certain it was still secure. Then the same man said, "Belt's OK, Billy, 'n she can't scream or anathin'."

The next sound also came from behind her—a slapping sound followed immediately by, "Hey!"

Hurried whispering: "Tol' ya not ta say our names, stupid!"

"Sorry. Won't do it agin."

"Don't hafta," was the response, still in a hoarse whisper as if the speaker thought Verry couldn't hear them talk. "She's heard it oncet already."

The van made a sudden right turn, went over some bumps, then came to a halt. The motor stopped, the front passenger door opened, someone got out, and the door quickly slammed shut.

"Yes, sir?" came a man's voice. "What'll it be?"

"Reg'lar unleaded. Full." was the response. Deep baritone voice, a slight tremor.

Probably the driver. Probably scared. Kidnapping's a federal offense. Another, even more frightening thought. *So's murder!*

Verry heard the gas filler cap door open, the cap being unscrewed, and the hose being put into the filler tube.

Either that guy is blind or he can't see me. More thought. *If he can't see me, this is probably a hard-sided van, not a passenger one. Or has really dark windows. They did a lot of planning. Wonder why? What've I done to—*

Her experiences in the weeks immediately before and after their wedding flooded over her. *These guys are after Lee! They've kidnapped me to get to Lee. And the silver spoon! I thought Lee stopped the Gerits from trying to force him to give up the spoon.* A bigger thought hit her. *But what about my babies?*

CHAPTER 7

The Demand

Lee had no sooner hung up after receiving the call from Verry's doctor's office than it rang again. He answered it after the first ring.

"Kaaler?"

"Yes."

"We got yer wife. If ya want 'er back alive, listen carefully. I'm only sayin' this oncet."

In spite of himself, Lee could feel panic growing inside him. "Is she OK?"

"She's OK. Fer the time bein'. Now *listen*! Ya got something else we want. If ya want yer wife back 'n unhurt, just give it to us. 'N don't call the police, 'cause that'll make us do somethin' ya *don't* want. Understan'?"

"I understand. How much money do you want?"

"We'll get plenty of money when you give us what yer guardin'. We'll call you soon so you c'n tell us how you're gonna git it to us."

Before Lee could say anything more, the caller hung up. *Another attempt to get the spoon? I thought I'd taken care of that once and for all.*

He breathed deeply several times to calm himself and help his heart stop pounding. When he saw the Cascades out the picture window, a memory broke his train of thought.

FarCaller! I used to talk to him while I looked out this window. I should call the police, but if these are the same guys who tried to get the spoon before, they'll probably hurt Verry without worrying about police. He thought back to when his parent's house was set afire. *One of Gerit's guys let himself be sent to jail just so he could get a message to me. How'm I going to fight that kind of dedication without knowing who I'm fighting? One thing's certain: it couldn't be the Gerits.* A few seconds of quiet thought. *I think.*

CHAPTER 8

Sensings

He began walking around the house, noticing anew things that Verry had done to make it theirs: bouquets of dried flowers, pale yellows, reds, blues and pinks. Knickknacks. Throw rugs. Paintings and prints in frames on the walls. Photos of their wedding reception right after they arrived in Bend. Shots of Verry and both families.

Without intending, he found himself back in his office, where he'd been compiling the Kaaler family tree before the two calls. The spoon was in his safe. When he brought it into view, the familiar curves and balance brought back many memories. Memories of the fun times when he and FarCaller were learning about their Gift and how to use it: of the serious times, when one needed the other's help; of the dangerous times, when lives were at stake; and of the last time he used it from his home. That was when FarCaller watched their homecoming party through his silver plate and Lee's silver spoon and presented to Lee and Verry his own wife and their twins—twins named after each of them.

That was wonderful, and a good time to stop such close contact. It let each of us live our private lives without constant concern about the other. A very deep breath. *But now things are different: Verry's been kidnapped. The police found her car just a mile or so from our place, with no damage or indication of a struggle, so whoever they are, they must have been watching us for some time.* After a short pause to change his train of thought, Lee added, *I had to do a lot of talking to explain why Verry left her car out on the road without telling me. Didn't want to have to explain any motive for a kidnapping, 'cause I couldn't talk about the spoon.* He shook his head both in disgust and in the unbelief that a kidnapping could happen to someone in his family. *It's time to do some serious Guardian work again.*

Lee followed habit, sitting in his recliner, looking out the living room window to the constant yet ever-changing vista laid out before him. *I'll have to let FarCaller see the sunsets. He won't believe how incredibly beautiful they are. But enough of that.* He closed his eyes, visualized his faraway friend, and mentally called his name.

It was nearly an hour before he felt and heard the familiar presence.

"Lee, long has it been." Inside the spoon, Lee could see his friend, a few gray hairs sneaking into his mustache, but the same eyes and the same smile. Same friendship.

"Yes, my friend. It's good to see you again."

"That also share I, but most unexpected is this."

"Did I catch you at a bad time?"

FarCaller looked at Lee for a few seconds before responding. "You did not at all 'catch' me. But—" He stopped talking, looked away for a short time, then returned his attention to Lee, wearing a slight grin. "Ah, my friend, something new said you. That 'captured' me meant you not. When you found me it might have inconvenient been, meant you?"

Lee couldn't help smiling. "Yes, exactly. What time is it in your home?"

FarCaller looked away, either at a clock or out a window before answering. "About an hour before sunrise think I."

"I'm sorry, FarCaller, but—"

"Be not sorry, my friend," FarCaller said, interrupting Lee. "Any time we talk, enjoyment is it." He looked more carefully at Lee before saying more. "But this call fear I about pleasure is not."

Lee's mouth went straight, his nostrils opened, and his eyes became slits. "You're right. Today someone kidnapped Verry. I needed to talk to you and I may need your help."

FarCaller's eyes widened in shock, then watered in sympathy. "But why such a beautiful woman would anyone steal? I understand not." His eyes suddenly widened, as if something suddenly became clear. "Unless—"

"Precisely, my friend. Unless the same enemies we thought we had defeated have somehow come back to attack me. But I don't think that's possible. The two leaders of the group that was seeking my spoon were so terrified after I used the golden plate that I don't think they would ever try to resume their search. No," Lee said, looking around the room, seeing everything but paying attention to nothing, "I think it is someone I've never met but who knows a lot about me."

"How help you can I?"

"I'm not certain," Lee admitted, "but I'd like to know what you might see in my future. And also, if possible, what you might see in Verry's future."

FarCaller looked thoughtful for several seconds before responding. "Into your future to look can I. But that to do for Verry, not certain am I. The Guardian she not is. And—"

"But you said yourself that she is Gifted, that she can communicate with me using the spoon. And she and I proved that for ourselves."

"Then into her future, why look you not?"

Lee looked at his friend several seconds before answering. "I'm afraid to. I'm afraid I might see something bad for her, or for the babies."

"Babies?" FarCaller's face instantly lit up. "Babies have you? Afraid was I that never would you children have."

Lee had to smile and laugh. "Once again, FarCaller, we're caught in the time differences between your world and mine. She's having twins. Like your first children, they will be a boy and a girl."

FarCaller looked a bit pensive, and then shook his head slowly. "Hard to remember is it that our times at different rates pass. Five suncircles here has it been since we last talked, and three more children have we. Three girls and two boys, all together. And just starting are you."

"Yes," Lee said, deciding at the same time to bring the conversation back to the reason for having it, "but that isn't so important as finding and saving Verry. She's due to have our babies in a few weeks, and I want those babies born here, in safety, with good doctors, surrounded by family and friends. Not in some awful place as a captive."

FarCaller expression changed from thoughtful to angry. "Right are you. First help you must I, then talk can we."

As was FarCaller's normal practice, he placed his hand against the silver plate that was the counterpart to Lee's spoon, closed his eyes, and stood still, preparing to receive whatever was to come. He stood still for over five minutes, then opened his eyes, took his hand down from the plate hanging on the wall of his great room and looked back at Lee.

"Indeed something sensed have I, Lee. How to describe it I know not."

"Just tell me, FarCaller. Usually we can figure out what it means."

"Very well, but most unusual was it, and in two parts. The first involved you. I saw you a golden plate in your hands holding, and into it looking as if something, or someone, seeking. Then shocked seemed you, after which smiled you, then into the plate peering, continued but with much more purpose. The second part Verry involved." He looked serious now, obviously about to change the subject.

"Never before anything which didn't involve you directly Sensed have I. But in a room Verry saw I, with two babies, suddenly around in shock looking, then into tears breaking. To someone talking started she, but in the room no one else was. In the midst of that, to hear something that distressed or upset her seemed she. Talking stopped she, and sat down, at the door of the room looking as if someone to enter expected she. Then faded the Sensing." Again FarCaller looked confused. "That to you this understandable is, hope I, because I understand it not. Much like when the machine that looks like a grasshopper saw I, and that it flies, said you."

Lee smiled when he recalled how, almost two years earlier, FarCaller had Sensed that Lee would escape constant surveillance when he first wanted to meet Verry. It involved having a helicopter land at the Bend airport and spirit him away from the men who had his home under constant observation.

"I remember," he said, unable to keep a smile from his face in spite of the seriousness of his present situation. "And I will think about what you said. Perhaps I can make sense of it after thought."

FarCaller looked relieved, then said, "And now, help me can you?"

FarCaller wanted me to sense his future. I got so involved in my own mess I forgot that he needed help, too. "Of course." Lee closed his eyes, held his spoon very tightly, and let FarCaller's face fill his thoughts. After a few very long minutes, he finally felt the uplifting he associated with Sensing. Letting the vision flow over him, he saw a large mountain, its top bare rock but not snow-covered. At the base of the mountain was a small village, surrounded by what seemed to be lush farmland. One large house sat higher on the grass-covered slope than the others, looking much like a large Swiss chalet. It was late afternoon; the sun was just starting to sink behind the large mountain.

Far back in the distance, several miles from the edge of the lush fields, he saw a group of men slowly and surreptitiously approaching. They were armed with spears, swords and daggers, occasionally brandishing them as if in response to some kind of challenge or dare. Then the vision faded.

Lee opened his eyes and returned them to the spoon, where he saw his friend anxiously looking at him. "It was very strange," Lee began, "but first I must ask a question."

"Do so, my friend."

"Have you moved since we last talked? I saw a village at the base of a small mountain, not the house you lived in before this."

FarCaller looked very interested. "Yes. When you the valuable rocks and ores for me found, to improve our first house able we were. But with three more children, a bigger home to build needed we. At the back of our property a large hill is, and on the side of that hill our new home built we. Many of our friends joined us, hoping from our good luck benefit they would, think I." He stopped his rambling, then looked sharply at Lee. "Why ask you?"

Lee then described to FarCaller exactly what he Sensed, ending with, "I think you are about to be attacked. Just after sunset some evening."

FarCaller's expression now turned grim.

"Expected it should have I." He looked around the room as if in thought, then back again at Lee. "My brother some very bad friends had. Like him, from anyone to take anything they could, believed they. What Sensed you may indeed an attack on this place be. Defensive preparations today start will, and what happens tell you will I. In the meantime, please in touch with me keep. I, too, much Verry love, and want no harm to her or your babies come."

There was nothing more either could say, both recognized it and cut the contact at the same time.

Lee remained in his recliner and kept trying to make sense of the scene described by FarCaller. *I'm using the golden plate, but not as a weapon. In the next scene, Verry suddenly gets excited and starts talking to no one. What can that mean? And where is she? And how can she have the babies already?*

Wait a minute! Maybe she's talking to someone FarCaller couldn't see!

The more he thought about FarCaller's sense of the future, the more he realized something had changed. *FarCaller didn't see the next few hours like always before; he saw a week or more into the future! That's how the babies could be there.*

What or who controls these visions? Why would they have been just a few hours or a day or so in the future when we first started Sensing, and now, suddenly, see much further ahead?

CHAPTER 9

Memories

"Ben honey, this is Etta."

Floretta Rosita Perez was Ben Gerit's most trusted contact in the Pacific Northwest. She was an expert burglar and a former lover. She used these skills to both of their benefits when Ben was trying to coerce Lee into giving him the "power spoon," as he called it. Etta lived in Bend, Oregon. She and Ben spent much time together in the past, for both personal and professional enjoyment but, with the years and distance, their personal relationship cooled. They retained great trust and respect for each other, however.

"For cryin' out loud, Etta! Haven't talked with you in a coupla years. How *are* you?"

Etta was a short, athletic, bosomy, Hispanic woman with flashing dark eyes, classic facial features, and jet-black hair. "I'm fine, Ben honey. Still looking for you to show up so we can have some quality time together."

They both smiled at their memories of the past when, consumed with desire and energy, and time wasn't pushing them, they could teach each other magical things about their bodies and what they could be made to feel and do.

"Well, Etta, you know how that is."

"I know you're not planning to come see me, or you'd be more specific."

The older, richer man nodded to himself. *As usual, she has it right. That's why I hired her so often.* Not rising to the bait, he asked, "And *I* know you'd not call unless something bothered you, Etta. What is it?"

That told her he was in his "business" mood. *Maybe later he'll find some personal time.*

"Rumor has it, Ben honey, that some of your people are doing things up here again."

Her words reminded Ben of their attempts to get the Guardian to give them that spoon—the device that his family journals reported had the power to make its owner richer and more powerful. Ben Gerit loved power and, two years earlier, finally found the Guardian. Just outside Bend. He was close to getting that spoon when that awful thing occurred.

The balding man still remembered the day that unseen and unheard power grabbed him and filled him with panic and fear whenever he heard or felt someone tell him never to try to get that spoon again. Moreover, how, from that moment on, whenever he even thought about the spoon or the Guardian, or heard a name sounding like "Kaaler" those awful memories returned to haunt him. The pain was so bad, and the terror so deep, that he blanked every thought of it from his mind and gave up the quest entirely, literally fearing for his life. Now Etta, from out of nowhere, calls and reminded him of that search, the search that resulted in such an all-consuming pain. Before he could stop her, Etta continued.

"A couple of my guys saw four of the men you sent up here after that Kaaler guy. They seemed confident about something were going to do, and how much money they were going to get."

His chest began to tighten. It took so much energy to breathe that he couldn't speak enough to tell her to stop talking about Kaaler, or anything regarding that chase.

"After a couple of beers, the guys mentioned a 'plan,' and how they were going to finish the job you and Jeff sent them on. To get the Kaaler guy. Then one of 'em told the others to shut up.

"Now they've disappeared, Ben honey, so I checked up on your Mister Kaaler. He seems OK, but his wife hasn't been seen in a couple of days. She's over eight months pregnant, and word is that her husband's frantic. Surprisingly, the police aren't involved, at least not yet. You didn't intentionally try to hide this from me, did you, Ben honey?"

Her alto voice was soothing, but each of Etta's words brought stabs and spasms of intense agony. By the time she stopped talking, Ben Gerit lay on the floor of his bedroom, unable to speak, crawl, or even breathe deeply. Suddenly his chest seemed to explode, and everything disappeared into a kaleidoscopic display of blues, purples, and black.

CHAPTER 10

Natural But Odd

"Is this Jefferson Gerit?"

I hate telephone solicitations! "Yes. Who's calling, please?"

"Sir, This is Sergeant John Mastersen, of the Chicago Police Department. I'm calling in regard to Ebenezer Gerit. He's your father, is that not so?"

"Yes, of course. But why would the police be calling me about my father?"

"Well, Mister Gerit," the slow-speaking man continued, "I fear I bear bad news."

Now Jeff was interested. "Is he in some kind of trouble?"

"Not exactly, sir. I'm afraid he's dead."

Jeff was momentarily stunned. *I didn't really like Dad, I'll admit. Nevertheless, he is—was—too young to die.* "How did it happen, Sergeant?"

"It appears, sir, that he had a heart attack and died while involved in a telephone call. There was no evidence of foul play, and no suicide note."

"Sir, was he under any particular kind of stress recently? Was he worrying about anything?" His voice changed from sympathetically simply giving information to officially requesting it.

Jeff frowned at both the question and the effort to follow the Sergeant's train of thought. "He had a heart attack about two years ago, as you probably know, Sergeant. Right after that, he slowed down everything he did, concentrated on long-range planning for his company and left the routine pressurized stuff to his staff. I don't know of anything particularly stressful that he was doing. But I'm not very deeply involved in Gerit Pharmaceuticals."

No sooner had he completed his response than Jeff felt the Sergeant's question was a bit peculiar. "Why did you ask that, Sergeant?"

"Well, sir, he looked particularly stricken, if you get my meaning."

"No, I don't. Explain 'stricken'."

"Well, Mister Gerit, instead of looking as if he simply passed away rather calm-like, he appeared to have died while suffering great pain." A short pause, then, "He looked terrified, sir. That's not what we normally find."

What would scare Dad to death? Jeff let his mind wander around in that vein, and then realized he might know the answer.

"Sergeant, you said he was on a telephone call when he died. With whom?"

"From Oregon. From a Miss Floretta Perez. In a town called Bend, sir. Do you know her?"

The word "Oregon" started the tendrils of panic inching through Jeff's body. He found his chest slowly tightening. Carefully controlling himself, he slowly and carefully asked, "Do you have her number handy, Sergeant?" *God, let this terror go away! I'm not doing anything to deserve this!*

"It's 541-555-4515, sir. Miss Perez she says she had no idea what happened. She admits calling your father, but says he stopped talking in the middle of the call—never hung up. When she hung up and tried to call back, his line was busy." *It has to be Etta!*

"Thank you, Sergeant. Now, is there anything else you need from me?"

"No, sir. I expect your father's lawyer will call you regarding final arrangements. But we're satisfied you father died from natural causes, sir."

"Thank you, Sergeant." As Jeff hung up, one thought kept hammering at his mind and body. *Not natural!*

CHAPTER 11

Jail

Verry was hot, tired, sweaty, afraid, alone, and surrounded by four men who seldom spoke. She was reduced to defecating and urinating in a van, blindfolded, where the four men could watch everything she did on the small portable RV toilet they provided. The odors seemed to her to permeate everything, so there was no relief even when her captors opened the front door windows because the air in the back of the van, where Verry sat, never really smelled much better.

The ride involved long, boring, and frightening hours punctuated with eating hamburgers, tuna sandwiches, and burritos, except the breakfasts. They were either stale cinnamon rolls or a lukewarm English muffin with sausage, cheese, and fried egg. The only tasty item was the cold orange juice. It was refreshing and useful: orange juice acted as a clock—two orange juices meant two mornings. At noon of the second day, Verry noticed a decrease in their speed and different roadway sounds. *We're off the freeway!*

Another long ride, another deceleration followed by a slow right turn. Shortly thereafter, the road surface changed to gravel and the noise inside the van became louder and harsher. After several several more hours on that road, the van slowed down, turned left, and stopped. It was immediately obvious that the trip was over because one of the men carefully helped her out of the van, telling her just where to step, how best to move, and when she could stand up.

She'd been sitting, blindfolded and sometimes gagged with duct tape, and her captors wouldn't let her even stretch out to sleep. Even moving out of her chair hurt. Every muscle in her body seemed to complain about having to move at all.

Once carefully out of the van, letting her muscles stretch and start to become accustomed to being released from their uncomfortable positions, Verry anticipated finally breathing fresh air. The air might have been refreshing, but it was so hot that Verry couldn't determine if it was refreshing. Besides that, the hot air and direct sunlight felt as if a heavy weight was pushing down on her. It was as hot or hotter than summers in Des Moines, where she grew up.

She opened her mouth and nostrils, trying to catch any clues that might help her determine her surroundings. *I've got to be in California! I'm not in a desert—doesn't feel right. And it's too dry to be near the ocean, too hot to be in the mountains. Plus I don't smell trees: I smell hay or something like that. And cattle manure.*

A dog barked and yelped excitedly, then Verry heard one of the men start talking to "Brandy." *A dog with a low bark—probably big. Friendly. Accustomed to people.*

It seemed everyone was ignoring her. To test it, she slowly raised her hands toward her mask, then suddenly found them grabbed by a large man's hand and almost casually pushed back to her side.

"If ya wanta play games, we'll tape both hands to yer body again," her escort said. "But in just a bit you can take off your mask 'n even take a shower. How's that fer hospertality?"

He's mocking me! She stopped thinking about herself and thought about the man who just spoke. *His voice came from above my eyes, so he's over six feet two or three. His hands are big and strong—probably a laborer. He's thoughtful, so he's probably used to being around a woman—probably married.*

Her thoughts zeroed in on herself. *Oh God, where am I? Why is all of this happening?*

Her escort took her right elbow and slowly led her over gravel for twenty steps—*Fifty or sixty feet.* Verry couldn't fight back, but she could try to remember everything that happened or that she noticed, just in case she ever needed to pass it to someone she trusted. She memorized details around her from seeing interviews with former prisoners of war—it helped them maintain their sanity.

Her "guide" helped her step up onto a concrete porch, take four steps, and pass through a doorway into a heavenly cool room. While she was enjoying the first cool air she'd experienced since these men grabbed her, her escort led her into what was obviously a long hall, then eight steps down to a landing, a half turn and another eight steps.

The air was now both cool and damp. *A basement!* Four steps straight ahead, through a door, then five steps more, and her escort stopped.

"OK, ma'am," he said. "As soon as I get my face covered, I'll help you outta your bindin's." A few seconds later someone carefully pulled the tape off her wrists—along with some skin, and then removed her domino mask. She saw

Oakland Raider logo on many of the items in the room: curtains covering a small window high on the wall behind her, a bedspread, and a pillowcase on a twin bed directly in front of her. Cheap beige carpet on the floor. Posters of Raiders on the walls. A single light fixture flush against the ceiling.

A young boy's room.

On the bed, a dark red bath towel, a matching washcloth, a bar of soap, and a clean white terry cloth robe.

"Your shower and toilet are over there, ma'am," the big man said, pointing to his right.

Verry was so engrossed in seeing again that she forgot to look at her captor. Startled slightly by the intrusion into her thoughts, she turned around to look at him. *Six foot three, sun-bleached hair, deep blue eyes, muscular shoulders, strong arms, and big hands. Dirty blue jeans, a non-descript orange tank top, dirty cowboy boots, and wide western belt with a big silver buckle bearing the silhouette of a man riding a bucking horse.* Around it were the words, "Merced Rodeo, 1st Place, Bronco Busting, 1988." A red bandana covered his nose and mouth. *Just like the outlaws in old western movies!*

"When are you going to explain why I've been kidnapped?" she asked. "I have no money. I can hardly move I'm so pregnant—why?"

"Ma'am," he said, "we don't wanta hurt you or that baby. Yer husband's got somethin' we want, and yer what's gonna make him give it to us."

Before she could say anything more, he turned around, walked out of the room, and shut the door. Then she heard a hasp slapped against the front of the door and a padlock inserted, closed, and pulled to insure it was locked: she was in a comfortable cell.

If they know enough to kidnap me on the road from our home to town, why don't they know I'm carrying twins?

CHAPTER 12

Ready, Willing, but . . .

Lee opened his eyes, finally admitting he was still awake after hours spent in his recliner trying to sleep, but without some answers about Verry, his mind wouldn't let him relax, so his body suffered. *It's been two days! No more word from Verry or her kidnappers. Could mean any number of things, some of 'em bad. It could also mean they've been moving around and either couldn't call or were waiting for something before they called again.*

He began pacing around his living room, oblivious to the beauty surrounding his home as well as that within. He'd only slept when his body couldn't stay awake, and even those periods of sleep were short and exhausting: not restful.

If I don't hear from her today, I'll have to call in the police. He leaned forward and let his headrest in his hands. *Dear God, how can this be happening to us?*

Forcing himself to slow down, he walked into their kitchen, its brightly tiled counters and red Mexican tile floor failing to add brightness into his life. He removed a gallon of orange juice from the refrigerator, poured himself a large glass, and forced himself to drink it. Not until it hit his empty stomach did Lee realize how hungry he was. It made him think about the number of meals he'd missed since that call from Verry's captor.

Haven't eaten in two days! How can I help her if I'm too weak to think straight?

Grazing through the reefer, he found bread, butter, sliced ham, a one-pound block of sharp Tillamook cheese, hard-boiled eggs, salad mix, at least six different kinds of dressings, and half an apple pie. Almost without thinking, he grabbed and bit into two slices of ham, tore off a corner of the block of cheese, then threw together the salad mix, some roma tomatoes and shredded carrots, and drowned it in ranch dressing. After washing it down with close to a quart of iced tea, he nearly inhaled half of the pie. After a moment to inhale deeply, he realized he had helped himself feel almost normal. Another glass of tea and he felt like a new person.

"Help" reminded him of how he used the golden plate to seek out the men who had hounded him and arranged the accident that injured Verry's right arm and left leg, and killed her best friend. *Now, that kind of "self-help" I do well!*

Quickly putting the dirty dishes and utensils into the dishwasher as Verry had trained him so well to do, Lee took a long, hot shower, shampooed his dirty hair, and shaved. When he was again in his comfortable brown shorts with their six pockets and elastic waistband, and his extra large white tee shirt, he was ready to fight.

For most of his adult life, Lee had an uneventful life. That all changed when he found himself the target of an intense search by the Gerits, trying to obtain the Kaaler silver spoon passed to Lee by his grandmother less than ten years earlier. He had barely begun to understand its amazing powers then, the most useful being his ability to learn something about his short-term future from FarCaller.

Much had happened since then, both good and bad. One of the most significant, besides meeting and marrying Verry, was the gift to him of a second matched set of spoon and plate with special powers. That set was gold instead of silver like the spoon and plate Lee and FarCaller used to contact each other. It allowed the Kaaler Guardian to find anyone whose face he could visualize. It also contained the awful power to let him talk directly into the minds of the person he saw, usually terrifying them just hearing words come from nowhere. Nevertheless, it also let him instill such fear and dread into those people that they would never again do anything against him or his family. It was so effective against the Gerits that they couldn't even *think* about him or their efforts against him without bringing great terror upon themselves.

The golden plate was under his desk in its original wooden case, wrapped in red velvet. He put the case on the desk pad in front of him, then opened it and unwrapped the plate. As he carefully and lovingly removed the plate and held it up to look at, a feeling of calm once again infused itself into him. *I'd use this against her kidnapper right now,* Lee thought, getting more and more angry as his search for Verry became more frustrated, *but it wouldn't help me find her. But when I do—.* He let that thought drop. *This isn't the time to be thinking about vengeance or payback. It's time to find Verry, five a.m. or not!* Jaws clenched, mouth a firm line, eyes radiating his anger; he looked into the center of the golden plate. *Now, Mister Kidnapper, let's see what a Guardian can do.*

CHAPTER 13

To Find Her

Lee looked into the golden plate, first seeing only his reflection: serious expression, eyes intently staring back at him, jaw clenched. He concentrated on Verry's face and, with that, how much he loved her and detested whoever it was that kidnapped her, trying to direct the plate's search. His image in the bottom of the plate wasn't flattering. *Nothing soft in my expression, and that's exactly how I feel.*

The reflection remained in the plate for nearly thirty seconds, at which point Lee was ready to give up the effort to use it to find Verry. Just before reluctantly rewrapping it, his reflection disappeared in a swirl of colors and textures, spiraling inward, almost drawing him into the center of its vortex. Then the abstraction disappeared, replaced by the scene of a bathroom: old white ceramic toilet; white sink jutting out from the wall, its chromed plumbing clearly visible; a cheap chrome-trimmed medicine cabinet and mirror right above the sink. To its left a tub, with a dark red shower curtain drawn, preventing him from seeing who was using it, but affording a clear view of the cloud of steam generated by the hot water. Then an arm reached out from behind the curtain and grabbed the red towel hanging on a chrome towel bar on the wall next to the shower.

At first Lee felt caught between wondering why the plate's powers were showing him this particular scene and the almost voyeuristic fascination with the person behind the shower curtain. Just as the arm and towel disappeared from his view, he noticed a bracelet on the bather's right arm. It was a gold bangle bracelet, its surface covered with a design that looked like single-globed leaves joined end to end, but when the wearer turned her arm, the light seemed to spiral up or down off the bracelet, presenting a fascinatingly simple yet unique display.

That's Verry's! I bought it for her during one of our trips to New York.

Just as he was about to wish she were with him, the shower curtain parted and a familiar, globular body stepped out. She had already wrapped herself with the towel as a sarong. *She's always done that, whether anyone's around or not. Found her!* His joy was short-live. *How can I talk to her? All I've ever done is scare people with this thing.*

Another memory. *I always said or thought things to scare the Gerits, and they always acted as if they heard me. Can't waste this moment. I have to let her know I'm with her.*

He looked at this lovely woman, carrying their son and daughter, now using a second towel to dry her hair. *Verry!* Lee fairly screamed at the plate. *Can you hear me?*

She looked wildly around, obviously looking for him. He could read her lips: "Lee!" she was saying, "Where are you?"

He spoke aloud, forgetting the plate, the distance, the wonderful weirdness of this whole experience. "Are you OK?"

She started talking rapidly, clearly almost raving.

"Stop, Verry! I can't hear you. Speak very slowly."

Verry stopped talking, but her face and body reflected her thoughts: "How can I talk to you?"

"Mouth your words slowly. Let me try to read your lips."

Her response was almost instantaneous. "I love you, Lee. And I'm scared!" she mouthed.

He nodded, forgetting she couldn't see him. "I love and miss you, too. But where are you?"

It took several attempts before he could understand her answer: "California."

"Do you know where?"

She wiped mock perspiration off her brow.

"It's hot," he responded. "You're in a hot area of California."

She nodded, now excited and hopeful.

"Do you know where?"

She shook her head.

"Can you give me any clues?"

After ten minutes of playing charades, both knew they were making no progress. Then she hit her forehead with her flat right hand, showing him she felt stupid about something. She began writing in the condensation on the on the medicine cabinet mirror.

"Boy," Lee said, "am I glad you're smart, Lady. It was right there and only you saw it."

She wrote: HOT. FARM. COWS. 4 MEN, ONE NAMED BILLY. FARMHANDS. CHASED YOU BEFORE. BILLY, I THINK, WORE

WESTERN BELT BUCKLE: "MERCED RODEO, 1ST PLACE, BRONCO BUSTING, 1988."

Just as she erased those words with her washrag and started to write more, she suddenly looked away from the cabinet toward the bathroom door. To Lee her actions were unambiguous: someone was coming.

Verry began yelling out at whoever was at the bathroom door.

Apparently, she got a response she could accept, because she quickly exchanged her towel sarong for a white terry robe. Wrapping her hair in another towel, she waved at the spot where she thought Lee's eyes might be looking at her, then opened the bathroom door and waddled out, her swollen belly leading the way.

CHAPTER 14

Final Agony

"Etta, this is Jeff Gerit."

"Jeff, it's good to finally talk to you." A short pause, then, "I'm really sorry about your dad's death. He was . . ." She stopped. Beginning again, she said, "We were really close, Jeff. For a long time."

That's quite an admission, he thought. *She might have pretended they were only casual friends.* "So I figured," he said. "And it looks like you were the last person he talked to."

She nodded, forgetting he couldn't see her. "I guess so. The police sergeant said your dad must have died while we were talking."

"Told me the same thing. But did he tell you how Dad looked?"

"How he looked?" Clearly, she was at a loss. "I don't understand."

Can't give too much away! "Let me put it another way," Jeff said. "Can you tell me what you talked about?"

A half-smiled sneaked onto her face. "Everything?"

"No, Etta. Nothing personal. But what else?"

When their conversation ended, Jeff understood exactly what happened. He also felt much of the pain his dad must have suffered, pain that almost certainly killed the older, frailer man.

Chapter 15

No Plan

Verry's "visitor" was a woman. Short, a bit dumpy, almost as bosomy as Verry in her advanced stage of pregnancy. But where Verry's hair was auburn, the other's was black as lava. Where Verry's eyes were hazel, her visitor's were so brown as to be black. Verry wrung her empty hands nervously; the other woman carried a tray of food in hers.

"You are hungry?" The woman's voice was deeper than Verry's, and revealed a different fear than Verry's.

She's afraid I might do something to her. Verry thought about the differences between their two situations and could find no reason a woman with at least four men to protect her should fear anything from their prisoner. *Unless she doesn't want anything to do with me. Unless she feels like she's also a prisoner.* Verry's mind raced through a series of possible scenarios and settled on one. *Maybe there's a way to get her to help! If I can only find her soft spot.*

"Yes," Verry replied, moving over to sit on the bed. "I haven't had very good meals for two days."

"This good food," said the woman, an unmistakable Spanish accent coloring her voice. "Good for you and baby." She smiled as she spoke about Verry's "baby."

She's got a family! No wonder she's nervous. Probably afraid all of that riding and lack of sleep might hurt my—" The impact of the woman's words then hit Verry. *She doesn't know I'm carrying twins either! These people are either stupid, go off half-cocked, or are over their heads.* She thought about the Hispanic woman again. *She had tears in her eyes when she talked about my "baby".*

Before Verry could say anything more to the woman, the small Latina put the tray of food on the end table by the head of the bed and quickly left the room. As she moved out the door, Verry saw a man, his face hidden behind a bandana covering his nose and mouth, look in at her, then close the door. Immediately thereafter, she heard the hasp close, the padlock snap shut, and the familiar tug on the padlock to insure it locked. Then near silence. Except Verry could hear country music coming from somewhere in the house.

As she placed the tray on her lap and smelled the wonderful aromas of homemade Mexican food, two thoughts hit her, one good, one bad. *These people couldn't have known how much I love Mexican food. What's more, they don't seem to have any real plan about what to do with me.*

When the impact of that conclusion struck her, Verry's apprehension began maturing into fear.

CHAPTER 16

Recruiting

"T.K.? This is Lee."

"Well, brother-in-law," came the familiar voice, "it's about time we heard from you! Seems you guys forgot us. Haven't heard from you for over two months."

"I'm surprised you have enough energy to count that far," Lee taunted. "In fact, we doubted either of you had come up for air yet."

Lee and T.K. Pajaro were college friends and classmates. It wasn't until Lee asked T.K. to help get Verry into a place safe from Ben Gerit's hired hands, two years earlier, that Lee learned T.K. was also a Kaaler. Moreover, it was then when T.K. met Verry's sister Dorella—"Drella". T.K. and Drella also were the only witnesses at Lee and Verry's wedding in that same old, small but safe place. When T.K. and Drella, too, were married, Lee and Verry switched roles with them: Lee was T.K.'s Best Man, and Verry was her sister's Matron of Honor, maternity clothes and all. The most amazing thing about that wedding: how everyone there said both couples fairly glowed with happiness.

"And how's your very pregnant wife, Lee?"

How do I tell him all of this? Lee pondered. But only momentarily. "That's exactly why I'm calling, T.K. Verry's been kidnapped."

Fifteen seconds after T.K.'s gasp of astonishment, he had partly recovered from his shock and disbelief. He then called Drella to the phone to hear the story, and Lee was finally able to explain why he called. "First, you two have to keep this *absolutely* to yourselves. I need you to network with nearly every Kaaler you know, to try to find reliable Kaalers in Central California. I'll email you my list of Kaalers there: you find someone willing to help us on this, but you can't tell them anything about Verry's kidnapping or her pregnancy, or any of that. Not yet."

"But what about calling the FBI, Lee," Drella asked. "That's their job, isn't it?"

"Sure, but what'll I tell them about the ransom? How do I explain what I'm Guardian of? Or what a Guardian is? We'll wait a bit, Drella, until I've learned more."

Ten minutes later Lee was off the telephone and had emailed T.K. and Drella four pages of names and addresses. He then picked up his golden plate and again visualized the woman he loved.

CHAPTER 17

Dreaded Memories

Jeff Gerit found himself in a quandary the likes of which he could never have imagined. His father was dead, probably from a panic attack brought on by Etta's talk with him about the hunt for the Guardian. She said she told his dad that Kaaler's wife had apparently disappeared. That could only have increased his dad's pain. Now the dread Jeff felt whenever anyone even mentioned Bend or Kaaler was coming upon him. He remembered it starting a few days after his men lost the trail of the Guardian in the Des Moines air terminal nearly two years earlier. The impact of that hit with a thud: *If Kaaler thinks I had anything to do with her disappearance, he might come at me again.* He had to find the men who worked for him in Bend and tell them to make no attempts to renew the search for Kaaler's power spoon, knowing he couldn't tell them it was a spoon. Moreover, if any of them had anything to do with Kaaler's wife's disappearance, they had to release her *immediately*. Otherwise, the consequences might include *his* death! However, Jeff didn't know where his former agents were.

I don't know how or why, but I'm certain that all of the panic I'm feeling is that Guardian's doing. If he ever finds whoever who took his wife, heaven help 'em. And if he thinks I had anything to do with it, heaven help me.

Chapter 18

Nightmare?

Benji couldn't explain what happened, but it thoroughly frightened him. Never in his ten years of life had he had such a realistic dream. *It was a man's voice telling someone how much he loves her. And asking where she was—like he made a telephone call to someone he knew, but didn't know where the other person lived.*

He wanted to talk to his Mommy and Dad about it, but wasn't sure what to tell them. It sounded like a dream, except he was awake when he heard the man. Worse, he didn't really *hear* him so much as *feel* the man's voice inside his mind.

The man called the other person "Very." *Very what? What kind of name is that?*

Benji *knew* the experience was real, that the man was really talking, and that the woman was somehow talking to him, but he had never heard *her* voice. It seemed she was afraid, she was in California, and it was hot. *Just like here!*

It wasn't quite a nightmare.

Chapter 19

Keep 'Im

The three men sat around the dining table in Barnaby Snoyl's home, their meal finished, their table cleared by his wife, and the aromas of chili and corn and onions still engulfing them. It was "beer time," when they usually stayed around and swapped lies. Or ideas.

Doug was a better listener than thinker. He usually didn't make suggestions but always had questions—as if he was always afraid of something. "Barn, I got a question."

"You always got questions, Doug, 'specially at meals."

"What're we gonna do if the guy in Bend don't come across purty soon? That woman's 'bout to bust!" Doug again proved he wasn't stupid—his question went directly to the significant part of the problem.

Barnaby liked telling people what to do, liked talking them into supporting his schemes, liked being looked up to. He didn't like questions about ramifications, because he seldom thought that far ahead on anything. When asked a question he couldn't answer, he resorted to the time-honored tactics of the unprepared; he bounced the question back so he'd have time to think up his answer.

"Wha' d'ya mean?" he asked. "She'll just have the kid 'n' we'll be able to put more pressure on Kaaler."

Doug wouldn't let go. "But havin' a baby costs money! Who'll get the doctor, 'n' who'll pay him, 'n'—"

The moment he stopped to breathe, Billy jumped in. He'd been thinking about the same things, but not as thoroughly as Doug had. "She's gonna need diapers, 'n' baby clothes, 'n' all kindsa creams 'n' stuff, 'n' formula, 'n'—"

Being questioned about his project angered Barnaby, but while his friends talked, he thought. And he found answers. "First," he said, speaking with exaggerated patience, "I got a nephew who's a doctor. Second, we got more'n 'nuff baby stuff right here. Rose kept 'em after we got Benji, hopin' to have one 'f her own some day. Third, we c'n get diapers anywhere. No one'll question us if we shop in Fresno 'stead of 'round here 'cause no one knows us there." He was frowning while he spoke, but his face now wore a smile.

"As to what we'll *do* 'bout that kid, if Kaaler don't come 'cross with that thing he has, we'll send his wife back but *keep* his kid. He'll *never* find it."

CHAPTER 20

Separated

"Verry, can you hear me?"

She was lying on her bed, thinking about all that had happened, and Lee's voice wrenched her out of her pity party. Her natural first reaction was to look around to see him, but when she realized he was still in Bend but talking to her though the plate, she felt embarrassed.

Speaking aloud, even though she knew he couldn't hear her, she said, "Yes."

"Can you find something to write with?"

Criminy! I forgot to see if there's any writing material here. "Just a minute."

Pawing through every drawer, cupboard, and closet, she found nothing. Looking up at a spot in front of her—where she imagined Lee's viewpoint was—she simply shook her head. "I'll just use the bathroom mirror again."

She waddled into the bathroom. Since there was no steam this time, she had to improvise. She found a bar of Ivory soap and tried using it on the mirror like chalk on a blackboard. It worked.

"First," Lee said, "I love you and really miss you."

His obvious sincerity brought tears flowing everywhere. She knew it would make Lee feel worse, but it helped her rid herself of some of her apprehensions. *I'm not really alone—just separated.*

After telling her about his talk with T.K. and Drella, Lee went directly to his point. "Anything more about where they're holding you?"

She shook her head. No need to write her response.

"How're the babies?"

Verry patted her abdomen, and then held up her right hand, thumb, and first finger touching in the familiar OK symbol. Then she smiled.

But that reminded her of something. On the mirror, she wrote, DON'T KNOW ABOUT TWINS.

"The kidnappers don't know you're carrying twins?"

She nodded in reply.

A pause, then, "That's odd. You'd think they'd have done enough research to know that."

Another nod.

"OK, then," Lee said. "Anything you think we should do?"

She turned to mirror and wrote two words.

CHAPTER 21

Unfair

It was the same voice, talking the same way, to the same woman: someone named Very. Benji couldn't hear her words, but the man acted like he did. Her story was sad. Someone took her away from her husband, she was going to have twins, and she was afraid. Her husband was trying to get help through some of his relatives—possibly some living in Central California.

Benji Snoyl was an intelligent young man who loved his Mommy and Dad, loved to play with their dog, go to football games, and walk through the cotton fields. He liked seeing the pheasants hunker down whenever anyone interrupted their dinner of cottonseeds—more interested in eating and hiding than fleeing. He liked fishing with his Dad in the lakes and big irrigation ditches. His favorite foods were all cooked by his Mommy—chicken enchiladas, peach cobbler, sopapillas with cinnamon sugar and strawberries and whipped cream, and she was teaching him how to cook.

He even almost liked the music his dad always listened to—Reba, Garth, Willie, Dollie, and Crystal. But he didn't like being afraid of the man's words echoing inside his head, because he thought he knew what the man meant and whom he was talking to. And why.

Ten-year-old boys are supposed to play. They're supposed to have fun, not worry about their moms and dads doing wrong things. And they're supposed to be able to talk to their folks about things that worry them, not be afraid to say anything.

It isn't fair.

Chapter 22

Almost Clueless

"Lee, this is T.K."

"Well, how's my favorite brother-in-law?"

"I'm your *only* brother-in-law, Lee. But aside from that, how's Verry?"

He always cuts through the small talk. "About as well as you'd expect, I guess. She wants out of there and the babies are apparently OK. So she's also OK, considering. But how are you doing on that task I gave you?"

"Drella and I've gone over the list you emailed me. It's really a big bunch of names."

"Any luck?"

"We found some willing to help, some who might, and some who don't want anything to do with this."

"About what you'd expect, I guess."

"Actually, Lee, I thought we'd get more offers of help. This being a Kaaler family thing and all."

It was now Lee's turn to cut through the small talk. "Any suggestions?"

T.K. seemed to miss the irony. "We've found Kaalers in most of the big towns in Central California: Sacramento, Merced, Fresno, Bakersfield."

"And?" Lee asked.

For the first time in the conversation, T.K. didn't answer right away. "Well, uh, Lee, I uh—I sorta thought you'd have some ideas on what to do next."

Lee was silent a few seconds. "All I know is that she was taken by four men—one named Billy. They were in a green eight-passenger van that might have either very darkly tinted side windows or none at all. They drove almost straight through from here to there, and it's hot farm country. What can we do with that?"

"Not very much."

"That's what I was afraid of."

CHAPTER 23

How to Frustrate a Lawyer

"Clem," Lee said into the secure telephone like the one he bought his lawyer nearly two years earlier, "I need some serious legal advice. But you have to promise you'll tell no one what I'm about to say."

Clem just shook his head. *How many times do Ah have to explain the lawyer/ client thing?* Then he thought a few moments more. *He understands it already. What would make him ask me again? Stress? What kind of stress would Lee ever be under?* "Ah'll tell no one without yoah prior approval, Lee. Ah'm not allowed to do anathin' else."

"Right," he said. He took a moment to decide exactly how to tell Clem what happened and decided on the direct approach. "Well, then, Verry's been kidnapped."

Clem Maestre had been an attorney for over fifteen years, starting as an Deputy District Attorney in Portland. Deciding he'd rather practice a wider range of legal issues than just criminal law, he settled in Bend, the largest community in Central Oregon. One of his firm's best clients had been Lee's grandmother, a strong-willed woman who knew exactly what she wanted done with her will and how those things affected Lee. After she died, for some reason unknown to Clem, Lee began searching for her papers. As a result, Lee had become a good friend as well as a reliable client. But kidnapping?

"Lee," Clem began, "Ah hope y'all're kiddin', but Ah feah y'all're not."

"I'm not," Lee responded. "She was taken a few days ago and is probably in one of the big farm valleys in California."

"Is that what the FBI told y'all?"

"They don't know, Clem."

"Lee," Clem began, carefully picking his words, "did the FBI say they didn't know, or do y'all mean y'all haven't told them Verry was kidnapped."

"I didn't tell them."

"Y'all didn't tell the FBI?" Clem was so surprised and upset that he stood up at his desk and fairly shouted into the phone, oblivious to the fact his secretary could hear nearly every word he said. "Yoah tellin' me y'all haven't told the one group that can best help both of y'all? How can y'all justify that in y'all's own mind, foah God's sake? What gives y'all the audacity to think yoah helpin' her by leavin' the FBI out of this? Lee, you're smarter than that!"

"No, Clem," Lee said, softly and very slowly, "I'm not."

Under normal circumstances, Clem would have continued ranting and railing at a client who'd acted as Lee did. *Ah'd tell him how stupid he was, how much he was endangering his wife, how much more difficult it would be to help her. But Lee already knows all of this and he's done all the wrong things anaway.*

Clem slowly sat back down in his comfortable dark brown Cordovan overstuffed office chair, then looked, unseeing, at the walnut paneled walls of his office, wallpapered with framed diplomas, certificates, and photos of some of his accomplishments. *Somethin' is verrah wrong. And it's not Lee's common sense and intellect.*

"What can y'all tell me?" he said, surrendering, for the present, to the fact he wasn't going to change Lee's mind with ravings about what Lee 'should' have done.

Lee quickly reviewed what he knew, leaving out all references to his Guardianship and anything involving Kaaler affairs.

"Can y'all tell me why y'all think she's in a hot part of California, and not, say, Nevada or Arizona? That might help me and anyone willin' to help us feel they're not on some kind of wild goose chase."

"No, Clem," Lee said, his voice clearly reflecting his discomfort with that response. "I can't. But I'm absolutely certain of it."

"Well, then," Clem said, again assuming his 'lawyer' role instead of that of a good friend, "why call me? Ah know of no legal issue Ah can help y'all with if y'all won't go to the FBI with the matter of Verry's disappearance."

"I was wondering," Lee began, "what you might do if you called me one day, like next Monday, and couldn't make contact. Say it had to do with an unspecified legal matter where timeliness was critical. Maybe something you knew I wanted to do and was waiting for you to complete some paperwork on.

"Perhaps, if that happened, you might even get my Dad to let you into my house because the matter needed my immediate action and you were concerned that I wasn't there, waiting for you, like I said I'd be. You feared I might be hurt, or something."

Before Lee could finish his hypothetical story, Clem interrupted, "And Ah found both you and Verry were missin', and maybe some notes or somethin' which pointed at central California as a possible startin' place for the authorities to search for y'all."

Both men were now smiling, even though they couldn't see each other—communications were clearly established.

"They wouldn't be searching for *me*," Lee corrected. "They'd be searching for *us*."

*   *   *

"Momma," Benji said to his mother after breakfast that Saturday, "you've been taking food down to the basement every day for almost a week. Why? Who's down there, Momma? Can I see? Can I help you? Why is the door locked, Momma? Are they really sick or something? Did you call a doctor yet?"

CHAPTER 24

I Want That Thing!

"Mister Kaaler?"

Lee immediately recognized the voice—*Verry's kidnapper*! His heart began thumping in his chest, his stomach tightened as if he was about to vomit, and his face and hands immediately began perspiring profusely. "Yes," he managed to say with his thickening tongue.

"Ready to trade yet?"

He wasn't so upset that he'd lost the power to think. *I've got to make this guy think I really don't understand what this is all about.* "Excuse me?"

"No games, Kaaler! We got yer wife, she's 'bout to burst, 'n we want to trade—her for that thing of yours." Barnaby wasn't accustomed to working with "customers," had never owned a business, and always shopped at discount stores. He couldn't negotiate for anything but used pickup trucks, and didn't really know what Lee owned that was so valuable to the Gerits. Now, when he was trying to make a deal to get whatever that was, he didn't know what to do or how to do it.

As soon as he heard Barnaby's words, Lee thought, *This man is really uneducated—not faking it—and probably out of his element. Maybe I can use that weakness to help Verry.* A short pause, letting reality bathe his hopes. *But I can't do anything that might put her in more danger.* "I have some money," he began, "and a couple of new cars. Are they what you want?" *It's a chance, but maybe it'll work.*

"Are you tryin' to kid me?" Barnaby shouted, his fear of being a kidnapper now compounded by Lee's apparent stupidity. "I tol' ya what we want—that thing the Gerits're after."

"You know," Lee lowered his voice, trying to sound reasonable as well as trying to calm down the caller, "I never met the Gerits, or even talked with them. But one of them left me telephone messages and never said what he wanted. Honestly, sir," he said, trying to sound seriously confused, "I don't know what Gerit wanted, so I'm not certain what you're after, but I want my wife back. Now how much money do you want?"

Barnaby slammed the telephone handset down on the pay telephone box, accidentally breaking the circuit. When he realized what he'd done, he got even angrier, but he wasn't sure why. *How can that man be so stupid?* As he calmed down, he realized neither he nor his three co-conspirators ever learned the Gerits' real target. *I'll git it outta Kaaler's wife.*

CHAPTER 25

Only Once

"Mommy," Benji Snoyl said, a slight amount of insistence in his voice, "Can't I help? You don't have to take all those meals to whoever's in my bedroom. I can help. Why won't you let me?"

Rosa Snoyl wasn't experienced in dealing with really smart kids, but she knew Benji was one. He'd always learned things quickly, earned good grades in school, and paid more attention to the Discovery Channel than Nickelodeon. Now he suddenly bursts out with questions that told her that Benji'd been watching her without saying anything and knew a lot more about what they were doing than she ever imagined. *Where's Barnaby?* She shouted in her mind. *Benji's asking questions Barnaby should be answering, but Barnaby's probably out with his buddies.*

"Mommy?"

Benji's voice broke into Rosa's thoughts again. *Can't lie to him. Never could.*

"Benji," she began, "Daddy has something special planned, and part of it makes someone stay downstairs in your bedroom. I know you don't like having to lose your room for a while, but don't ask your Daddy about it. You know he doesn't like to be asked about some of his projects, and this is one of them. It makes him nervous, and he sometimes gets angry." *He ALWAYS gets angry, and he usually hits me when he's angry.* "This is a *family* secret."

Benji was smart enough to know that once he got his Mommy talking about something, he could get a lot of information. Moreover, he could maneuver her into doing things she really didn't want to do.

"OK, then, Mommy," he said, finishing his breakfast and stacking his milk glass and cereal bowl so he could take them to the sink, "I'm old enough to keep secrets, so let me help you."

Rosa looked at her son—her adopted son and only child—and wondered what his first parents were like. He was a handsome kid, so they must have been good-looking. He was still slim, had started to eat an alarming amount of food, so he'd probably be a tall man—taller than even his Dad. *His step-dad,* she thought, correcting herself.

It was time to take breakfast to the woman in the basement. She couldn't hide this from Benji because she now knew he already knew she was doing it. So . . . "OK, Benji," she said, knowing she was going to do something Barnaby wouldn't like. Nevertheless, she felt compelled to. "You can help—once. Before you can do it again, your Daddy has to OK it."

CHAPTER 26

Goodbye, Bend

Lee never imagined he'd ever re-use the false identities and disguises he'd used when he escaped surveillance by Gerit's men in Bend to go to Iowa to meet Verry for the first time. Then a second time, when they left Des Moines after they were married. Nevertheless, here he was, again doing it. First, he withdrew ten thousand dollars in cash from his local bank. Then he bought a nondescript but reliable used Honda Accord from a man selling it through a classified newspaper ad. Next, he drove to a nearby drug store and purchased some black hair dye and a roll of paper towels, then to a party store where he bought a realistic false mustache and false sideburns. Finally, he stopped at the SPCA Thrift Store and bought a blue plaid Western shirt, a cowboy hat, and a pair of old cowboy boots that barely fit. Completing his new wardrobe: a pair of dark sunglasses and a black backpack. Then he gassed up the car. In the service station's restroom, he rinsed his hair black, drying it with most of the roll of paper towels. That took over ten minutes, then he stuck the false black moustache onto his lip, donned his new clothes, and headed south on US97 towards California. Next to him in the front seat, hidden beneath an old denim jacket, was the wooden case containing the golden plate. In the left breast pocket of his shirt was the silver spoon that let him communicate with FarCaller; in his billfold were three false ID cards.

The rest is up to Clem and the FBI.

CHAPTER 27

Open It

"Rosa," Billy asked after refusing to unlock the door to the room where they kept Verry, "does Barnaby know you're bringing Benji down here?"

Rosa wasn't a good liar, but she was a good wife, mother, and cook, and knew Billy for many years. He was a good friend of both her and Barnaby—they'd even dated a few times in high school. "No," she admitted, "but Benji knows we've got a 'guest.' And he knows we feed her three times a day, and he knows how to keep secrets. Today he asked if he could help, and I agreed. After this, he'll probably bring some of her meals when I'm really busy or tired, so I've brought him down today. "Now," she said to the much taller man, "are you going to unlock this door or do I wait until Barnaby comes back before I feed the woman? Remember, Billy," she said, a tinge of scolding in her voice, "in her condition, our 'guest' needs good food."

Billy just looked at Rosa and Benji, quietly standing behind her carrying the breakfast tray. Finally, Billy just shook his head in surrender. "Barnaby's not gonna like this."

She flashed a big smile at Billy, accompanying it with a conspiratorial wink. "But he'll get used to it, don't you think?" Her implication was clear to her friend and former occasional lover: if she needed to, she'd use sex to get Barnaby's cooperation.

'N' she's really good! Billy thought. *Barnaby prob'ly don't have a chance.*

Verry was lying on the bed, trying to get comfortable. She sat up when she saw Rosa, then smiled at the boy carrying her food tray.

Rosa said nothing, just smiled to acknowledge Verry's unspoken query: Yes, Benji was her son.

After putting the tray down on the small bed table, Benji whispered, "Are you Very?"

Her eyes nearly bulged out of her head in surprise and shock. No one, since her capture, had ever called her by her first name, let alone her nickname. Before she could respond, Benji whispered a word that nearly made Verry faint from shock.

CHAPTER 28

He Knows!

Lee stopped in Redding, California that night, tired from the strain of the drive but anxious to talk with Verry. First, he put the black backpack containing his meager belongings onto the dresser in the $18/night roadside motel, and then removed the golden plate from its case. Sitting in the cheap tan upholstered "living room" chair, with its square arm rests, square back, square silhouette and square cushion, he stared intently into the plate and fairly screamed his wife's name. It took only a few seconds for her image to appear.

She sat on her bed, head in her hands, tears running down her cheeks, shoulders shaking, sobbing. Lee felt terrible. His first impulse was to blame himself, but he knew that wasn't useful: he hadn't kidnapped her and had done as much as he could to find and recover her.

I'm here, sweetheart.

She instantly sat erect, instinctively looking around for him even though she knew she couldn't see him. "Lee," she said, "I've been so lonely. And scared."

He couldn't hear her, but by now, he could read her lips pretty well. "Lonely" and "scared" were obvious. "*Has something more happened? Why do you look so much more frightened?*"

"What do you—" she started saying, then realized that he couldn't hear her, but her captors could. She rose from her bed and waddled into the bathroom, her hands pushing hard on the small of her back, trying to ease the constant ache she now felt.

Once there, she picked up the bar of soap and wrote on the mirror, HURT, LONELY, SCARED!

"*I understand,*" Lee said. "*Your body hurts, there's no one to talk to, and you don't know what's going to happen to you.*"

She nodded, then wiped the words off the mirror with the washrag and wrote, BOY CALLED ME VERRY.

Lee stared at the words, shocked by what they might mean. *"Someone called you by your first name?"*

She nodded enthusiastically, happy that Lee nearly understood, and then held her right hand so it was barely five feet above the floor. On the mirror she wrote, W/ MOTHER. BROT FOOD.

"A child?"

She nodded again, her lips forming the words, "BOY."

"But how could he know your name?"

She shrugged, and then wrote WHISPERED IT on the mirror.

"He didn't say it aloud, he whispered it? Like he didn't want his mother to hear what he said?"

She nodded.

"That's strange," Lee slowly said. *"Why would he do that?"*

Verry again shrugged her shoulders.

All Lee could say was, *"I don't see how he could possibly know your name."*

Verry quickly erased those words and wrote four more: ALSO KNOWS ABOUT TWINS.

Chapter 29

No One's Home

As he and Lee had planned, the following Monday Clem called Lee's house and, as he expected, received only a telephone answering machine message. He then called Lee's dad, told him that Lee hadn't shown up to sign some important papers, and asked if Lee's dad would meet him at Lee's house so they could check to see if Lee was sick or something. Fifteen minutes later, both arrived at Lee's house, his dad opened the door and turned off the security system, and then both searched for Lee. When there was no sign of him, and after a short discussion, Clem called the sheriff's office to come there, because he feared something bad might have happened to Lee.

"Bill," Clem said to the sheriff's deputy who responded to the call from Lee's dad to go to Lee's house, "Ah only know Lee was supposed to be here to meet me on an impoahtant matter that needed his signature. This morning. We've been working on it foah some time and he couldn't have forgotten it. When Ah got heah, the place was all locked up—not like Lee at all. And Verry didn't seem to be heah either.

"So I called his dad and he let me in. Lee and Verry are both gone. And there's this note, in Lee's handwriting, that Verry missed her last doctor's appointment."

He looked at Lee's dad, then back to the deputy. "She wouldn't do that unless something was wrong, Bill."

Lee's dad nodded full agreement.

Clem continued. "She's anxious and excited about having twins, and wouldn't do anything to threaten theah health. I'm afraid something's happened to both Lee *and* Verry."

CHAPTER 30

Another Sensing

"Lee! For many suncircles not talked had we, and now in only a few months twice meet we! Such a wonderful surprise is this! But concerned look you, my friend."

"I am, FarCaller. Verry is still with the people who took her, and I still don't know where that is. She told me where she thinks she may be, and I'm driving there so I can be close in case we find her soon."

FarCaller couldn't hide his smile. At first Lee thought FarCaller felt something was funny about Verry's kidnapping, but quickly discarded that idea. FarCaller's next words explained the expression. "In that house on wheels you had when to marry her went you?"

Now Lee smiled, in spite of the seriousness of the situation. Almost two years earlier, he had contacted FarCaller while driving a rented motor home through Idaho on his way to marry Verry. To help FarCaller see more of America and this world, Lee attached his silver spoon so it pointed at the road and then at the inside of the vehicle. FarCaller had never seen anything like it, and now associated Lee's travels with driving a motor home. "No," he said, smiling as he remembered that trip and FarCaller's amazement. "I bought a small car and I'm driving it. I'll be there tomorrow, if all goes well."

"Close is it then, Lee?"

"I think it is about 700 miles or so from my home—an easy two-day trip."

FarCaller shut his eyes and shook his head back and forth. "To hear you travel such distances so fast, strange is," he said. "Twenty miles a day to be fast consider we." Then he changed his demeanor. "But to talk about motor homes you did not so soon back call me. The reason for this contact, tell me."

"I need you to Sense my future," Lee said, now also deadly serious. "No one knows where I am yet, but if there's something bad in what you Sense, I'll have to tell my best friend. So, please, Sense ahead for me."

FarCaller nodded once, then put his hand on the silver plate that was his link to Lee's silver spoon. He closed his eyes as if in thought, held that posture for a few minutes, then his eyes snapped open, radiating fear.

"Lee," he began, "A room with bars in the doors and windows see I. In that room are you, your face and arms wrapped in white bandages are, and a man a dark blue shirt wearing and dark blue pants with a gray stripe down the legs near you stands. As if he is on guard it is, but no weapon see I. On his belt a leather pocket is, and in the pocket what looks like part of the horn of a goat is, only shorter and fatter. On his shirt, by his left breast, a piece of silvery metal cut like a star is." He blinked several times, adding, "With you talking seems he, but as a friend not." FarCaller then looked squarely at Lee. "That Sensing understand I not, Lee. Do you?"

Lee idly looked around his cheap motel room. Double bed covered with a dark brown bedspread; end table and lamp with a yellow shade painted with rodeo scenes in silhouette; TV set on a small, low dresser, both brown; bathroom door with a dressing mirror on the side facing the bedroom. Brown rug with a tweed-like pattern. *A depressing place and a depressing Sensing.* After a few moments, he said, "You've Sensed me in a jail, possibly after either a fight or an accident. A policeman or sheriff is talking to me. That's all bad."

FarCaller was obviously distressed. "So sorry am I, Lee," he began, "but—"

"No need to feel that way. Remember, I asked you for this, and it's a good warning."

"Well, then, now you will what do?"

Lee smiled wryly. "Change every plan I've had about this trip."

CHAPTER 31

D & D

After closing with FarCaller, Lee first sold his car to the motel owner for five hundred dollars, acting as if he had no idea of its real value. Then he called a private aviation company in Redding and chartered a plane to take him to Woodland, paying with cash. Once in Woodland, he rented a room in another cheap motel, under another false name, got a few hours sleep, and contacted Verry via the golden plate.

In contrast to the small bedroom he expected to see, he saw a brightly lit room and Verry in a birthing bed, feet in the stirrups, face covered with sweat, seemingly every muscle in her body under strain.

She's having our babies! At first, Lee felt jubilation, quickly followed by remorse because he wasn't with her, then anger at the reason for their separation.

He saw her stop straining for a moment, and then spoke to her, very quietly. "*I'm here.*"

Her eyes widened in surprise, then she winced as another, harder contraction overcame her. Lee saw her strain as he'd never expected to see, then her whole body relaxed. Pulling back from the scene, he saw a doctor hold up a newborn baby, say something to Verry, then hand it to her. Crying in both joy and pain, she held the baby against her chest, kissing it. Lee saw her open her eyes, look up at where she was certain he was observing the miracle from, and then hold the baby up. Her mouth formed the word, "Dannice."

Lee thought to her, "*Thank you for that lovely gift, Verry. Our Dannice is a beautiful little girl.*"

She couldn't say anything to him, but smiled, blinked back her tears, and held on to their daughter, refusing to let the nurses clean her, but allowing them to clean out little Dannice's nostrils and put something in her eyes.

Then Lee did another difficult thing: he stopped looking at his kidnapped wife and their new daughter and looked around the room, trying to find something that might tell him where they were.

Stenciled on the nurses' surgical gowns, on their left breast pockets, were the words, FRESNO PEOPLE'S CARING HOSPITAL.

"Verry," he fairly yelled at her, "*I found you! You're in a hospital in Fresno—isn't that right?*"

Verry was, at that very moment, in the middle of another massive contraction, but she forced herself to nod her head up and down, vigorously mouthing the words, "Yes! Yes!"

Then she relaxed again, the contraction momentarily easing.

"*I'll be there in no less than three days,*" Lee thought at her. "*Things are a bit tricky on this end, so don't expect to see me for a while. But I'll be in touch.*"

Just then she stiffened and trembled in pain, her legs shaking with the effort, her hands gripping the arm rest handles as if her life depended on it. Then she totally relaxed, and he knew, from how she looked, that it was over.

A few seconds later, the doctor handed her a second baby. Verry took the little one into her arms, kissed it, then again held a baby with outstretched arms, and said, "Daniel."

CHAPTER 32

The Best One

It took Lee several minutes to recover from the joy and regret he felt in seeing his children born. Tears cascaded down his cheeks like small rivers flowing onto the front of his tee shirt, leaving him exhausted from seeing his wife strain so hard to deliver their children, and from knowing he should be with her but wasn't, and regretting it deeply. After a few minutes, he regained enough control to wipe his face dry with a handkerchief, and think about his next stop. Taking a deep breath, swallowing hard to regain some semblance of control, he retrieved his cell phone from his backpack and pressed one of his often-used numbers. After two rings someone picked it up.

"T.K., this is Lee."

"Cripes, Lee," his brother-in-law nearly screamed, "Where are you? The FBI was here and said you might have been kidnapped!"

"I'm OK," Lee said, making his voice intentionally calm, hoping it would calm down his friend. "I'm heading for Fresno—Verry's there. *She's* the one in real trouble. But I don't know exactly where in Fresno she is, so I need your help."

"Anything. You know that."

"Who's your best Kaaler contact near Fresno?" After a few seconds, Lee added, "Make this fast, T.K. Your phone may be tapped and I don't want anyone to know where I am."

"The best one is a single schoolteacher in Clovis: Doris Mooradian. I'll tell her to expect a call."

After T.K. gave him Doris's telephone number, Lee broke the circuit without any niceties. *Now I've got to get to Woodland. Then Sacramento. Then Fresno. After that I don't know what I'll do.*

CHAPTER 33

I'm Not Crazy

As soon as he heard that man's voice in his head again, Benji stopped playing with his dog and ran into the house, closeting himself in the upstairs bathroom. There he quickly pulled down his pants and underwear and sat on the toilet, just in case his mother checked on him. *Going to the toilet Mommy would understand. Listening to a man's voice in my head would scare her to death.* A few seconds, Benji added, *It kinda scares me, too.*

It took only seconds for him to realize two things: "Very" was in the hospital—probably to have her babies, and that man, almost certainly her husband, was coming to Fresno. Then a truly frightening thought struck the young man: *What's he going to do to Daddy?* Benji didn't realize he'd accepted as fact that the man married to "Very" would somehow find where they lived and come for his father.

Then a second, more frightening thought: *Daddy and Mommy won't believe I heard a voice in my head telling me about "Very" and twins and her husband coming here. So how can I warn them?*

CHAPTER 34

A Plotter?

"Mister Kaaler?"

"Yes. Who is this, please?" Lee's father responded.

"Special Agent Fallerou, from the FBI, sir. We talked a few days ago about the disappearance of your son and his wife."

Lee's father didn't know whether he wanted to hear the agent's message, fearing it might be bad news. He closed his eyes, steeling himself for the worst, then said, "Of course. Forgive my momentary memory lapse. What can I do for you?"

"Well, sir, we wondered if you'd heard from either your son or his wife since reporting their disappearance."

"No. You asked me to inform you of any such contacts, I agreed to do, and I haven't had any. So far as I know, they're just gone."

The agent's voice remained calm, almost a monotone. "Yes, sir. Well, we have some indication they didn't disappear *together*, if you know what I mean."

"No, sir, I don't" the older Kaaler said, trying to disguise the frustration that was building inside him. "What are you saying? That there were two kidnappings?"

"Not at all, sir," the drone-like voice responded, "Quite the opposite, as a matter of fact."

"I still don't understand, Agent." Now the frustration and exasperation began coloring his voice. "Can't you just tell me straight out what this is all about?"

There seemed to be no reaction whatever on the part of the Special Agent. His response was still slow, his voice still barely inflected. "Sir," he began, "it looks to us like your son left on his own."

"Without telling anyone? Is that what you're saying?"

"Yes, sir. Exactly that."

"That's ridiculous! Why would Lee do such a thing? What could be gained? Besides, isn't that kind of skirting the law? Faking a kidnapping?"

"Directly doing so is, sir," the agent said. "But just disappearing and letting his friends or parents *assume* he was kidnapped—well, sir, that's not the same thing."

Lee's father felt himself getting more and more angry at this call. His wife, curious about the call, first noticed the tenseness in his voice, then the reddening of his face, and then the clenching and unclenching of his fists. "Why would you think such a thing?" he barked at the agent, not attempting to disguise his concern, frustration, and resentment at the implications of the agent's comment.

"Well, sir," the man continued in the same, steady voice, almost as if he was refusing to show any emotion about the supposed event, "we found a place that might have sold your son some used clothes the day after his wife's apparent kidnapping. And we have reason to believe he bought a car—for cash, that same day. Those aren't the actions of someone who's been kidnapped, sir."

Lee's father took several deep breaths, letting his left hand, and the telephone it held, drop to his side for a few seconds, as he tried to digest what he'd finally learned from the FBI agent. Then he raised the handset back up to his ear. "And what now, Agent?"

"Well, sir," the man said, still droning, "we have several options. What we've done is put out an FBI bulletin announcing both your son's and his wife's disappearances, but as two related and separate events. We're hoping that might gain us some help."

"What if the kidnappers told Lee not to call the authorities or they might hurt her? Or even—God forbid!—kill her?"

"We're keeping it within law enforcement channels pretty much, sir. Just because of the very things you said. I merely want you to know we're on this matter, consider it serious, and want you to tell us if anyone contacts you on this matter."

"But you already did that several days ago, and I agreed! Why are you telling me this again?"

"Well, sir, because before this we thought your son was a victim. Now we're not so certain he's not part of the plot."

CHAPTER 35

The Voice in my Head

Things were happening too fast for Benji. First his Daddy and three good friends bring a stranger into his home and turn Benji's room into a jail. Then he hears a man's voice in his head, a voice that sounds like it's a man talking to his wife. *Could that mean there's a woman down there? And her name is "Very"?* He hears the man talk about twins. *Mommy and Daddy never mention twins.*

Benji talks his Mommy into taking him to see the woman, and when he whispers the name "Very" to her: she looks shocked and frightened. But when he mentions twins, she turns pale—like a ghost.

A few days later, the man's voice talks to "Very" about their babies being born—like he's watching it. In a hospital in Fresno. Earlier the same day his Mommy and daddy rushed "Very" out of the house and drove away without even saying goodbye.

Now she's back, with two babies, and Mommy's up all hours of the night helping "Very" take care of the little ones.

Why is "Very" here? Locked up? And how can I hear that man's voice when no one else can? Or, he suddenly thought, *Maybe they can hide it and I can't.* More thought. *No, Daddy couldn't hide something like that. He'd be yelling and swearing and trying to beat up whoever was doing it.*

He was losing sleep over this, glad only that school hadn't begun, because his grades would be so bad his parents would *know* there was something wrong with him.

I still don't know how to tell them about the man's voice. Or if I should.

CHAPTER 36

Spinning Downward

The whole world seemed to be conspiring to remind Jeff Gerit of his efforts to locate the Guardian and obtain what he and his dad, and generations of forefathers, believed was The Answer to their dreams of power and wealth. Since Etta called from Bend, barely a day passed when something didn't remind him of those ill-fated efforts. With every instance came the overwhelming feelings of dread and terror that drove him and his dad to abandon their effort to find the Guardian. Today was no exception.

Since his dad's death, Jeff moved to Chicago and began assuming more and more of the duties of running Gerit Pharmaceuticals. He never really wanted to—he just wanted to spend the profits. But it seemed to be the only way to keep from thinking about that spoon and again suffering the awful feelings that accompanied those memories. Today's reminder of Jeff's past life came with a seemingly innocuous telephone call.

"Mister Gerit, this is William Donover, in Accounting."

"Yes, Mister Donover," Jeff responded. "How can I help you?"

"Well, sir," the small man began, "it's about your personal finances. You asked us to check them and make certain they were in order."

"I remember that. It seemed best to insure there were no loose ends, so I could devote my time to running this company."

"Yes, sir," the man answered. "Well," he continued, "we found some unusual current charges appearing on one of your credit cards, sir. And when we looked into them, we also found what seem to be related expenditures from one of your bank accounts."

"I don't understand. 'Unusual'?"

"Yes, sir. Car rentals in central Oregon, motels, meals, and gasoline in southern Oregon and northern California, and what appear to be fairly large salaries or retainers over twenty-seven months for four people in Fresno, California."

Before the accountant could complete his report, the terrible pains returned, and Jeff's chest tightened so much he could barely breathe. Then his office began spinning around. And around. And around.

CHAPTER 37

No buses, planes . . . .

L ee ambled toward the bus depot in Woodland, still in disguise, intending to buy a ticket to Sacramento to continue his trip to Fresno without being recognized. When he turned the corner of the front of the bus depot, he noticed several official-looking men in civilian clothes carefully checking the identification documents of everyone entering the depot. He was both puzzled and frightened.

Can they be looking for me? he thought, stopping cold in his tracks about a half block from the depot. *If they are, my fake IDs, as good as they are, won't fool professionals like them. And if they're not looking for me, they'll find me by accident. That eliminates buses, airplanes, probably taxis, and motorcycles as ways for me to get out of this place.*

So how do I get to Fresno?

CHAPTER 38

A Bit Harder

The household was turned completely upside down with the return of "Very" and her babies. The first thing Barnaby realized was that he couldn't keep her, and them, locked in Benji's room, because those twins were too much work for their mother to handle alone. So Rose was up and down the stairs at all hours of the day and night helping care for them. Control of his household had been wrested by two babies!

Now he sat alone at the small dining table, eating a breakfast he had to prepare for himself: four microwaved pancakes afloat in maple syrup. He didn't really like them, but he liked dry cereal even less, and at least he could drive a microwave oven.

If Rose didn't keep telling me she HAD to help that broad, I'd bet it was all faked. But it's been only two days 'n they're going through diapers like they was Kleenex, 'n havin' to wash everythin' two 'n three times a day, 'n I'm havin' to fix some a my own meals! 'N th' house is already startin' to smell like baby crap. This has gotta stop!

Barnaby had no idea how to stop it, and he couldn't think clearly because he hadn't gotten a full night's sleep since the babies arrived. *Gotta do somethin', and soon! But if my nephew Jeremy wasn't a women's doctor, there'd been hell to pay jus' findin' a place for that broad to have 'em. Then, after Jeremy kicked me out of the room jes before she drops the brats, and she ups n' uses their* real *names on th' birth certificates, I can't 'dopt 'em out like I planned.*

He thought more while he stuffed another forkful of hotcakes into his mouth. Then a small smile oozed its way onto his face. *Now it'll jus' be a bit harder.*

Chapter 39

You Wouldn't Believe

Discipline had deteriorated to the point where Barnaby and his friends now guarded only the three entrances to his house: front, back, and garage. Further, Benji now could take food down to "Very" at least once every day, usually when his Mommy was trying to catch a nap. That meant the downstairs had no people in it other than the mother and babies and, today, Benji.

The first few times Benji took food to "Very," he said little even though he really wanted to. The third day, however, he couldn't wait any longer. After putting her food down on the end table, he backed up a few paces then stood facing her, clearly not intending to leave.

Verry was so hungry she didn't notice he hadn't left, and simply began eating right away—nursing made her hungry and thirsty almost all the time. About halfway through her tamales, when she had finished her Mexican rice, she glanced up and noticed the slim, light-brown-haired boy quietly standing just a few feet away, but out of her usual line of sight. "I'm sorry," she said, hastily wiping the warm, spicy sauce from her mouth, "I didn't notice you." She quickly looked around, trying to learn if they were alone before saying anything to the boy. "Your parents aren't here?"

"No, ma'am. Mommy's asleep and Daddy's out working on the tractors."

Verry craned her neck, trying to see if there was anyone else in the basement, but saw no one. She really didn't want to get up if she could help it, because her stitches still hurt quite a bit.

"What's your name?" she asked.

"Benjamin, but I'm called Benji."

"'Benji' what?"

"Snoyl," he answered.

"How old are you, Benji?"

"Ten," he answered, then looked down, apparently embarrassed about something. "Almost ten, anyway."

He was a bit hesitant for some reason, so Verry decided to change the subject. "Would you like to see the babies?" She couldn't keep motherly pride from her face and voice.

Benji hadn't yet moved, but now he shyly returned her smile. "Yes'm," he said. "If it's OK."

"Go right ahead," Verry said, pointing at the makeshift cribs made from two drawers taken out of Benji's chest of drawers. "They're asleep right now, so go right ahead and look, but don't wiggle their beds or anything."

Not quite sure how to approach two brand new babies, Benji tiptoed the few feet to where they lay, sleeping on their stomachs. One had blue booties, the other pink.

He carefully put out his hand and pointed to the pink shoes. "Is that Dannice?" he asked.

This time Verry didn't reveal her surprise as much as before, partly because she felt he wanted to say more. "Yes, it is. Do you know the boy's name, too?"

He turned around to look directly at Verry. "No, ma'am."

"It's Daniel," she told him. "Daniel Kaaler."

Before he could say anything more, Verry asked, "How did you know Dannice's name, Benji?"

Again Benji ended their meeting by doing something totally unexpected: he colored slightly, mumbled, "You wouldn't believe me," then turned around and almost ran from the room.

Chapter 40

Shared Tears

"*I'm here, Verry,*" Lee said to the image in the golden plate, trying hard to hold it steady against the vibrations and weaving of the truck he was riding in.

She had been catching a quick nap, trying to recover her strength from both the ordeal of birth and of trying to care for her two little ones. Before responding, she pushed herself to a sitting position, trying to reduce her pain from the stitches, carefully rose from the bed, walked over to the door, and quietly closed it. Next, she tiptoed into the bathroom, where she picked up the bar of Ivory and prepared to "talk" with her husband.

It took over a half hour to catch each other up on what had happened since they'd last talked—while she was giving birth. Near the end of that time, Verry finally asked Lee where he was and when he'd get to Fresno.

"*Actually,*" he began, "*right now I'm in the passenger cage of a semi truck taking a load of furniture from Woodland to Sacramento.*" His voice dropped conspiratorially. "*The driver thinks I'm talking to my girlfriend on a cell phone.*" A short pause, then, "*He's half right, I guess.*"

Verry ignored his attempt at humor. On the mirror she wrote, WHY TRUCK? WHY NOT PLANE?

"*Because,*" he began, "*I think the FBI thinks I was kidnapped, too. If they find me without you, they'll likely think I'm more of an accomplice than anything else. So I'm in disguise and keeping a low profile.*"

Verry didn't like what she heard, but it was too difficult to try to get all the explanation when she was forced to write on a wet mirror.

Then Lee asked, "*What about the boy who knew your name? And about the twins?*"

Verry immediately brightened up, then wrote, TALKED TODAY. WOULDN'T SAY HOW HE KNEW MY NAME. SAW BABIES. BENJAMIN SNOYL. She erased those words and wrote, WANT TO TALK TO HIM. HE'S AFRAID, I THINK.

"*What's he afraid of?*" Lee asked, clearly getting excited. "*Benjamin Snoyl? We should be able to find someone with that name.*"

Just then Verry heard a noise at the door to her room. She turned from the mirror and moved to the bathroom door, getting ready to ask who was there, but she was so startled that she nearly fell down.

Just outside the bathroom door, tears streaming down his face, stood Benji.

Verry quickly pulled him close to her, giving him a strong but loving hug. At first, he kept himself stiff and didn't respond, but after a few seconds, he put his arms around Verry's hips and began softly but deeply sobbing.

"What's happened, Benji?" Verry said, her voice soft, her right arm around his waist, holding him close to her. "Tell me why you're crying."

It took nearly and hour, during which Verry cried *for* Benji and *with* him. What she learned distressed her for reasons she couldn't have imagined before being kidnapped and jailed in a small house in the farmlands west of Fresno.

CHAPTER 41

The Hospital

"Doris Mooradian?"
"Who's calling?"
"My name is Lee Kaaler."
"Really? You're Lee Kaaler?"
"Yes, ma'am," he responded. "This may sound odd, but would you please Challenge me?"

She was silent for a moment, apparently thinking about what Lee asked. "OK, I'm looking for a different career path, and think I may have found a new calling."

The words of the Kaaler Challenge came easily to Lee, even though he hadn't spoken them in over two years. But they were drilled into the brain of every Kaaler.

"A new calling can be very hard to find," he said, every word precisely spoken and exactly right. "Did you have any preferences?"

Lee was intently listening for how Doris pronounced the next key word in the Challenge because, again, the plural was important: the word had to be "distances," not "distance." "Something in long distances," she replied.

"World-wide, I presume," he said, completing the litany.

With that formality correctly completed, Doris' tone of voice immediately changed from serious to happy. "It is so good to speak with you, Guardian."

"Thank you," Lee said, "but I prefer Lee."

"OK, Lee, how can I help you?"

"I need to know the address of Fresno People's Caring Hospital. My wife just had twins there."

"Well, congratulations," she said. "Let me check the phone book and I'll get that address for you."

Lee knew exactly what he saw when observing his children's birth, and the words were indelibly branded in his memory: FRESNO PEOPLE'S CARING HOSPITAL. He could feel his hunt closing in on the prey.

After less than thirty seconds, she returned to her phone. "Lee?"

"Yes."

"There's no such hospital in this whole valley."

CHAPTER 42

He Hears What?

Later that evening, Lee arrived in Sacramento and rented a room in a hotel near the river. He knew some nice places to stay while in that city, but they weren't in the cards this trip. He sat in another of the cheap square chairs that seem to inhabit every cut-rate or seedy hotel and motel in America. Unlike the Redding hotel, which was decorated in shades of dirty brown, this room was done in varying shades of dirty blue. But the telephones worked the same in either city.

"Doris, this is Lee."

"Hi, Lee! Sorry I couldn't find that hospital for you when you called yesterday, but it just isn't here."

He sighed in exasperation clouded with frustration, was silent another moment, and then spoke. "I know. Let's not worry about that right now. I'd like you to locate someone named Snoyl. Benjamin Snoyl. Boy about ten. See if you can get me an address." Then he hung up.

Removing the golden plate from its case, Lee held it so one edge rested on his knees, letting him look straight into it. *Verry,* he aimed at her, *Can we talk?*

Her face appeared almost instantly in the center of the plate: she was clearly waiting for his call, but she didn't look particularly happy to see him.

"What's wrong, Verry? You look—upset, or something."

She took one long breath, then reached over to the bed table, and withdrew a child's Magic Slate from the drawer. Pulling the stylus from the tube holding it, she started writing. FOUND THIS UNDER THE BED. After writing a few words, she turned the slate so Lee could see them. BABIES FINE. EATING WELL. GOT RUN OF HOUSE. I'M MISERABLE. Tears started trickling down her cheeks from what Lee now noticed were very red eyes.

"*Honey,*" he began, desperately trying to find something to make her feel better, "*I'm in Sacramento now, and with luck I'll be in Fresno tomorrow. I think we'll see each other pretty soon, and we'll get you out of that place.*"

The tears now flowed so hard that it was clear she could barely see, SOMETHING AWFUL HAPPENED. She wiped her cheeks and eyes with the sleeve of a pink, flowered housecoat the woman of that house had obviously given her.

"What? What's happened?"

BENJI HEARS EVERY WORD YOU SPEAK TO ME,

Lee just looked at his wife's image in the golden plate, suddenly unaware of his surroundings and totally confused by what he just heard. "*I don't understand. I don't even say anything aloud when I'm in touch with you—I just think it. Besides, he doesn't even know where I am, and—*"

As her husband spoke, Verry began writing on the slate. When he stopped she held it up for him to see. HE HEARS EVERY WORD YOU SAY. IN HIS HEAD. She started crying again, but somehow found a tissue and blew her nose. HE THOUGHT HE WAS GOING CRAZY.

Lee was essentially struck dumb. *Someone else can hear what I say to Verry when I'm using this plate?* More thought, almost unconsciously watching his wife crying yet not feeling anything, so lost in thought was he. "*I thought the only people who could hear me were those I thought about. Who is he?*"

Verry regained enough composure to be able to write more and cry less. ADOPTED SON OF OWNER OF THIS HOUSE. HIS DAD WAS ONE OF THOSE WHO KIDNAPPED ME. PROBABLY RINGLEADER. She pulled up the plastic sheet covering the base of the "tablet", making her writing disappear, then began writing some more. HE'S SMART AND SENSITIVE. NOW PROBABLY MORE SCARED THAN EVER.

"*What should we do, then?*" Lee asked.

She was ready for that question. WHILE YOU'RE HUNTING ME, CHECK HIS BIRTH RECORDS IF YOU CAN. THERE'S ONLY ONE WAY I CAN THINK HE COULD DO THIS.

"*Absolutely true,*" he responded. "*I think I can take it from here, Honey. Now let me see my children.*"

She immediately recognized what he was doing: changing the subject both for their benefits and for Benji's. Since he hadn't repeated much of what she wrote on the slate, Benji couldn't deduce what she wrote, so now, at least, they had some privacy.

When she moved over to the babies, both were beginning to wake, arms moving, little fists trying to rub sleepy eyes, probably sensing dirty diapers. In a few minutes, they'd be completely awake, crying for attention, and hungry. As much as Lee wanted to see his wife nurse their children, he knew he had things to do, and couldn't wait around for all the cleanup and preparations to be completed.

"*I'm going to work on some things now, Verry,*" he said. "*But we made beautiful babies.*"

She smiled, but was becoming engrossed in caring for Dannice right then, and he was no longer getting much of her attention.

"*Love you, Verry. I'll be in touch tomorrow.*"

She nodded and he broke the connection, then let the plate lie flat on his knees and thought about what he'd just learned.

CHAPTER 43

Dangerous Game

Jeff Gerit opened the next company mail envelope in his IN basket and immediately felt the familiar terror build inside his chest. He even felt sweat start to break out on his forehead and in his palms—unmistakable warnings that he should stay away from the subject of the Kaalers and the Guardian and anything to do with them. *I have to put an end to this!* He decided to fight against fear and panic just long enough to complete this one remaining item from that part of his past.

Inside the envelope, as directed, were four names and addresses. He recognized each one. *Hate to do this to old "friends" but I've got to.*

He hurriedly wrote instructions to Donover, the man from Accounting who prepared the list, then put the sheet back in the envelope, crossed out his own name and office symbol, and wrote Donover's. *I just hope those guys are smart enough to leave well enough alone. They've got no idea what they're playing with.*

CHAPTER 44

Hiding in Plain Sight

Before leaving Sacramento, Lee changed his identity once more. He picked out the ID he used when driving from Boise to Des Moines on the way to his wedding. *This worked well enough to let me rent an RV and get to my wedding. It should work for the same thing now.*

Next he called Clem Maestre on his cell phone. When Clem answered, Lee said only, "Please rent me an RV in Sacramento, same as before. I'll call for specifics."

Leaving the hotel, Lee walked to the nearest bank, asked for the manager, and arranged for a funds transfer from one of his numbered Swiss bank accounts. He never gave the manager his name, hadn't shaved for two days, wore his dark sunglasses, and mostly wrote instructions, faking difficulty in speaking. The banker's first reaction was something Lee hadn't expected.

"Sir, I'm afraid I cannot accomplish this transfer until you show me a photo ID and remove your sunglasses so I can confirm you are the person pictured on it."

Lee had to smile, because that mistake was so elementary that he couldn't believe he'd forgotten about the amount of identification that might be required for a bank transfer, especially one in the amount he'd requested. "Of course, sir," he replied as he removed the offending glasses. "I forgot."

After that, the transfer went as Lee hoped. It was clear to him that the man would remember the process and the bank's fee much more than Lee's appearance.

After doing the same thing—correctly—at two more banks, Lee went to a pay phone and again called Clem. Finally convincing Clem's secretary to let him speak to Clem even though he refused to give his name, Clem came on the line.

"This is Clem Maestre," Clem said, in his smooth, calm voice.

Lee again wasted no time. "Got the specifics?"

Clem's voice quality immediately changed from smooth to business-like. "Yes. Want them now?"

"No," Lee said, "fax 'em." Giving Clem the fax number of the small drugstore from which he was making the call, Lee then said, "Thanks, friend. I'll fill you in later."

Two minutes later his fax printed out on the drugstore's fax machine. Paying the four dollars for the two pages, Lee thanked the manager, an attractive pharmacist in her mid-30s, and left.

An hour later, with $50,000 in his pockets, he was on the road to Fresno in a thirty-four foot motor home, luxurious beyond his belief. *Clem's smart. If the FBI and police are really looking for me, they won't expect me to arrive in anything so conspicuous.*

Six hours later, he arrived in Fresno, found an RV park, hooked up the vehicle, and paid a week's rent in advance. Then he took a taxi to Clovis.

CHAPTER 45

Yes, He's Angry

Benji was tired of playing with his dog, tired of not being able to share his concerns with his parents, and ready for some changes in his life. But at ten he couldn't think very deeply or see what he would need if he changed his life.

If I left home, I could go to Allen's house, but then his folks would call Momma and Dad and ask why I left, and I'd have to come back here. If I don't leave home, I stay here and worry about Dad going to prison for kidnapping Very—what a strange name! If that happened to Dad, where would Momma and I live? Would I have to quit school and go to work? What kind of work can a ten-year old kid get?

He didn't like where his thoughts took him, so he decided to talk to the only person who seemed interested in what he thought: the woman with the strange name.

When he came to the door to what was his bedroom, he noted it wasn't locked, then remembered his dad had told his friends to keep it unlocked, because the babies took so much care that it was stupid to keep it locked. Benji gently knocked on the door. Hearing nothing serious, he slowly pushed the door open and very carefully looked in, not wanting to bother either Very or her babies. He also knew that, if he saw her, her husband wouldn't be talking to her, because he couldn't hear words coming into his head.

She sat on the bed, her back leaning against pillows propped against the backboard, holding one of her babies. The room was very quiet, the silence only broken by the hum of the air conditioner and by some slurping sounds the baby made. As he moved to get a better view of Very and the baby, she saw him and smiled.

"Come on in, Benji," she said. "Dannice's just about done." As Verry spoke, the baby jumped, as if she was startled by something, then nuzzled against Verry's breast, resuming her meal.

Benji had never seen a woman nurse a baby before, but he'd heard women talk about it, and knew their breasts held the baby's milk. He'd never been this close to that process before, and he didn't know if he was supposed to be embarrassed, or what. Verry didn't seem to care what he saw, but she did keep Dannice's blanket over much of Dannice's face, so he didn't really see much except the side of Dannice's head and the swelling on Verry's chest. It was still a really neat scene, because she looked so happy, and the baby seemed to enjoy it, and—

He couldn't describe why it looked so neat, but he knew it was. He also believed he was one of the few kids he knew who had ever been this close to a nursing mother. *Except Molly. Her mom's had about six or seven kids, and she knows all about those things. Plus she's a girl.*

"Sit down, Benji," Verry said. "Dannice's done now." Saying that, she pulled the baby away from her breast and held her erect, head resting atop her shoulder. Then Verry very gently tapped on Dannice's back. In just a few seconds, Benji heard what was, to him, a monstrous burp. At first, he was embarrassed, but Verry held Dannice close to her face and said all kinds of sweet things that he could almost hear, but not quite. Then Verry pulled her robe closed and got off the bed, walked to the chest of drawers, and laid the baby down. She tapped the baby's back a few times more, then turned around, a smile glowing on her face.

"That's the best time," she said to him as she resumed her place on the bed. "There's a lot to raising a baby, and I only know a bit about it, but nursing them is just marvelous." She was quiet a few seconds, clearly thinking about something, and then her eyes began to water up. "I just wish Lee could be here to see it," she said, choking back more tears.

She wiped her face with her robe sleeve, and then said, "But you didn't come here to watch me cry, did you, Benji?"

Now what do I do? My problems aren't as big as hers at all. Why would she want to hear what I think? He was going to leave the room, but something made him decide to stay. Still, he hadn't said much at all yet.

She broke the silence. "Benji," she asked, "why haven't you asked more about the voice you heard inside your head? You know it's my husband talking to me because I told you that. But you haven't mentioned it at all since that first time. What do you think about it?"

He thought a minute, then said, "It's still scary, ma'am. I know your husband isn't mad at me. He's mad at my daddy, though."

Verry just nodded. After a few seconds to think about how to respond to Benji, she said, "Does that surprise you? That my husband is angry with your Daddy?"

Benji shook his head, but said nothing.

"What do you think my husband should do?"

He just looked at her, obviously afraid to say much.

"Come on, Benji. We both know what you heard Lee say to me, so you know that he's trying to find me. Is that what you'd do if someone kidnapped *your* Mommy?"

His mouth tightened into a straight line and he looked at the floor, clearly having thoughts about the subject but still unwilling to say anything.

Verry didn't miss the significance of his silence, and began talking again. "Let's talk about my babies. If you were a baby boy, growing up here in the Fresno area, what would you want to be when you grow up?"

An hour later, they were talking easily, sharing ideas, thinking, speaking without being judged. Benji had never had such a conversation before and found he liked it. Much later that day, when he was getting ready to sleep, he realized that "Very" was the first person to ever treat him like an adult. He knew he'd never forget it.

CHAPTER 46

Iced Tea and Questions

The door to the modest home in Clovis opened slowly and tentatively. A woman in her mid-fifties looked out, carefully sizing up the man standing on her small porch. He was slightly over six feet high, slender, had a dark mustache and dark brown hair, and carried what looked like a wooden attaché case.

"Yes?" she asked, her voice a bit cautious.

"Are you Doris Mooradian?" the man asked.

"I don't know you," she said warily, still keeping the door only partially open, her right foot solid against the door just in case that man tried to push it open.

"I'm Lee Kaaler."

Her eyes widened in both shocked surprise and pleasure. "Lee! Please come in." She pushed aside the screen door, and held both doors open.

His first impression of her home was neatness and cleanliness. Everything seemed to be exactly where it should be, and was spotless and dustless. The motif was American Southwest, the colors various earth tones, and the furniture mostly made of roughly turned posts and leather-like upholstery. In the center of the room was a Navajo rug, obviously receiving both great care and deserving of a place of honor: she probably spent what was, to her, a large amount of money for it.

The walls were decorated with small rugs and southwestern scenes: Grand Canyon, the Petrified Forest, Bryce Canyon, and photos of buffalo, pronghorns, and yucca cacti. A warm, friendly, pleasant place.

"Please sit, Lee." She pointed to a large chair facing the wall next to the front entrance. "That one is pretty comfortable." As he walked over to it, she asked, "Can I get you some iced tea? Coffee?"

All Lee could do was smile at the hospitality shown him. "Doris," he said, "I'd love a nice glass of iced tea, but please don't go to any pains on my account."

She flashed a quick smile and then stopped her motion towards the kitchen. "Lee, you're the most important person in the entire Kaaler family. The fact that almost no one outside of our family knows you even exist doesn't make this less an honor for me, so if I want to go to pains on your behalf, I will!" Another smile and she disappeared from his view.

Nothing I can do about it, so I might as well shut up and enjoy it. I still don't like it.

The last thought was more for his own benefit than anything else, because he began to suspect he'd receive this same type of treatment whenever he attended any Kaaler family meeting, no matter how big or small. Unless he could keep his role as Guardian a secret.

Doris returned carrying a silver tray with a gray-blue porcelain pitcher and two large glasses of the same color and design. Setting them down on the small, rustic coffee table directly in front of him, she poured his glass full of what appeared to be tea, and then poured herself one. She sat and then held up her glass in a small toast. "Welcome, Guardian. Welcome to my home."

Lee sipped the tea, finding it deliciously refreshing. "Fresh lemons?" he asked.

"Right," she said. "From my tree. I think it really improves the tea."

"You're right, Doris. It does." He took another long swallow, then put the glass down on a coaster woven like a Navajo rug, and looked up at her. "But I didn't come here for just a pleasant visit, Doris. You must know that."

Another quick smile. "I do. Nevertheless, I'm not going to let you spoil what is a thrill for me. Now that you've drunk some tea, the floor is yours."

He appreciated her candor, recognizing it, too, was a kind of compliment to him. "Tell me what you learned about Benjamin Snoyl."

CHAPTER 47

Too Loud

"I'm gettin' tired a this!" Barnaby yelled, pounding the shaky bar table to emphasize his frustration. Doug and Billy understood and agreed, but said nothing. They'd learned not to interrupt Barnaby when he was in one of these moods: just let him slowly wind down before even attempting to insert their own thoughts into the conversation.

Barnaby's pounding on the table got Jerrilee's attention. As the proprietor and only employee of the small rural bar, she'd known all three for years and knew their habits, likes and dislikes. Without bidding, she brought three more bottles of beer to the table. Barnaby and the others were so accustomed to this kind of service that they barely noticed her, so Barnaby continued his tirade without stopping to think about even keeping her from hearing what he said. "We bring this broad here, tell her husband what we want, 'n what happens? He says he don't know what we're talkin' 'bout, 'n then she drops twins!" Before continuing, he launched into a stream of invectives, and then said, "What more c'n happen?"

He stopped talking for just a moment, enough time to take several deep breaths and deep swallows of the cold beer Jerilee brought them. At that moment, Billy spoke. Slowly, his voice low, but his tone intense. "Barnaby, yer talkin' too loud."

Barnaby at first was angry, but before he said anything, Doug nodded his agreement. So seldom did either disagree with him, or challenge him, that Barnaby realized that—maybe—just maybe—they might be right. This once.

Chapter 48

Think Fast!

After leaving Doris' house, Lee taxied back to the RV. He considered it a marvel: the dining/living room expanded over two feet, instantly adding real living space instead of just room. It was fully carpeted, had oak cabinetry throughout, a TV and VCR in both the living room and bedroom, and excellent air conditioning. In the San Joaquin Valley in summer, AC wasn't a luxury.

Lee's favorite color was blue, but the RV's main color scheme was deep maroon. First, he thought it looked too "feminine"—not knowing exactly what he meant by that. However, after only a few hours, he found he liked the luxury that maroon seemed to convey, and the ways the designers had pulled every aspect of the design together around maroon.

He decided to contact Verry, but rather than start the contact by saying something, he simply thought about her, let her image appear in the center of the golden plate he held before him on his knees, and looked at the scene before him. It was the first time he'd really watched her nurse his child. It was such a special moment that he said nothing at all, but sat in silence in the upholstered chair in the RV's living room, tears running down his face.

After watching Verry nurse one of their children, then put it down in its drawer bed, Lee wiped the tears from his face, then spoke, very softly. "I'm here, Verry. That was wonderful!"

At first startled at the sound of his voice, she immediately smiled, then opened the bed table drawer and withdrew the Magic Slate so she could "talk" to him.

I LIKE IT, TOO, she wrote. WONDERFUL.

"You look good," he said "Must be getting more sleep, or eating well, or all of them."

ALL, she wrote. ROSE HELPS MUCH.

"Rose?"

BENJI'S MOM. WANTED 2ND CHILD. KEPT BENJI'S BABY CLOTHES. HUSBAND SAID NO MORE KIDS. OUR TWINS ARE WEARING THEM.

"His name?"

BARNABY. AND DOUG AND BILLY, AND JIMBO, I THINK. NO FAMILY NAMES.

Now we're making progress!

Knowing Benji could somehow hear what he said, Lee carefully chose his next words. "How's Benji? Last time we talked you said he was sensitive, smart and sad."

Verry looked up at where she thought Lee's "camera" might be, and smiled at him.

She knows I'm trying to get information about Benji without asking directly.

BETTER, she wrote DIFFERENT FROM STEPDAD. NOT AN ATHLETE—HIS DAD'S SOLE INTEREST. She swept her hand around the bedroom, reminding Lee that everything was decorated in Oakland Raiders logos and products. Then she pulled up the erasing sheet on her slate and resumed writing.

DAD'S IDEA OF A BOY'S ROOM. BENJI LIKES SCIENCE, ESP SPACE FLIGHT.

"Any personal background?"

NOT REALLY. ADOPTED WHEN A FEW MONTHS OLD. BIRTHDAY APRIL 6. DOESN'T KNOW BIRTH NAME.

"You seem much more relaxed, Verry."

TREATED MORE LIKE VISITOR THAN PRISONER. STILL CAN'T GET TO TELEPHONE. She looked up "at" Lee, then down at her slate. PROBLEM: I WAS KIDNAPPED. A FEDERAL CRIME, BUT DON'T WANT TO HURT ROSE AND BENJI. She "erased" the slate and resumed writing. I'D LIKE BARNABY AND HIS BUDDIES TO PAY A LOT, BUT SOMEHOW PRISON SEEMS WRONG.

"Stockholm Syndrome, Verry?"

She smiled at the reference, knowing she hadn't changed sides to support the kidnappers, yet recognizing she was no longer so desperate.

MORE LIKE COMPASSION.

"Do you know how close we are to each other?"

WE'VE GOT TWO KIDS! The words made it look like she was angry, but when she showed him the slate she was smiling.

"I'm acutely aware of that," Lee said, "but I meant in hours."

She shook her head.

"You start writing numbers. When you get to the right one, I'll tell you."

5, she wrote: he said nothing.

4. Silence.

3. More silence.

With each number that received no response from Lee, Verry felt excitement rise and, along with it, hope.

2. *Dear God! He's that close?*

1.

"*Stop.*" Lee thought at her.

Her eyes widened and began watering as she wrote, GET ME OUT OF HERE!

"Soon," he said. "But first I've got to think about things like the FBI and police and Barnaby and his friends."

She nodded once. THINK FAST!

Chapter 49

Who's We?

After talking with Verry, Lee left the RV and called T.K. again. "Can you come to Fresno—soon?"

"I think so, Lee. I'll have to take some vacation time, but that shouldn't be a problem." He thought a few moments, then asked, "Why? And why Fresno?"

Lee reviewed what he knew. "So," he said in conclusion, "I need someone to coordinate Kaaler help for Verry."

"What about the FBI? Won't they keep looking for Verry? And you?"

"Probably, but I can't control what they do. All I can do is try to stay out of their sight. One of the reasons I want you here is so that details won't tie me up.

"OK, Lee, we'll do it."

"We?"

"As short a time as we've been married, do you honestly think Drella would let me come to California alone?"

Chapter 50

All I Know

At noon the day after Barnaby finally realized he couldn't keep Verry locked up all the time, Benji paged her to come upstairs for lunch. She had been resting, a process which hadn't yet become easy. Or long enough.

After eating tuna fish and cheese sandwiches with sliced fresh tomatoes, then topping them off with BBQ-flavored potato chips and milk, Verry felt better. However, Benji looked nervous.

"What's wrong?" she asked. "You look like you're concerned about something."

He smiled shyly at her comment. "I didn't think you'd notice, Verry." Benji felt a bit uncomfortable calling a grownup woman by her first name, but Verry had insisted. In addition, she had shown him how to spell her name correctly: two Rs instead of one.

Verry slowly looked around the room, checking to see if anyone was listening. She saw no one, but didn't trust herself. "Can we talk freely?"

Without hesitation, he nodded. "Daddy's out in one of the cotton fields, and Mommy's asleep."

"Then I'd like you to tell me what you know about your birth parents. Anything at all."

His quizzical expression told Verry he didn't understand why she'd be interested, but he trusted her more than almost anyone, so he simply shrugged.

"My birth mom," he began, "was from the Mid-West someplace. My birth dad lived around here—somewhere. They put me up for adoption when I was about six weeks old. Something 'bout my mom's health, Mommy says. Dad said they weren't married and couldn't pay their bills." He frowned as he thought some more, and then added, "My mom went to college, but I don't know where. My dad worked on a farm. Or in somethin' related to farmin'. The papers were signed in Sacramento." He blinked a few times in thought, then said, "That's 'bout all I know."

CHAPTER 51

Humbling Help

When Lee returned to Doris Mooradian's home that evening, it didn't look like the same place he'd visited two nights earlier. Instead of the neat, clean, beautifully organized place he'd seen before, it looked more like an invasion target, or a messy command post staffed by eight people sitting around Doris' dining table. Every flat spot held a tablet, and to that tablet was attached a pencil held by the hand of someone Lee had never met. All held cell phones to their ears, and no sooner would they put them down than their phones would chirp again. It sounded like an aviary full of birds gone mad. "What's all of this, Doris?" he asked, sweeping his hand around the room. "Looks like a political fund-raising convocation." She took his hand and led him into the middle of her living room, from where they could better hear each other. "Who are these people?" he asked. "What're they doing?"

"They're all Kaalers," she responded. "Every one. They're trying to help find your wife and babies and their kidnappers." She looked him straight in the eyes. "They'll do whatever you need them to do."

"But," Lee said, "my brother-in-law called a bunch of Kaalers in this area, and you were the only one who gave any sign of being willing to help. What happened to change their minds?"

She couldn't hide her smile and, he noticed, several of the others openly smiled at his question. "Because," Doris said, "they didn't know your brother-in-law from Hogan's goat. But they knew *me*, and when I told them the Guardian needed help, they came." She turned back toward the people in her dining room and smiled back at them. "I didn't get halfway through my list of Kaalers until I had as many as my place could hold." She turned back to him. "And here they are."

He looked around again, noticing a sudden drop in the noise level as they turned to look at him. "This is very humbling. I don't know how to thank you."

"Don't try," she said. "We're enjoying this—most exciting thing most of us have ever done."

Lee took a few steps toward the dining room, and saw more of the same, except there were two men interspersed among six women operating cell phones.

"*Two* men?"

Doris's face turned grim. "Seems most of 'em weren't interested in doing family tree things—that's what we called this when we tried to get help."

She turned back to look at him. "One thing's for sure, Lee. The next Kaaler family reunion will be something else!" Her smile was contagious. The women around her, who were listening to the conversation as much as they could over the phone calls they were taking, also broke into smiles. A few added, "Right on!" and similar expressions.

"I'm more than pleased, Doris. But there's one thing T.K., my brother-in-law, forgot to tell you—an important thing." His smiled dissolved into a serious expression: mouth straight, brows slightly wrinkled, eyes locked on hers.

With his sudden change of mien, Doris' eyes widened in surprise, then concern. "Have I done something wrong? I thought I was *helping*."

"You *are*, Doris. More than I could have imagined. It's just that I wanted to keep my identity as Guardian as much of a secret as possible, but now all of these people know I'm it." He then realized all the talking had ceased and everyone was looking at him. *I've got to tell them more than I planned. Brackafrass!*

He made a sweeping gesture towards the people seated around the dining table, indicating they were to join him and Doris in the living room. When all were seated on the sofa, chairs and on the floor, he moved to stand in front of the TV set and began speaking. "Can I trust you to keep secret everything I tell you now?" Before they all began nodding, he added, "What I'm going to tell you is a Kaaler family secret, just as secret as the Challenge." His audience stopped nodding and sat still, eyes now fixed on him. "Will all of you promise to honor this? It's vital that you do."

A few exchanged glances before doing anything else, but in a few seconds everyone in the room had nodded or spoken their agreement.

"Thank you. Now listen to what I have to say and tell *no one*, even spouses. Can you do that?"

The room remained silent. Everyone, including Doris, again nodded to indicate their willingness to cooperate with Lee.

He then told of the attacks made on him, Verry, and their friends just because someone *suspected* he was the Guardian, and included the death of

Verry's best friend. When he finished, he said, "I don't want *anyone*, including you and your families, to be objects of such threats and fear as I have been. One way to prevent this from ever happening again is to tell no one who the Kaaler Guardian is—even if they are Kaalers." He stopped, nodded once as if to put a period at the end of his words, then said, "Understand?"

In unison, everyone else in the room nodded their concurrence.

He broke into a smile. "Good. Then let's all get back to work." Just as they began moving, he added, "And thanks for your support."

When they had returned to the dining room, Lee returned his attention solely to Doris. "So tell me," he said, bringing the visit back to the subject at hand, "what's all of this getting us?"

Doris noticed his concern and responded quickly. "First, we've located Barnaby Snoyl's house." Lee's heart leaped up, but before he could ask, Doris continued. "The doctor who delivered Verry's babies is Jeremy Snoyl, Barnaby Snoyl's nephew. He's an OB in one of the local hospitals." Anticipating Lee's next question, she held up her hand to cut off his question. "I already told you there was no such place as 'Fresno Caring Community Hospital'."

He nodded impatiently; she continued.

"This Dr. Snoyl is apparently a really funny guy, a jokester, and somehow the idea of 'Fresno Caring Community Hospital' arose some time ago—as a joke. So he and his team had their surgical pajamas stenciled with that false logo to wear when they work together."

"How'd you find him?"

"Birth registration. One of our gals checked birth records in Fresno County for the past two weeks and found those he signed. Went from there."

"How 'bout finding Barnaby Snoyl's place?"

"He's listed in the phone book; got his address there. Then we checked for the Kaaler nearest his place and found Jerrilee Perez—her grandmother's maiden name was Kaaler, but Jerrilee doesn't carry it. Asked Jerrilee for her help and got it. She turned toward the dining room and gestured toward a slim, Hispanic-looking woman, who rose and approached them.

"This is Jerrilee Perez, Lee." They shook hands while Doris continued her report. "She runs a bar west of town. Jerrilee," Doris said to the woman, "tell Lee what you heard."

Jerrilee described the conversation between Barnaby and his friends when they talked about taking a woman who subsequently had twins, how distressed Barnaby was about the whole thing, and then how he shut up when his friends warned him to stop talking about something like that.

"So," Doris said, "we're sure he's the right guy and your wife and the kids are at his place." For the first time in the report, she smiled. "One more thing. The Snoyl's have a son named Benjamin. Goes by 'Benji.'"

Lee looked closely at Doris, partly because he was surprised, partly because she seemed so happy, partly because his mind was turning very fast. He continued looking at her until it was obvious she was becoming nervous about his lack of response to what she thought was good news.

"What's wrong, Lee? Did I make some kind of mistake?"

He shook his head quickly back and forth. "No. Not at all. I'm a bit overwhelmed by what you and your friends have accomplished in just a few days. Plus I've been thinking about what I can do to help Verry now that we know so much more." He looked away from her, his eyes blinking from heavy thought. After several seconds, his eyes cleared, his blinking stopped, and he looked directly at her. "Do you have any friend who actually *knows* Benji Snoyl?"

Now Doris lapsed into momentary deep thought. Then, "I'm not certain. Why?"

"Because, if you do, or if you can find someone who is *absolutely trustworthy*, we might be able to get something to Verry that will make things a lot easier for everyone."

CHAPTER 52

It's Empty

Early evening, Lee returned to his RV and, immediately after a light, microwaved supper, went to bed early. Just after he had fallen asleep, his cellphone chirped. He was sleeping so soundly he had difficulty clearing his mind enough to recognize the unfamiliar and unexpected sound as his borrowed cellphone. After a few groggy seconds to clear his mind, he picked it up, flipped it open, and slowly said, "Hello."

"Lee, this is Doris."

"Yeah, Doris," he said, his tongue feeling large and clumsy. He was so sleepy he didn't sit up in his bed to answer the call, but stayed on his back, holding the telephone in his right hand, covering his eyes with his left. "I'm sorta awake now. What's up?"

"I sent a friend to Barnaby Snoyl's place to make certain we had the right house—things like that. It's the right house, but the lights are out and there's absolutely no one there."

CHAPTER 53

The Hunt

What Barnaby never realized was that, if Lee knew what he looked like, there was no way, wherever he was, that Barnaby could hide from The Guardian. When Lee finally woke enough to think rationally, however, that was what *he* realized.

It was not yet dawn, but Lee was still wide awake. Out of habit, he wore his short, light blue, cotton pajamas with their loose, pullover top. They were comfortable and usually helped him relax, but what Doris and her friends had already learned about the Snoyls kept him awake. On his lap now lay the golden plate. Checking the time, Lee prepared himself to search for his wife. *It's still dark around here—only five o'clock, so I won't be able to see much. In addition, I'll probably wake that boy Benji if he's with Verry and the kids. But I can't wait.*

*   *   *

Barnaby was tired of worrying about taking care of two screaming kids, a woman who had completely taken control of his lifestyle just by dropping a couple of kids, and a wife who was more interested in those kids than in fixing his meals. It was taking so long to get that Kaaler guy to come across with whatever power thing he had, that Barnaby was beginning to worry abut someone becoming suspicious about never seeing Rose any more, or how Benji seemed to stay at home a lot more than normal for summer vacations. He decided to do something different, something he controlled completely.

What better time to take a fam'ly 'n "guests" to see the great outdoors than late summer? Barnaby thought, chuckling to himself. *Fresh air, bootiful stuff ta see, 'n no way fe'r anyone to find us!* He raged into his living room and yelled,

"Come on! We're going to have some family fun!" Even as he said it, he knew the family wouldn't have as much fun as he would.

It took over two hours for Rose and Benji to get clothes packed, get out the sleeping bags, pick up the broad's baby stuff, and pack it all into his van. Once everyone was finally in, and in spite of how much the babies screamed, he sped away from the house and down the bumpy gravel road toward the highways leading to the foothills of the Sierras. In addition, the more the babies screamed, and the more Rose asked him to slow down, the faster he drove. After several hours of aiming his car east, he found the road he sought and turned off the pavement onto an old logging road full of holes and bumps, but leading to a hunters' cabin where he could finally be in charge of his own life, and where no one could find them.

A particularly rough patch in the gravel road, the Suburban still twisting and turning, interrupted his self-congratulations as they headed further north and east and away from Fresno. In the background he could hear the twins squalling as they bounced back and forth, adding to their discomfort from lack of sleep. To help calm them, Verry held Daniel and Rose held Dannice, but the road was so bumpy it was a losing cause. Barnaby didn't care, but everyone else, including Benji, did. He was holding on to the handhold by the front door of their vehicle, glancing at his dad between bumps and swerves. Barnaby was driving as fast as he dared over the barely-improved road, thoroughly enjoying himself. For the first time since they kidnapped Verry, everyone was under *his* control. It was his kind of heaven.

Chapter 54

Listen Carefully

When Lee looked into the golden plate and the initial colored vortex of cloudiness faded away, he thought he was riding a roller coaster. He could see Verry, but she was bouncing up and down and back and forth so much it nearly made him sick just to see it. Then the motion stopped and she let her head drop back against the headrest—*Head rest? She's in a car!*

Rather than say anything then, he pulled his view back a bit and so he could better see what was happening. Verry held one of their children, obviously crying loudly, its little face deformed by its discomfort and, probably, exhaustion, hunger, and dirty diapers. She sat next to a Hispanic woman holding another baby, also squalling and moving about, unquestionably for the same reasons.

Pulling his view back even farther, Lee could see the entire car in the dim early morning light. The driver's door swung open and a man stepped out. Caucasian, late thirties, strong, dark hair, coarse features, denim pants, wide leather belt. He appeared simultaneously tired, angry, and smug.

What a strange combination! Lee thought, still watching the man he expected, one day, to teach a very big lesson. The man looked around, as if checking his surroundings.

The other front door opened and a boy emerged. Blond, slender, slightly awkward. Tired, his cheeks streaked from tears and dust, also looking around, checking where he was. The older man said something, apparently sharply, because the boy's head snapped around to look at the man, then he nodded and moved to the back of the vehicle, pulling down the tailgate and releasing a large dog that joyously jumped out. He then began pulling out sleeping bags and small overnight bags, setting them on the ground. Behind them, still inside the car, Lee could see boxes, apparently food. While the boy did his chores,

Verry and the other woman got out of the car and moved away. Verry had to go around the car to join the other woman, each carrying one baby.

Lee then turned his view around, and saw a grey-weathered cabin beneath the large trees surrounding the area. *I'll bet Snoyl believes no one can find them there.* He thought some more. *And he's right. Just because I can see Verry doesn't mean I know where she is.*

Verry and the woman—Rose?—entered the cabin, went directly to a small bedroom, put the babies down on the bare mattress and began changing the babies' diapers and wet clothes. Once they cleaned the babies, the Hispanic woman closed the door and Verry sat back on the bed, unfastened her blouse, extracted her swollen breasts from her nursing bra and began nursing both babies. She lay back against the backboard, holding one baby in each arm, letting her head sink back against the top of the rustic rail at the top of the headboard, tears beginning to slide down her cheeks.

Tired and depressed. Maybe I can help lift some of that. "Verry," he called to her in his mind, "*I'm here.*"

Her eyes instantly flew open, and then she seemed to remember Rose was also in the room, and merely nodded very gently. Mostly, her actions seemed designed to keep Rose from noticing anything unusual. *However,* Lee remembered, *she could also be trying not to upset the babies any more.*

"*Do you know where you are?*"

Her head shook slightly.

"*Do you have even a general idea?*"

A nod.

"*I'll name direction, you nod when I hit the right one. They're all from Fresno.*"

Another nod, and a slight smile began to crease her face.

"*North?*"

No reaction.

"*South?*"

Same result.

"*East?*"

Slight nod.

"*That puts you in the foothills of the Sierra Nevadas, East of Fresno.*"

Another nod, this one slightly more definite than the others.

"*That's all I can think to ask you.*"

Another nod.

Then a new thought struck Lee sharply. *Verry, do you think Benji knows where you are?*

A slight shrug, then she looked to her left and said something to Rose. From the manner in which they moved their lips and looked intently at each other,

Lee felt they were whispering. After about a minute of that, Verry mouthed the words, "Thank you," then closed her eyes and nodded just a bit.

Lee decided to try something that, until that day, he'd have considered impossible.

"Benji," he thought while still looking at Verry, *"If you hear me, please knock on the door to the room where your Mom and Verry are and ask if they need any help."*

Verry's eyes opened wide as she realized Lee was talking to *Benji*, not her. Neither Lee nor Verry said anything, waiting, hoping, then doubting the experiment worked. A few seconds later, someone knocked on the bedroom door.

At the sound of those knocks, Verry's eyes snapped toward her left. Recovering slightly, she said nothing, but merely smiled.

Thanks, Benji," Lee said to the boy.

Verry began bouncing on the bed slightly, then she looked to her left.

"Is Rose going to the door?"

One slight shake of Verry's head.

"Is she talking to Benji?"

Another nod.

Verry then said something to Rose, a smile on her face. Lee pulled his view back a bit. The Hispanic woman reached down beside the bed and picked up her purse.

"Good girl, Verry! You asked to see a picture of Benji."

Nodding only slightly, Verry smiled just a bit.

Rose retrieved a small photo album, flipped past several pages, then held it up for Verry to see.

"Have her hold it closer, Verry. I need to see his photo clearly."

Verry said something, then Rose moved closer to her, holding the photo about a foot and a half from Verry's face, right in Lee's vision.

"Got it! That's confirms who Benji is. I was pretty certain when I saw him get out of the car, but I didn't want to make a mistake and scare someone else when they heard my voice."

As Verry was talking to Rose, Lee stopped concentrating on Verry and thought about the boy in the photo. The image in the golden plate clouded again, then that boy's face, slightly older than in the photo, and considerably more unkempt, filled the image.

"Benji," Lee directed his thought at the boy, *"can you hear me? If so, just nod."*

A sudden look of terror flashed across Benji's face when he recognized Lee could see him. Then that expression disappeared, replaced by a shy smile, and he nodded.

"Wonderful. Before I go any further, Benji, I want you to know how much I appreciate how nice you've been to Verry and our babies."

Benji nodded once, then looked across the room, clearly afraid of something.

"Is your dad in the room with you?"

Benji nodded, smiled, and pointed to his left.

Lee's first thought when he saw the boy act that way, *I think he's having fun.* Then, to Benji, *"Do you know where you are?"*

A definite nod.

"Could you point it out on a map, or write it on a piece of paper or something, so I could read it?"

The boy looked around the room idly, not seeing, but thinking. A smile, then another nod. He made a fist, extended his pointer finger, and then wrote in the dust on the table Lee just realized Benji was sitting at. SHAVER LAKE.

Lee noted the name. *"That's the nearest town?"*

Benji nodded.

"Is it very big?"

Benji looked confused, frowning in his effort to understand Lee's question.

"Benji, this is important If there's a doctor there, I think I can do something to find all of you. I just want you to try to remember if you ever saw a doctor's office, or a hospital, or a clinic, or—"

At the word "clinic," Benji's face lit up, he smiled broadly, and nodded vigorously.

"Terrific, Benji! Now listen carefully, because I don't want you to be surprised or to misunderstand what's going to happen soon."

Chapter 55

Unexpected Excitement

Lee shifted his attention from the image in the golden plate to important things right in Fresno. Again the used the borrowed cell phone. "Doris, this is Lee."

"Hi, there! Any word on Verry?"

"I think we can find her," he said, unwilling to reveal anything about the golden plate and its powers. "Right now I've got some things working."

"Anything I can help you with?"

"Yes, as a matter of fact. I need photos of Barnaby Snoyl's closest friends, Doug and Billy. Don't know their family names."

"We're working on it, Lee. Jerrilee knows 'em. She's checking to see if her bar has any pictures of them taken at parties there. With luck we'll know later today."

"I need to know as soon as possible after you get them. It's very important to this whole thing."

"OK, I'll tell her. Anything else?"

"Yes. Heard anything from T.K. Pajaro yet?"

"He's the guy from Omaha, right?"

"Right. What've you got?"

"He called. Said they'll be here tonight. Route 66 Motel on Blackthorn."

"Leave a message for him to call me on my cell phone when he gets in."

"Done. That it?"

"That and my undying appreciation for your help."

"Don't even think like that. I haven't had this much excitement in decades."

CHAPTER 56

Fix Your Own

"Rose!" Barnaby yelled through the closed door to the bedroom where she, Verry and the babies were sleeping. "Get up! 'S lunch time."

At his voice, the babies immediately woke and resumed the crying they'd been doing for most of the time since they arrived at the cabin. Both women and Benji had been up almost all night; Barnaby slept on the couch in the small living room.

Rose and Verry exchanged angry glances, then Rose got up from the bed and went to the door. Opening it just a few inches, she looked up at her husband and glared at him. "We've been taking care of babies ever since we got to this filthy place, Barnaby, and you've been snoring away out there. Fix your own lunch and let us rest!"

Before he could say anything, she shut the door in his face.

CHAPTER 57

Checking with FarCaller

It was noon the day after Barnaby took Rose, Benji, Verry and the twins to the mountains, and Lee was back in the RV for privacy, thinking about how to help Verry. Unfortunately, there were too many variables to allow him to even get a feel for what might happen. *This is so darned frustrating! I'm so tied up using the golden plate that I forgot about my first weapon—the spoon Grandma willed me that started this whole Guardian thing. It's why I'm the Guardian. If I had half a brain, I'd be dangerous.*

He took the spoon out of his shirt pocket, caressed it just a bit, then held it in front of him, looked into it, and called FarCaller.

"I'm here, Lee," FarCaller said. "About Verry and your children, tell me."

"They're still with their kidnapper, FarCaller," Lee began, "but I've been in contact with Verry almost the entire time."

"How is that possible? Another silver plate like mine there is?" His voice confirmed the confusion coloring his facial expression.

"Not that I know of." Lee then reviewed the story of the golden plate and spoon set given him by the doctor who treated Verry in Des Moines, and how he'd learned to use it both as a weapon and as a way to communicate with Verry. FarCaller listened in amazement.

After Lee stopped his story, FarCaller just looked at him. "Never would I have imagined such a thing." He thought a bit more, then his face brightened. "Now, why you *really* called, tell me."

"I need to know what you Sense in my future, FarCaller. Things are happening so fast I need every bit of help I can get."

Saying nothing, FarCaller put his hand on the silver plate mounted on the wall next to his fireplace, and closed his eyes. After only a few moments, he opened them and earnestly looked up at Lee's image. "In great danger are you if, where you are, you stay. Two men, with those small weapons that like goat horns look, your house on wheels approaching, saw I."

CHAPTER 58

Flee!

Panic was something Lee had heard and read much about, and even caused it in others when he used his golden plate as a weapon. Until this latest warning from FarCaller, he had never before experienced panic. *The biggest problem: I don't know who my enemy is. Barnaby Snoyl's friends? With guns? Or maybe the FBI or police. How do I fight them, for Heaven's sake?*

As he fretted about his possible confrontation with armed men, he was already acting. He ran out of the RV and disconnected the water and electric hookups. Then he closed all the valves from the gray and black water holding tanks, leaving the connecting hose on the ground. Running back into the RV, he made no effort to clean up the sink or put loose things back into their storage spots, he just started the engine and put the vehicle in gear. As soon as it was running, he headed out of the RV park, intent only on getting away from the threat FarCaller warned him about.

I hope FarCaller's view of my future didn't start from the moment he told me about it. If it did, my efforts to get out of this place are doomed to failure. Worse, if I don't succeed, any chances for anyone else to find and rescue Verry and our kids will almost certainly fail; no one else in the world has any idea where they are.

CHAPTER 59

Certifiable

Lee drove through and around Fresno for several hours after fleeing the RV park, not really knowing where to go or what to do. He knew he had to do one thing as soon as possible: change where and how he was living. One stroke of luck made his search easier: he found an RV consignment lot just south of town. Betting that there'd be no one there so late at night, he parked his RV as close as he could to one of the used RVs at the back of the lot, then shut everything down, including the air conditioning, and tried to rest. He was thoroughly surprised when he woke up about six a.m. and realized he'd actually slept.

He immediately drove to a lot that would accept an RV they hadn't rented, turned it in, and paid the fee for the lost water and sewer hoses and driving the RV back to where he rented it. He then packed his few belongings, including the golden plate and its counterpart spoon, into a black garbage bag. No longer wearing his false mustache but now sporting the start of a real goatee, he took a taxi to Doris' house in Clovis, arriving just as Jerrilee Perez was walking down the porch steps.

Lee was surprised to see her, but neither she nor Doris expected to see him at that hour, especially looking so harried. Once seated at the dining table, Lee began talking seriously. "I've already told you about Verry's kidnapping, and Jerrilee and your other friends know about the babies and our need to find them quickly and quietly."

Doris nodded, aware that something even more serious was at hand.

Lee took a large bite out of the fresh-basked frosted cinnamon roll that Doris gave him, having forgotten that he'd not eaten breakfast. He was suddenly ravenously hungry but unable, out of courtesy, to eat as much or a fast as his body was demanding. After quickly chewing the tasty chunk he'd nearly torn off the bun, he washed it down with a large gulp of the piping hot coffee and resumed his tale. "I need some more help, but a different kind, I'm afraid."

Doris simply said, "Just ask."

He looked at her, a new friend deeply and willingly involved in his life and this crisis, offering help however he needed it, no questions asked. His eyes immediately filled with tears of joy compounded by a feeling of humility: it was hard for him to accept that he had earned such loyalty. "Now," he said, going to the crux of his visit that morning, "you know I haven't contacted the FBI or any other police agency on this because they'd want to know what I have that would make someone kidnap my wife. You don't know what it is, but you'd accept it. If I told *them*, they'd think I was certifiably crazy. However, if I don't contact them, I'm breaking federal law. So, if they can prove the latter, I could go to jail whether Verry and my kids are found or not." When he stopped, the room was silent except for the nearly continuous background hum of the air conditioner.

Finally Doris spoke. "So what do you need, Guardian?"

From that Lee recognized that she not only believed him, she was awestruck. *This is not the time to tell her not to call me that.*

"First," he said, starting down his needs list, "I need a safe place to stay." Before she could offer him her home, which was what he expected, Lee said, "It must be safe, away from family members, but easy to get to and from." Again speaking before she could respond, he said, "Next, I need to know where Doug and Billy are. Not because I'm going to meet them, but because I'm going to scare them to death, and I don't want anyone to see it happen." His voice was now low, determined, and intense. "Third, I need a cell phone that can't be traced to any Kaaler, and I need it right away. Last, I need a private room, Doris, so I can do some things that I can't let anyone see—Guardian things."

Doris blinked several times, obviously thinking hard about what she'd just learned. "You can use my guest room. It's safe and private." Thinking more, she added, "Jerrilee should be able to find Doug and Billy and keep me posted on their whereabouts." Another moment of thought, then, "A neighbor of mine bought a cell phone to use when she travels, in case of accidents or things like that, and doesn't use it at all otherwise. I'll borrow it."

He couldn't restrain the need to smile at how quickly this solved his "problem." "That'll work well, because if anyone tried to trace calls from her number, none would point to me. Be sure to tell her we'll pay all the costs we run up."

"I'll tell her, but she won't care. They were insurance poor when her husband died. She got his jewelry business and a whole pot full of money."

Lee's expression quickly turned grim. "OK, it's a deal. Now please show me the guest room."

CHAPTER 60

Not Missionaries

Clem Maestre had seen and worked with criminals and police long enough to be able to recognize a law officer in a split second. That happened when three strangers entered his office. The two men wore dark gray suits, white shirts, and dark maroon ties. They were both above average height, with athletic bodies and serious expressions. The woman was dressed in a suit of gray pinstripe wool, white blouse, yellow bow. Her shoes were black pumps with one-inch heels so she could run if she had to, yet still look like a businesswoman when walking. She carried a large black leather purse with a shoulder strap and large gold-plated buckle. Clem guessed she was no more than five feet three. And armed.

Definitely not missionaries. Probably FBI sending three agents on some kind of power play. He decided not to play their game, so he quietly watched as they entered his private office and responded to his gesture to be seated. *Trying to bluff me.*

"Now, Agents," he said, opening the meeting by showing them he wouldn't play their game, "what can Ah do for y'all? Surely y'all don't need legal advice." Clem was smiling, but knew his guests wouldn't share the humor.

The woman responded for all three. "Mister Maestre, do you know a man named Faerleigh Kaaler?"

"Ma'am," Clem responded, "do y'all have identification? Ah'll not answer *any* questions about mah practice unless Ah know who y'all are and am satisfied that Ah should answer y'all."

"Of course," she said. With a quick nod, she opened her purse and retrieved one of the familiar black badge and ID cases. Her compatriots retrieved theirs from their left shirt breast pockets, and all three held them out for Clem's review.

"Let me see," he said, coming out from behind his desk and checking each badge against its holder, "ya'll are FBI Special Agents Darlene Schneider, William Manser, and George Williams. Is that correct?"

Three nods; no words.

Clem returned to his chair. sat down, and leaned forward on his elbows, hands together in front of him. "The answer to yoah question, Agent Schneider, is 'yes.' Lee Kaaler is both a client and a good friend, but Ah expect y'all already know that."

She ignored his inference about their research on Lee, and referred to a small notepad she kept in her coat pocket.

Something's wrong here, Clem thought. *This is too much like an old movie.*

"When," she began, "did you last see him?"

"Ma'am," Clem responded, "is he the target of an investigation? If so, Ah must remind y'all of attorney/client privilege. If not, y'all need to tell me what this is *really* about."

His visitors shared another quick glance, then she began again, but Agent Schneider's attitude seemed to have softened. "We have reason to believe Mister Kaaler's wife was kidnapped," she began, "and that he is trying on his own to find and recover her. Do you know anything about this, Mister Maestre?"

Clem liked many things about the practice of law, and knew that successful lawyers had to be able to think on their feet and to debate well. He was not in a courtroom facing these three, but it helped to think of this confrontation as a kind of trial. Except there was no judge interrupting things when the exchanges became really interesting.

"Ah knew Lee was out of town. Ah don't know if he is with Verry or not."

"Verry?" Agent Manser, the tallest visitor, asked.

"His wife, Vera. She goes by 'Verry'."

"And you don't know where she is." This question came from the third agent, Williams.

"Ah don't know where *either* of them are. But that's the norm. Lee doesn't keep me informed of his whereabouts unless there's some special reason to do so. So far as Ah know, this is not one of those times."

It was a lie, but the attorney/client privilege prevented Clem from telling the agents that Lee told him Verry had been kidnapped—and what advice he gave to Lee when told that. If and when Lee released him from that restriction, he could answer such questions without resorting to rationalizations.

No one spoke for a few seconds, then Agent Schneider said, "Mister Maestre, are you aware of the penalties for withholding information from government agents involved in a major investigation?"

Now the threats finally come! "Yes, ma'am," Clem said, his face calm, his pleasant smile locked in place. "But Ah don't know that this is a 'major' investigation and, even if Ah did, if Lee told me anything about a kidnapping and Ah learned it in my role as his attorney, there is no way Ah would violate the attorney/client privilege by telling y'all anything Lee told me on that matter. Y'all know full well that doing such a thing could get me disbarred—at the very least."

He looked at his "guests" and decided to end all of their misery.

"Let me do this, Agent Schneider. If and when Lee next calls me—and Ah assure you Ah have no idea when that might be, Ah will discuss this matter with him. If he has any information regarding a kidnapping of Verry or anyone else, or if there is an attempt on his part to try to find those kidnappers without cooperation from appropriate authorities, Ah will strongly recommend he tell y'all anything he knows about any such matters. But, you understand, Ah cannot force him to do anathing."

From the expressions on the faces of the three FBI agents, it was clear the meeting had concluded.

CHAPTER 61

Wanted Pics

Just after Lee went to the guest room, a knocking at her front door surprised Doris. One reason was that almost all visitors used her doorbell; the other was the visitor herself. When Doris opened the door and saw the caller, her eyes opened wide and her mouth dropped open. "Jerrilee! I didn't expect you so early, especially since you left here about eleven last night. Come on in!"

The day was still in its infancy, but it was already hot. Jerrilee wore her usual summer outfit: shorts and a tank top, accompanied by sandals. Today all were in pale yellow, accented by a ring of yellow ribbon holding her ponytail in place. With her medium dark complexion and bright red lipstick, she was just a few points less than gorgeous. Doris, however, wore pink pajamas covered by her favorite short-sleeved cotton robe, light pink with small flowers. Her sun-bleached hair was quickly brushed into place, her feet bare. "What brings you here so early?"

As they talked, they moved into Doris's dining room. Jerrilee sat while Doris went on into the kitchen and made both of them some instant coffee. Once settled, Jerrilee responded.

"I kept thinking about Lee's request for a photo of Barnaby, Doug and Billy—although I really don't understand why he'd want one."

Doris said nothing, but sipped her coffee and waved for Jerrilee to continue. *I'm not going to comment on what the Guardian does,* she thought, and then returned her attention to her friend.

"I looked through several boxes of photos we have of parties 'n' stuff, but couldn't find pics of either of them." A quick shake of her head: as if she thought herself stupid about something. "Then," she went on, smiling, "I remembered where they were." Now she looked up from her coffee and straight into Doris' eyes, a rueful expression on her face. "On the back wall of the bar. I had some pictures framed of a party for the last Cinco de Mayo, and Doug and Billy were in one of them, along with their buddy, Jimbo—don't know their last names. They were all juiced up, all wearing sombreros—having a good time."

She reached into her small, black purse and withdrew a rolled up photo. Pushing it across the table to Doris, she said, "Give this to Lee when you can. I really don't see how it can help him, but he's more than welcome to it. When I get back to the bar, I'll try to find a shot of Barnaby,"

CHAPTER 62

Shooting Barnaby

As soon as he entered Doris' guest room, Lee closed the door and retrieved the golden plate from his backtrack. He sat on the bed, put the golden plate on his knees, looked into it, and thought about Verry. He found her in the small bedroom he'd seen before, holding one of the babies, clearly having problems.

Verry, I'm here.

Her shoulders slumped, as if she had just been relieved of a great burden. She didn't try to say anything, but looked up at where she thought he might be and put her hand on the baby's forehead, then quickly picked it up, as if it were too hot to touch. Her message was crystal clear: the baby had a high fever.

She then turned to her left and looked at Rose, who was holding the other baby, a wash rag in her hand, washing the howling baby's face, also trying to fight the fever.

I understand. The baby's have fevers. Do you have any medicine for them?

She slowly but definitely shook her head back and forth.

You've told Barnaby?

Her face instantly reflected anger, and she gave a quick, almost nasty, nod.

And you're still there! Isn't he going to take you to the clinic?

For the first time in her life, he saw her look hateful.

OK, then let's see what I can do.

He changed his interest from her to Benji, and Benji's face suddenly appeared in the middle of the plate. He appeared to be outside, walking among the trees. Alone.

Benji, did you hear what I said to Verry?

The young man jumped a bit when he heard Lee say his name, then he smiled shyly.

You also remember I told you I might do something to convince your dad about some things?

Again he nodded, this time not so happily.

Well, Benji, I'm about to do just that. Stay away from the cabin for about fifteen minutes, and then go back. Your dad will have a bad stomachache—or something like that—by then, but I can make it go away. Just don't be surprised, and don't tell him I'm responsible? OK?

Benji's face was serious, but he nodded.

One more thing, Benji. If you hadn't told me about the clinic, those babies might get very, very sick. So I thank you for that. And I also want you to insist, to your mother, that the babies and their mother go to the clinic with your dad. Will you do that for me?

The boy nodded again, now walking among the trees.

You're a courageous young man. When we get the chance to meet, I'll thank you personally. Goodbye for now.

Benji nodded, then Lee changed his focus to Barnaby Snoyl.

When that man's face appeared in the center of the golden plate, it was obvious that he was outside, sitting at a table, smoking a cigarette and drinking a beer.

At ten in the morning? Lee thought. *That's not good for you, Mister Snoyl.*

Summoning his dislike for the man, Lee thought about a burning arrow and visualized it plunging into the man's beer gut. Almost instantly, Snoyl doubled over in pain, nearly falling from the chair, his cigarette and bottle of beer falling to the ground. From his facial expression, it was clear he was moaning and groaning, then he turned his head and apparently yelled the word, "Rose!" A few seconds later his wife appeared in Lee's view, seeing her husband falling over onto the porch in pain. She yelled at him and held her hand out for something. *She probably wants the car keys. Doubt he'd trust her with them after taking her into the boonies without any warning.*

He saw the man painfully reach into his pocket, retrieve the keys, and reluctantly hold them up so Rose could take them. Then she yelled something, and a short time later Benji ran up to her, looked at his father, paled quickly, and then looked around, as if trying to find Lee.

Rose said something else to her husband. He violently shook his head, and then Benji joined in the argument.

They're about to convince the man he needs to get the babies to the clinic.

Seeing Barnaby continue to shake his head back and forth, Lee shot another of his hateful arrows into the man's body, this time at his chest. Snoyl rolled over onto his back and held both arms against his chest.

Rose didn't let up her arguing, and Snoyl then nodded. She immediately turned and ran into the cabin.

Thanks, Benji. I'll talk to you in the clinic. And your dad will be OK. To himself, he added, *For now.*

CHAPTER 63

Cooperation?

Two normal days had passed since the FBI agents had visited Clem, but he knew enough about their practices to expect another contact soon. A telephone ring interrupted his thoughts on that subject. "Mister Maestre?" It was a familiar woman's voice—an unwelcome one.

"Yes, Agent Schneider. What can Ah do for y'all?"

She went directly to the point, no niceties, no pleasantries. "Have you had any contact with Mister Kaaler since we last spoke?"

Something's up! "No ma'am. Ah still don't know wheah he is, and he hasn't called me since y'all were heah. Why do you ask?"

"We believe he is in central California, or at least heading in that direction. I was hoping you might be able to help us. You'll remember that we're concerned that he may be interfering with FBI business."

As if I could ever forget! "Ah truly haven't see or heard from him, Agent. Nevertheless, be assuahed that, if and when we do have contact, Ah'll pass yoah words to him. As Ah said when you werah heah, he's both a good client and a close friend. Ah don't want him to get into trouble any moah than you want to expend resoahces on tryin' to find him."

"We appreciate you understanding, Mister Maestre."

The lined clicked off before Clem could even say good-by. *Ah'll just bet y'all do*

130

CHAPTER 64

Are You Kidding, Counselor?

After "talking" to Benji, Lee returned to the dining room, where Doris was talking on the telephone. She gave Lee a quick, small wave, continuing her conversation. Soon it was apparent she was talking to Jerrilee Perez. Much of what Lee heard was simply friends talking, not related to Verry's kidnapping. But just before hanging up, Doris said, "Wonderful! Just bring it over here as soon as you can."

As she pressed the STOP button on her cordless phone, she gave Lee a big smile. "This morning, Jerrilee found a photo of three of Barnaby's closest buddies—Doug and Billy, whom you asked for, and another, Jimbo. I don't think you know about him, Lee. Big guy, farm hand, does rodeo for fun. Good friend of Barnaby's. Wouldn't be surprised if he's part of this whole mess."

At the word "rodeo", Doris got Lee's full attention.

"Does he do bronco busting, perhaps?"

Doris looked astonished. "You know him?"

"Never met any of them, but one of the guys guarding Verry was tall, strong, and wore a Western belt with a buckle having words about bronco busting—in 1988. Maybe that's this guy Jimbo."

Doris looked at him for a few moments, saying nothing, obviously thinking. Then she asked, "How'd you know about this guy and bronco busting, Lee? With the possible exception of Jerrilee, I don't know anyone who could possibly know that."

"I can't tell you, Doris. Sorry, but it has to be that way."

Doris waved her hand, as if dismissing the whole subject. "Shouldn't have asked."

"No problem at all, Doris."

Still smiling, she handed Lee another photo. "This is the a photo of Barnaby's buddies. She just told me she found one of Barnaby and will bring it over in a bit."

"I'll thank her next time I see her." As he took the photographs from Doris, he said, "Were you able to get the cell phone I need?"

Her smile returned. Darting into the kitchen, she returned carrying a black cell phone wrapped in its charging cord. Handing it to him, she said, "Use it all you want. My friend says you can have it except when she goes on vacations, and that's not until Christmas."

It was Lee's turn to smile. He flipped open the instrument and started punching a telephone number onto the keypad. The call was answered in two rings.

"Clem? This is Lee."

His friend immediately began talking fast—for him, but Lee cut him off. "You know that cell phone I had you get for me? The one I've never used?"

A quick "Yes".

"I'll call you on it in one minute."

Before Clem could say anything, Lee broke the connection.

Lee's next call was answered after one ring.

"Lee? Where are y'all? Ah've been worried."

"Not to worry, Clem. I'm in Fresno with friends, and this cell phone isn't registered to anyone who knows me. However, before you say anything more, I want you to leave your office and talk from the sidewalk or parking lot. If the FBI is really serious about trying to find me—or us—they might bug your phone, or office, or both."

From Clem's silence, Lee concluded two things: Clem was having trouble believing the FBI would do anything like that on a "feeling" there was a kidnapping, and he would do as Lee asked.

"OK," came Clem's voice after about ten seconds, "Ah'm out in the summer heat, watching traffic drive along the Division Street bypass. Now, Lee, please tell me what's going on."

Thirty minutes later, Clem returned to his office, retrieved a business card from a large chrome paper clip on his desk, and then dialed the number printed on it. His call was answered after one ring.

"Agent Schneider, this is Clem Maestre, in Bend, Oregon. Y'all asked me to call if Ah had anathing which might related to the matter we discussed, remember?"

"Of course," was the businesslike response. "Does this mean you've heard from Mister Kaaler?"

"Yes'm. Just now. He's in the Fresno, California area, and his wife is not with him. He told me he in fact *has* done some checking around, and believes he has the name of a man who might give y'all some help on this." Clem paused momentarily, then added—as if an afterthought, "Oh, yes! He said his wife *was* kidnapped, as you suspected, and that one of the men who took her contacted him. They demanded a ransom, but it wasn't money, and they couldn't describe what they really wanted."

"Are you serious, Mister Maestre? Kidnappers who wouldn't define their ransom demand? You expect me to believe that?"

"It's absolutely true, Agent Schneider. Lee said he offered them money, but they said they wanted something else. Lee's really concerned, because if they won't tell him what they want, there's no way he can get Verry—and her newborn son and daughter—back."

"She has new twins?" Now she paused, and then continued. "You're stretching your credibility and my gullibility, Counselor." It was not merely a statement, it was a clear and scarcely disguised warning.

"Agent Schneider," Clem said, using his most honest-sounding tone of voice, "Ah know better than to lie to the FBI. What Ah told y'all is absolutely what Lee told me, and Ah've known him long enough and well enough to believe him. In all honesty, Ah said many of the same things to him. But he not only insists he's telling the truth, he sounds a bit desperate." Clem stretched the truth only slightly: Lee was exasperated, tired, frustrated, *and* a bit desperate.

"Very well, Mister Maestre," the agent said, "I'll take your word for all of this. But if it's not true—" She left the sentence unfinished; the conclusion obvious to both of them.

"Ah understand," Clem said. Then, almost innocently, he asked, "Do y'all want the name of the contact that Lee gave me?"

"Of course! Now that he's stopped playing policeman, it's about time we got something useful." She made no attempt to hide her belief that Clem knew all along that Verry was kidnapped and Lee had been trying, on his own, to get her back.

"The person Lee said would know who these men might be is Jefferson Gerit. He lives, or lived, in the San Francisco area."

"Of the Pharmaceuticals Gerits?" Agent Schneider now made no attempt to hide her feelings. This was pure astonishment. "You've got to be kidding!"

"Quite the contrary, Ah assure y'all. Jefferson Gerit knows these men and, Lee thinks, hired them to do some work in the Bend area a couple of yeahs ago. In fact, Lee believes they learned about him *from* Jefferson Gerit."

Now Clem went on the offensive, something he'd been longing to do ever since Agent Schneider and her two subalterns came into his office. "Agent

Schneider, Lee and Ah are fully cooperating with the FBI. He has confirmed his wife was kidnapped and he was contacted about a ransom. He has given y'all the name of a man whom Lee believes knows the men Lee thinks kidnapped his wife, and even told y'all wheah they might be found. I'd say, Agent Schneider, that the ball is in yoah court."

CHAPTER 65

Send a Message

From the events following his first attack on Barnaby Snoyl, Lee learned a lesson that would stay with him the rest of his life: never start something you can't stop or control.

Knowing the drive from Snoyl's cabin into the small town would be hard on everyone, especially his children, Lee thought it might be a good thing to lessen Snoyl's pain—applying mercy. Therefore, as everyone got into the Suburban, Lee used the golden plate to ease Snoyl's discomfort.

Rose was in the driver's seat, Barnaby in the front passenger seat. In the back seats were Verry and Benji, each holding a thoroughly miserable baby. The second Lee made some of Snoyl's pain abate, which was just before Rose put the car in gear, Snoyl opened his door and got out.

"Gettin' better, now," he announced, a slight victorious tone in his voice. "We're not goin'."

Verry couldn't believe her ears. Lifting the screaming Dannice up so Snoyl couldn't miss what she was talking about, Verry yelled at him, "What about my babies?"

He started walking around the car toward the driver's door, apparently to retrieve the keys from Rose. "They'll be OK," he announced, as if he were in control of their pain. "Now git out!"

Why, you selfish slob! Lee thought to himself, watching this episode take place. *You don't care about anyone or anything else!* Letting his growing dislike for the man feed the energy he was going to direct against him, Lee pointed another "arrow" at the man, this one aimed at his testicles. Watching Snoyl grab his groin then again collapse to the ground again, Lee lessened that pain a bit and added more to the man's chest.

Like it or not, Barnaby *Snoyl, you're taking my family to the doctor!*

Then, remembering Benji, fearing the effect on him of seeing his father in such misery, and his knowing, almost certainly, that Lee caused it, Lee concentrated on the young man. The image in the plate blurred slightly, but didn't disappear in clouds and then reappear. Then Benji's worried face filled the screen.

Benji, Lee said to the boy, *your dad's going to be OK. But I can't let him hurt those two babies. When you are all at the clinic, and a doctor has treated those babies, your dad's pain will ease and he'll feel a lot better.*

Then Lee changed his concentration to Verry, and her tired, drawn and worried face appeared. *I'll be in and out of touch with you all morning, but when you get to the clinic I'll stay there until you're satisfied with the kids' treatment.*

Again she nodded, her expression now calmer.

If you can, he continued, *try to get a message out regarding how you got there in the first place.*

This time her smile was broader, and she winked.

Chapter 66

No Escape

Rather than watch the trip all the way from the cabin to Shaver Lake, Lee lay back on his bed, put the golden plate beneath the unused pillow on his bed, and tried to relax. The next thing he knew, he snapped awake, felt a momentary panic attack from being in an unfamiliar room, then realized he'd fallen asleep and, just as quickly, regained his orientation and thought about Verry and his kids. Retrieving the golden plate from beneath a pillow where he stored it, Lee sat on the edge of the bed and looked directly into it. He concentrated on Verry and, almost immediately, her face appeared. She was in a bright room, looking down at something. Lee pulled the view back and then understood. She and their children were in an examining room, and she was watching a woman doctor examine one of the twins.

Verry looked both tired and relieved, but was paying extremely close attention to what was happening. After a few minutes, the doctor said something. Verry nodded, then moved away from the table. Before Lee could change the view, Verry reappeared holding the second child, still crying loudly, its face red, arms flailing about. The doctor, an older woman—gray-haired, slightly overweight, with a kind but concerned expression—took the baby from Verry, held it up to her shoulder and patted its back. A very short time later, the baby did something that, from the expression on both adults' faces, was probably a large burp. The doctor seemed pleased, then said something more to Verry, who was now smiling. She laid the baby down on the examining table, removed the diaper, and pushed with two fingers on the area just above the pubic bone. The little girl suddenly urinated on the doctor's hand, which she had held down as a shield against that very reaction.

While she wiped off both the baby and her hand, Lee directed his thoughts at his wife.

Verry, I'm here.

Again, her immediate reaction was one of surprise, then she smiled and nodded.

Are the kids OK?

A slight nod, accompanied by raising her hand to her throat and squeezing slightly.

Sore throat?

The same nod.

Stomach ache? Gas?

The nod, this time quickly done.

Serious?

Two quick head shakes.

Before Lee could say anything more, the doctor began speaking, and Verry turned her full attention to her. As the doctor spoke, she gestured slightly, once touching her throat, once her abdomen. She then said something else, and Verry began re-diapering Dannice, leaning over her, putting her face close to Dannice's, and smiling and talking, obviously attempting to reassure her daughter.

It was then that Lee realized there had to be a third person in the room—someone to hold Daniel. Again shifting his view around the room, he saw Benji sitting on one of the chairs, carefully holding the still-crying Daniel. Benji looked decidedly uneasy in this role, but was trying to do whatever he could for the little person he held.

Thanks, Benji. I really appreciate you doing this. Now I'm going to look in on your dad.

A quick envisioning of Barnaby's face, the plate blurred, turned cloudy, then the man's face appeared, looking straight up. Lee pulled his view back and saw that the man who kidnapped his wife was lying on an examination table. A male doctor was listening to Barnaby's heart with stethoscope, clearly concentrating very hard on what he heard. He said nothing, but moved the instrument around Barnaby's chest, listening more, eyes flitting back and forth, looking at nothing in particular.

Lee's first thought was to let the man suffer more, then he realized that Barnaby was also going to have to pay for his own examination as well as that for the twins, plus whatever medicines they needed.

I really don't want to add to this man's financial troubles, because it'll hurt Rose and Benji—they don't deserve more misery. His decision pretty well made for him, Lee aimed a thought at the man's chest, gently relieving the pain he had inflicted. He then did the same for Barnaby's groin—trying to keep some pain there, but not the disabling level the man was suffering.

Barnaby said something to the doctor, and then tried to get up. Surprisingly, the doctor pushed Barnaby back onto the examining table, said something quite sharp to the bigger and stronger man, and shifted his efforts to palpating Barnaby's abdomen. When that was done, he said something more, and Barnaby sat up and pointed toward something. The doctor then handed Barnaby a white tee shirt with the Oakland Raider black and silver logo in the middle of its front, and a red cotton short-sleeved shirt that Barnaby had been wearing.

While Barnaby put his shirts back on, the doctor sat down at the small desk and began writing on a prescription pad, all the while talking to Barnaby. The kidnapper said little, but clearly listened to the doctor, then got down from the table and reached out for the prescriptions, which the doctor handed him, an exasperated look on his face.

Barnaby said something else, apparently asking a question, and the doctor pointed out the door and then to the right.

He's going to look for Verry!

Shifting his thoughts back to his wife, the image on the plate clouded, then cleared. Verry was no longer in the examining room, but walking down a hall. She held one baby; Benji was next to her holding the other. Once into a bigger room, Verry went directly to a window marked "Pharmacy" and slipped two prescription forms across the counter to a woman about her age. The woman smiled at the two babies, made some comment that seemed sympathetic and understanding, then turned away from Verry and disappeared from Lee's view.

While the woman was out of sight, Verry picked up a pencil, pulled a small pad of paper toward her, and frantically began writing with her right hand, holding Dannice with her left.

Good, Verry. Give them something to help find you and the kids.

She nodded and continued writing. Just as she was completing what she was writing, a large hand clamped down over hers, and then a second pulled the pad from beneath her hand.

Lee pulled the view back and saw what he least wanted. The hand belonged to Barnaby Snoyl, and as he tore off the page containing Verry's note, he verbally lashed out at her. Then he grabbed her right arm and began pulling Verry away from the Pharmacy service window. Verry, now protesting, pulled her arm out of his grasp just as the pharmacist returned, holding two bottles of medicine, one red and one green. Grabbing the medicines, Verry yelled something Lee couldn't read from how her lips formed the words. Barnaby shouted something at her, then at the pharmacist, grabbed Verry's arm again and pointed to his head, moving his index finger in a circle. The message: that woman is crazy.

When Barnaby did that, Lee lost his self-control. Dislike for Barnaby Snoyl overcame logic, and he felt himself mentally punch the man in his stomach. Then, before his eyes, Barnaby's eyeballs glazed over and rolled up into their sockets, he doubled up, and fell to the floor.

CHAPTER 67

I'm Taking Daniel

Verry couldn't believe what happened and how fast it took place. When Barnaby grabbed her arm and took the note she'd written about her kidnapping, she thought all was lost. Then he rolled into a ball and fell to the floor, helpless. With that, her hopes again rose to the point where she could visualize freedom.

Suddenly, Rose gave Verry little Daniel to hold, which, combined with the crying and fidgeting Dannice, effectively paralyzed the new mother. While Verry tried to find some way to control and care for both babies at the same time, Rose and Benji helped Barnaby to his shaky feet. Then Rose put Barnaby's left arm around her shoulder and began walking him toward the clinic exit. Benji came to Verry, a thoroughly distressed expression on his face, and pulled one of her arms. Verry found herself having no options. If she tried to stay in the clinic, Benji could pull her arm enough to cause her to drop Daniel.

As Benji led her out the door, Verry began speaking loudly, quickly, and intensely. "Benji, you're making a big mistake. Helping your mom and dad keep me and my babies like this makes you part of their crime." She was so intent on how the situation had changed so suddenly that she missed a step, caught her foot on a small curb at the edge of a median strip in the parking lot, and began to fall. Benji's firm grasp on her arm prevented her from falling down and hurting the babies, but kept them moving toward the station wagon. When she fully regained her balance, Verry continued her efforts to get Benji's cooperation. "Benji, you've got to listen to me! You could go to reform school for this!"

She knew Benji could hear her, but he gave no sign he did or, if he did, that he cared about what she was saying. Her frustration so consumed her that she didn't realize they had reached the car.

Rose had already put Barnaby in the passenger's seat and was waiting for Benji so she could help Benji and Verry. Benji said nothing, but didn't let go of Verry's arm.

The first thing Rose did was to take Daniel from Verry and put him in the front seat, between her and Barnaby. Then she calmly started the motor and put the car into gear. Before letting up on the brake pedal, she looked across the car and out the right rear passenger door at Verry. "Come or stay, Verry. But I'm taking my husband, Benji and Daniel, with or without you and Dannice."

CHAPTER 68

Heart Pain

Jeff Gerit didn't want to lose the power he enjoyed as head of his people searching for the Guardian because every day was exciting, new, and challenging. It also let him party often, meet influential people, and date beautiful women. Then two things messed up his good deal. First, just when his people were about to capture Mister Faerleigh Kaaler, the man they believed was the Guardian, just when that man's power spoon was within reach, something awful and mysterious happened to both him and his dad. For no reason either could understand, whenever they even *thought* about the Guardian, immobilizing onsets of fear, panic, and terror struck them.

Secondly, they quickly learned that they had to immerse themselves deeply in other projects so they could concentrate on subjects in no way related to their hunt for the Guardian.

Then, recently, one of his dad's long-time girlfriends called Jeff's dad from Oregon and reported details of unauthorized Gerit activity in Bend, where Kaaler lived. Jeff absolutely believed that her call and the resultant pain from the memories it invoked, combined with his father's poor health, killed his father.

Jeff was now CEO of the company his father founded and built; a job Jeff worked years to avoid, and now lived in Chicago, a town he didn't like. With his Dad's death and the unexpected return of so many things reminding him of the Guardian and his powers, Jeff needed something to consume nearly every waking minute. That had worked for almost two years—until now, because he was about to meet some FBI agents. They didn't tell him the reason for their visit, but he believed it involved the Guardian. That thought, by itself, was enough to create chest pains and the onset of panic.

Chapter 69

Back from Freedom

Immediately after causing Barnaby's collapse, Lee thought the situation was under control and Verry and their children would be free. However, Rose's actions completely surprised him so much he didn't try to stop her. He therefore found himself helplessly watching his family pulled back from the edge of freedom and on their return to the woods.

Then he realized something about the Guardian's powers, something that made him smile—for the first time in what seemed a month: *I can stop them from going back to that cabin.*

*　　*　　*

Verry was in a minor state of shock from what just happened to her and to Barnaby, and now from Rose's sudden change in attitude. She sat in the back seat of the old Suburban, holding Dannice. For the first time in nearly a day, both babies were asleep, almost certainly because of the shots the doctor in Shaver Lake gave them. "Rose," she asked, "why are you doing this? I could probably have protected you from the punishment your husband's going to receive for kidnapping me. But now you're part of it. That means you'll possibly go to prison, too." As she spoke, Verry had to lean to her left and look into the rear view mirror so she could see Rose's face, a pretty face now dark with determination.

Daniel still lay on the front seat, sleeping. Barnaby sat next to him, doubled over, occasionally moaning. Since they'd left the clinic, he'd not voiced a single coherent word.

"He's my husband," Rose said, mouth still set, determination painting her voice, her fists holding on to the steering wheel so hard her knuckles were white from the effort. "I won't abandon him."

"If both of you go to prison, Rose, you'll have to." Verry kept her voice pleasant but insistent. Her goal was to convince Rose, not anger the clearly frightened woman. Then Verry added, "And who'll the court give Benji to while you're behind bars, Rose? Who'll raise him? Who'll go to his high school graduation, and send him off to college? It won't be you and Barnaby."

Rose's jaw muscles clenched and unclenched, but she said nothing. When Verry turned to look at Benji, she saw a frightened and confused boy—not a young man, his face now pale with fear, his hands held tightly together between his knees, his head down, eyes teary.

During the pause after Verry's attempt to convince Rose to change her mind, Rose slowed the car, preparing to make a right turn onto the narrow road leading to their cabin. As Rose began to turn the steering wheel, she suddenly cried out in pain, quickly stopping the car and grabbing her right elbow with her left hand.

When the car stopped, no one spoke. Even Barnaby now suddenly awake and alert, looked up, around, and then at Rose. She was bent over the steering wheel, teeth clenched in pain, holding her right arm close against her body as if doing so would relieve her pain.

In the midst of this sudden, frightening moment of pain, Verry heard something familiar and comforting, even though the words weren't.

Verry, tell Rose to drive straight ahead. Once she passes that turnoff, the pain will go away. Before Verry could say anything, Lee added, *And, Benji, say nothing at all! Do you understand?* Lee's voice was not the calming, loving, concerned voice both Verry and Benji had associated with this contact. This voice was serious and threatening.

Verry quickly glanced at Benji. He was now sitting erect, eyes wide in sudden realization that someone very powerful had threatened him. Looking back at Verry, his face still tear-streaked and ashen, he nodded twice.

Good! Now, Verry, tell Rose what I said. I'll be watching everything she does. If she tries any more tricks, she'll be hurt. And if Barnaby tries to interfere, he'll learn a lot more about pain.

CHAPTER 70

Revenge

The more Verry talked, the angrier Barnaby became. What at first was a distraction had become the center of his thoughts, and the initial dislike he felt for Kaaler's wife had become a festering sore that he couldn't treat. Now, with the pain he felt and the pain inflicted on Rose, he was beyond his limits.

One thought kept inserting itself into his mind, wedging itself through the pain and frustration her presence had placed in his life: *Get Kaaler.* As they drove down the highway, Rose being unable to turn off the road toward their cabin, and he finding himself unable to get out of his seat, let alone drive anywhere, his thoughts began crystallizing. He found himself starting to think straight.

First, he envisioned what had to happen and then where. When he had thought this through, he felt he'd come up with the best plan of his life. And it had to be, because what he intended to do to Kaaler's wife had to be something he believed Kaaler couldn't trace back to him.

CHAPTER 71

A "Nice" Threat

Jeff Gerit didn't know what to expect of his first meeting with the FBI, but this somehow fit the stereotype. Three agents, rather than two, one of them a woman, all well-groomed and dressed in gray business suits, all serious. None appeared threatening, but their mere presence constituted a threat—especially if he was guilty. *But I'm not, so they're after information.*

Terror and dread surround him like a soft robe; close enough to touch, but far away enough so that he didn't feel uncomfortable. Not directly. *This has something to do with Kaaler. Has to. Barnaby and his stupid cowboy buddies did something!*

After introductions and a minimum of small talk, the senior agent began. "Mister Gerit, we've received information that you have some former employees in the area of Fresno California."

Jeff could feel the level of dread rising and, with it, the beginning of abdominal and chest pain. *Gotta keep control! Can't show 'em anything about this. If I tell them everything, maybe they'll go away and I'll never have to think about Kaalers again.* "Yes, ma'am," he began. "They did some work for me a couple of years ago. I've not had any contact with them since."

She looked at her fellow agent, then back at Jeff. "None?"

"No, ma'am."

"Can I ask why you broke off contact with them?"

Bad question, lady! The thoughts that arose from hearing that question increased Jeff's pain level. By sheer force of will, he held it back enough to be able to remain sitting erect instead of doubling over, and to think clearly rather than not at all. "We—my father and I—decided to discontinue our project in Bend, Oregon—where we sent Barnaby Snoyl and some others. After that, we sent them back to their homes." His forehead felt cold and sweaty, but Jeff didn't want to wipe it off. *I probably look guilty already; don't want to make it worse.*

From her lower right coat pocket, Agent Schneider withdrew her note pad and began writing. After having Jeff spell out the man's name, she continued with her line of questioning. "You mentioned some 'others,' presumably friends of this man Snoyl. Do you remember their names?"

"Doug, Billy and Jimbo. I never knew their last names."

All three agents wrote them down, then Agent Williams asked, "Any more ex employees from the Fresno area?"

"I don't remember," Jeff responded, "but I don't think so. You can check with the Accounting Department on that, if you wish. They'll have whatever information we held on those guys. You're welcome to it."

"Is there anything more you think we might need to know about Snoyl and the others?"

Get out of here! Jeff thought. Then, "Yes, as a matter of fact. Barnaby's not very smart, so he usually reacts emotionally when stressed out, rather than with his brain. I'd hate to have him hurt because your people didn't understand that about him." Another thought slapped his brain. *I should have asked this first.* "Agent Schneider," he said, continuing, "you haven't told me why you're interested in Barnaby. Is he in serious trouble? Or is this part of an investigation of someone else?"

She looked at her compatriots, then back at Jeff. "This involves him directly, we believe, Mister Gerit. And, yes, it is serious."

"Can you tell me what kind?"

"Possible kidnapping," she said, her eyes looking directly into his.

At those words, Jeff's growing pain and dread overcame his commons sense, and he blurted out, "He kidnapped Kaaler?" Then he realized what he'd said, and how it probably looked to his visitors.

It got their attention, clear from their sudden change of interest level from "normal" to "intense."

"No," Agent Schneider said, "not Mister Kaaler. His wife." She looked down while she wrote something on her pad. Returning her attention to Jeff, she said, "Why did you think it might be Mister Kaaler?"

Jeff slowly drank from his ever-present glass of ice water on his desk, trying to gain time to reestablish control over his mind and body, fighting off the pain and terror that always accompanied thoughts about Kaaler. When he replaced the glass on its crystal coaster, he could again speak calmly. "Because we thought Kaaler had taken something that rightly belonged to us," he lied. "When it was clear that wasn't the case, we ended our project there. Snoyl was one of our key men and didn't want to give up when we told him to."

Agent Williams spoke up then. "If he wasn't very smart, why did you make him one of your key men? Seems that might not have been in your best interest."

"Because," Jeff said quietly, "he'd do what we told him and almost nothing else. And he could control his buddies. Whenever he got ideas about how to 'improve' things, they were inevitably incomplete and usually stupid, so we didn't let him use his imagination at all." *And that's the God's truth!*

By the time his visitors left his office, Jeff was nearly unable to retain any semblance of control over his fear and pain. As his secretary closed his office door behind the guests, he sat down in his chair and then fell forward onto his desk, his stomach churning and his forehead and upper body sweating profusely.

On their way out the doors and down the steps of the skyscraper that held the headquarters of Gerit Pharmaceuticals, Agent Schneider quietly said, "I'd like to know what made Kaaler such a target."

Meantime, Jeff Gerit was barely able to pull his wastebasket out from under his desk in time to catch the fluids and solid remnants of his lunch spewing out of his stomach.

CHAPTER 72

APB

Deputy Sheriff Dawn Carrson tore the fax off the machine and gave it a quick scan: an FBI bulletin on a possible kidnapping. This one, however, differed from all the others Dawn had seen because it *really* involved Fresno County. She took it to the senior dispatcher in the control center, handing it to him without comment. Since she usually made some kind of remark about whatever message she brought, it made him read it more closely than he normally would.

Like all experienced law officers, he looked first to find the sender's name, then at the address list, and finally the subject and text of the message. Just as with Dawn, he was surprised to find it directly affected Fresno County and his own office.

"Know this guy Snoyl, Dawn?"

She simply shook her head.

"Ever heard of him?"

Same reaction.

"How many men do you think it'll take to keep this guy under continuous surveillance and not be seen?" It was a rhetorical question; both knew exactly what resources were required.

"Four or five each from both us and the Fresno police," she responded. "Three to keep him in sight, and at least one to supervise the recon, keep track of the people watching him, log their reports, send them to the FBI—that kind of stuff." She smiled at him, raising her eyebrows as a question. The meaning: "How'd I do?"

He smiled back and nodded acceptance of her answer.

"So," she countered, "who're you going to take off regular patrol to try to find and watch Snoyl, wherever he is?"

He answered with a smile. "I have absolutely no idea, but I'll do it right away!"

CHAPTER 73

What's He Look Like?

It took Rose barely five minutes to realize she was being "herded" back to Fresno. Every time she tried to turn off the highway, the excruciating pain returned. When she stayed on the main road, no matter how it turned, she had no pain. The things she most believed about the cause of her pain: it seemed magical, evil, or simply inexplicable. In all three cases, it was frightening. She wasn't thinking only about the cause of her pain and who was behind it. As she drove down the highway toward Fresno, she was making a very important decision. The worst part was that it would anger her husband so much she couldn't even guess how he would react.

Cries from little Daniel interrupted her thoughts. He'd slept for several hours, so he was wet, hungry, or both.

"Benji, please take Daniel and help Verry care for him." Her eyes didn't leave the road, but putting Daniel in the back seat helped her find a way to implement her idea.

As Benji picked up the fussy baby, Verry put Dannice down on the seat, and then took Daniel when Benji handed him to her. She said nothing to the boy, but smiled in thanks and laid Daniel down on her lap, supporting him between her thighs. As she pulled up Daniel's little gown and began removing his diaper, Benji surprised her by handing her a clean one without being asked. "Thanks, Benji. That was a big help."

He shyly smiled back, but closely watched Verry. In all the time Verry and her twins were prisoners at his house, he'd never seen her change a diaper, and the process fascinated him, especially because it took so little time. When Daniel's diaper was changed and his little suit snapped shut, Verry gently put him to her breast. Right after that, Benji heard a slurping sound. Once Daniel was nursing well, Verry leaned over him, kissing his head and murmuring things Benji couldn't understand but which sounded loving and reassuring.

The idea of "reassuring" made Benji realize, for almost the first time, the stress Verry had been under. *My Daddy actually took Verry away from her home. Then he brought her to our home in a van, and then locked her up in my bedroom—like a jail.* He again looked at Verry. She continued murmuring things to Daniel, occasionally caressing the top of his head and his cheeks. As before, it generated another distressing thought for Benji: *There's no one to make* her *feel better. My daddy took her away from her husband.*

Benji knew he was different from most people he knew and very different from his Daddy. Now he began to understand more about why this was so: *He's not really my Daddy. Someone else was my daddy: I was adopted.* A correlating thought then came over him, almost like a revelation: *Is that why I hear that voice in my head but my Mommy and Daddy can't?* Then another question: *I wonder what that man Lee looks like.*

CHAPTER 74

Drop the APB?

It was now clear to Agent Schneider and her team that Lee Kaaler had been the target of a *real* conspiracy, not an imaginary one. "But," she said to her two agents, "I haven't seen anything to tell us what Jeff Gerit and his dad thought was valuable enough for them to spend all that money to try to get."

"And then," Agent Mancer added, "suddenly give up their search and everything it cost."

"So what do we have?" the third agent—George Williams—asked. Before the others could reply, he began answering his own question. Holding up his right index finger, he began. "His wife was kidnapped." The second finger extended and he said, "He didn't report it right away—that's not a crime."

Holding up three fingers, he continued, the others comparing his conclusions with their own. "Then he went to California." Now a touch of uncertainty colored his voice. "I don't know why, for certain, but it was probably because of the trouble Gerit's people caused him a couple of years earlier. He'd learned they worked for Jeff Gerit, and Gerit was in California, so—"

"But in the Bay area," Agent Schneider interjected. "Gerit lived in San Francisco, but Kaaler went to Fresno."

"And he did it cautiously," Agent Mancer said. "We could probably prove he used false IDs getting here—that's a crime, but he's a victim. Makes no sense to push that on him." He looked at their supervisor. "Don't you agree?"

She nodded, and then shifted her attention back to Bill Mancer. "Go ahead, Bill. This helps a lot."

The youngest agent resumed his summary, certain now that everyone was listening and cooperating. Holding up four fingers, he said, "For some reason,

Kaaler went to Fresno in this search of his wife. From there he called his lawyer, told him what was happening, and told him to call us."

"I still think the lawyer knew about the kidnapping earlier," Agent Schneider said, "but we can't prove it."

"But," Agent Williams said, "we do know that Kaaler is a pretty careful guy. Remember," he reminded the others, "he wouldn't talk to his lawyer over the lawyer's office phone line—at least once. Then, when he did, it was a pretty sterile report."

"Almost rehearsed," Darlene Schneider commented.

Two nods in response.

"Now," Agent Williams said, "we've got a good line on the guy Gerit fingered, plus three of his buddies. All of 'em were out of town when someone kidnapped Missus Kaaler, and then they reappeared here a couple of days later. That was enough time to fly to near her home Oregon, rent a car, and then drive her to Fresno from there."

Before anyone could interrupt him again, Bill Mancer held up his right hand, all fingers splayed, plus his left index finger. "And shortly after that Missus Kaaler has twins in a Fresno hospital."

"So she's there," Agent Schneider said, "and Kaaler's there, the Snoyl's live just outside Fresno—everything's pointing to Fresno and them."

Agent Schneider nodded. "Kaaler's not doing anything to hurt our investigation and we know he wasn't part of the kidnapping. Let's cancel the bulletin on him."

CHAPTER 75

Still Prisoners

Lee spent almost the entire day in Doris's guest bedroom, eyes glued to his golden plate, guarding against any attempt by Rose to take Verry and the kids off the most direct path back to Fresno. Helping him was the fact that Rose was a quick learner: it didn't take many attacks on her arm for her to conclude why she was being hurt. Since the first half-hour's drive out of Shaver Lake, she'd made no other attempts to take the car anywhere except toward Fresno.

Occasionally, Doris would knock on the bedroom door, stick her head in to check on Lee, and occasionally bring him a glass of lemonade. Once she brought an open-face sandwich of lettuce, shredded carrots and cabbage, cucumbers, alfalfa sprouts, mushrooms and thousand island dressing. The dressing, like the bread, was homemade by Doris.

Lee's attention, however, remained fixed on getting his wife and children back to Fresno, where he had a better chance to find them. Right now Verry was either asleep or resting, her head leaning back against the headrest, eyes closed, breathing slow and relaxed. Both babies were also sleeping: Dannice on Verry's lap and Daniel on the seat between Verry and Benji. If Lee didn't know better, he would have thought the scene was peaceful. The appearances belied reality: Verry and the kids were still prisoners, and Lee still hadn't found a way to rescue them.

CHAPTER 76

Two More

It was getting late in the afternoon. They had driven out of the forests that marked the uninhabited parts of the Sierra Nevada foothills, and the road was now significantly straighter. It had fewer right turns—less chance of the pain recurring. Rose, however, wasn't thinking about anything related to that. Her mind consumed itself with trying to concoct a way to implement her idea without telegraphing her intent.

The problem she saw was that her husband noticed nearly everything she did, even though he often didn't say much until sometimes days or weeks later, when he was angry with her for something she just did. She had to preplan everything so, whenever she had the opportunity to make her move, nothing leading up to it would appear unusual.

Right now Barnaby appeared to be asleep, but he wasn't snoring: that told her that he was still awake. Benji, in his seat behind Barnaby, was leaning against the door, eyes closed, breathing slowly: almost certainly asleep.

Rose couldn't see Verry in her rearview mirror, but it was so quiet she knew both babies were sleeping. Verry, at the least, was resting, taking advantage of every chance to escape the pressures of tending to her babies.

Just two more hours, Rose thought. *Please!*

CHAPTER 77

No Common Sense

It was getting well toward nightfall, but the heat in the Valley hadn't let up two degrees. Fortunately, there was a slight wind, and as it passed through the screens separating the small bar from the insects, it cooled the customers. It was too early for the ranch hands to start arriving for their after-work beers, so there were only two customers and one employee: T.K. and Drella Pajaro, and Jerrilee Perez. They sat at one of the small tables, the newlyweds nursing their cold beers, Jerrilee drinking fresh lemonade.

Doris had given T.K. and Drella the photo of Barnaby Snoyl and his three friends. Their task was to find Barnaby's three friends and keep them under a close watch. Doris told them to start with Jerrilee.

"Those guys come here every day," she told her visitors. "If you really want to find them, just sit and enjoy yourselves. They're all working on the same job, so they should come together." Jerrilee checked her gold Mickey Mouse wristwatch, and then added, "I give them maybe thirty more minutes."

That gave them about twenty minutes to talk and get acquainted before their prey arrived, and they spent it mostly talking about Kaaler affairs, a very enjoyable time. By the time the regular customers started arriving, T.K. and Drella knew a lot more about Lee and the kidnapping.

Doug, Billy, and Jimbo arrived about an hour after T.K. and Drella, and they were everything Jerrilee told them to expect, and more. Strong, fairly good-looking, dust-covered, obviously hard working. From the content of their conversation, T.K. believed their world covered the area from Sacramento to Bakersfield, and Clovis to Oakland. It was hard to determine if the men were very smart because their conversations contained little of substance and almost nothing disclosing original thought. They liked football, disliked their foreman.

They liked pickups, disliked small cars. They liked fishing and hunting, disliked sightseeing. They liked women—at least talking about women, but weren't ready for marriage. There was only one thing in their conversation that might have related to Verry's kidnapping.

Very shortly, the three men were nursing their third beers, each having chuggalugged their first two. Their conversations covered the day's work, the day's complaints, and their frustration that there were no football games between Monday and Friday nights except high school, and it was too early for high school football. After those apparently obligatory subjects were covered, Billy said, "Haven't seen Barnaby for a while. Was by his house yesterday and no one was there. Where'd he go?"

Doug and Jimbo just looked at Billy. "Thought you'd know," Jimbo said. "You guys 'r closer 'n anythin' most a the time." He leaned forward conspiratorially and added, "'N I miss looking at that broad with the big . . ." He held his hands out in front of his chest: his meaning was clear. Both Doug and Billy immediately hit Jimbo on his biceps with clenched fists. Hard. They didn't like what he was doing, especially in public.

Jimbo would have been angry if he didn't hurt so much, but he was smart enough not to shout out or do anything to bring attention to their table because the pain got to his brain more than words might have.

"Ya ain't got any sense, Jimbo," Billy said. "When're you goin' to learn to keep yer big mouth shut?"

"Well," he started, defensively, "she's really got 'em, 'n I thought—"

"Wrong!" Doug said. "You didn't think. Now le's get outta here before you say somethin' else that's all wrong."

"But I haven't finished my beer," he protested as his friends rose and grabbed him by his arms, lifting him out of his chair.

"'N yer not gonna!" Billy said. With that, Jimbo gave up his fight and accompanied the other two out of the bar and into Doug's dirty, black, '78 Ford pickup. When Jimbo tried to climb into the cab, both men exiled him to the truck's bed, full of tool chests, chains, a welding machine, and a bale of hay.

As they drove off, T.K. and Drella rose, nodded their thanks to Jerrilee, and hurried out to their rented silver '99 Corvette. In seconds, T.K. had the car in gear, throwing out a cloud of dust and sand as they sped down the gravel road so they could keep their targets in sight.

CHAPTER 78

They're Gone!

At dusk, Rose arrived at the outskirts of Clovis, about twenty miles from their home on the other side of Fresno. Trying hard to conceal her plans, she carefully looked around to see what Barnaby was doing. At first, he simply looked asleep, breathing deeply without snoring. Then, as she listened more closely, she could hear light snoring sounds. *Just wait 'til his mouth opens,* she thought. *He'll sound like a freight train.* That part of her plan seemingly in place, she headed down the wide avenue toward the California State University Fresno campus and the service station just west of it.

This was the hardest part of the trip. Rose perspired freely as she neared her goal, and feared more than anything that her husband, the master of bad timing, would wake, notice the moisture covering her face and arms, and start asking questions.

Her greatest fear came when she had to stop at the light just a few blocks east of the service station. She feared the change in sounds from traveling to stopping might wake Barney, but he only moved slightly, his head turning enough for his mouth to open. The rasping sounds of her husband's snores had never before been so comforting.

Easing the car into motion again, she edged down the road, trying to keep near enough to the speed limit to keep cars from passing her, yet slow enough that she could do what she had to with the minimum of advanced notice.

Finally the station was in sight, several cars getting gas, but still a clear drive through it back onto the street. She edged the car closer to the curb, cutting off the traffic behind her, yet not signaling because she feared the new sounds would wake her husband. As she neared the turnoff into the station, she leaned to her right and looked into the rear view mirror so she could see Verry's face.

What she saw was a distressed woman, looking around and not seeing anything she recognized, again fearing the unknown.

Just as she pulled up the small ramp into the station, the motion jostled her husband. He looked around, saw the lights, looked back at Rose, then mumbled, "Good. Need gas," and dropped off to sleep again.

Once at the pump island, Rose opened her door and got out, but then turned and opened Verry's door. "Do you have to go to the bathroom?" She stood close to the car, so neither Barnaby nor Benji could see her head. As she spoke, she nodded enthusiastically to Verry. The message: say "Yes!"

Rose's sudden change of attitude surprised Verry and made her wary, but she felt she had nothing to lose. "Yes, thank you. And I have to throw out these used diapers and things."

"I'll go with you," Rose said, apparently more for her husband's benefit than anything else.

Both women, each carrying a baby, walked through the station to the back of the station office. Once they entered the women's room, Rose leaned over to Verry and said, "When we leave here, you go straight out the back, so the building is between you and our car."

"But what about you, Rose? What'll happen to you?"

Rose looked Verry straight in the eyes. "I don't know, but it'll be better than prison, whatever it is." She looked at Dannice, lying partially awake in her arms, then raised the baby to her lips and kissed her forehead. "Adios, Dannicita." She then leaned over and kissed Daniel's head as he rested in Verry's arms, then handed Dannice to her mother. "Now leave!"

As soon as Verry and the babies were out of side behind the building, Rose went into the station and paid for the gas, then quickly walked back to the car, started the motor and immediately sped out from the pump island onto the thoroughfare, and headed toward their home. Benji saw what happened and immediately knew what his Mommy had done. His only reaction was a slight smile reflecting both approval and pride.

When the car accelerated so fast, Barnaby immediately looked sat up and looked around. At first he looked down the road and around the street sides, orienting himself. Then he checked the back seat and saw only Benji. He slammed his fist against the dashboard so hard it dented it and scared both Rose and Benji, and then unleashed a stream of invectives so vicious and filthy that they shocked both his wife and son. Then screamed, "Where're the broad and her babies, Rose? What've you *done*?"

"They're gone," she answered, her head locked forward, hands gripping the steering wheel like it was trying to escape from her. "For good, I hope."

CHAPTER 79

Call 911!

Verry waited behind the service station until she saw Rose's car drive off, then entered the small combination cashier's station and convenience store. Going directly to the cashier, Verry said to the woman behind the glass security panel, "I've got to get to a telephone and call the police!"

"Sorry, ma'am," the woman answered, "I can't let you use our telephones. But you can use the pay phone outside."

Verry was too emotional, upset and filled with hope to stop there.

"Look, lady," she fairly shouted, "I've been kidnapped and held with my two new babies for two weeks. I want to tell the police where I am so I can have some protection and get back to my husband. Now, are you going to play games and let those people come back and try to get me, or are you going to call 911 and get a cop here right away?"

The cashier simply stared at Verry. When Verry turned around to tend to her babies, the cashier casually resumed ringing up gasoline sales.

CHAPTER 80

Come Now!

Lee snapped awake from an unintentional nap, *I've been asleep! What's happened to Verry? How could I let this happen?* He immediately picked up the golden plate and thought of his wife. She was neither in neither Barnaby's car nor in mountain cabin.

"Verry, I'm here. Where are you?"

She looked startled and then mouthed, "I'm OK." The pointed down at a counter at some writing: it was the name and address of the station.

"I'll be there in just a few minutes! Stay right there, where you can be seen and are around a bunch of people."

She smiled and hugged her babies.

Lee jumped off the bed, slipped the golden plate under the pillow to hide it, then ran out of the room into the kitchen. Doris was busy cooking something deliciously smelling of cinnamon and sugar and cream and onions and he didn't know what else. Even in his haste to get to his wife and children, it made his mouth water.

Doris was clearly startled at his sudden appearance, but before she could say anything, Lee asked, "Can I borrow your car? Verry just got free from the kidnappers and I've got to go pick her up."

Doris's eyes widened in surprise, then she pointed to a key rack next to the door to the carport. "Key closest to the door. Good luck!"

Lee grabbed the key and simultaneously opened the door into the carport, then pulled the 97 Honda's door open, got in, fastened his seat belt, and started the car. He backed out onto the street and then headed toward the center of Clovis and the main route to Fresno. When he got to the signal light, he made a quick near-stop right turn and headed down the road towards a reunion his wife and children. Less than a minute later, he noticed red and blue lights flashing behind him, checked his rearview mirrors and was surprised to see a police car behind him.

Brackafrass! What a time for this to happen!

He stopped the car and sat, impatiently, waiting for the police officer to come up to speak. Anticipating this, he opened the door window and looked back. The police officer was speaking on his police radio, obviously checking the license number or something. Finally, he got out of his car and approached Lee. He was short, stocky, and had a serious expression. Stopping at the car door, he said, "You seemed to be in a hurry, sir."

Lee sheepishly nodded. "Yes, officer, I am. My wife and kids were just kid—"

"You were going too fast, sir," he said, nodding to his partner still seated in the police car. "Is this your vehicle?"

"No," Lee said. "It belongs to Doris Mooradian, a friend in Clovis."

"May I see your driver's license, sir?"

"Of course, Officer," Lee responded, retrieving his billfold and pulling out his Oregon driver's license. *This is no time to play games with false IDs.* As he handed it to the policeman, he said, "I'm sorry if I was driving too fast, but I'm going to get my wife, and—"

The officer ignored Lee's excuse while reading the driver's license. "Mister Kaaler, is it, sir?"

"Yes. Lee Kaaler."

"Well, Mister Kaaler, I'd like you to step out, please. I've got a warrant for your arrest."

Chapter 81

. . . And Into the Fire

Barnaby couldn't believe either his eyes or his ears. "Wha'd'ya mean, 'gone'?" As Rose steered their car away from the gas station, Barnaby looked at her, then back at the empty seat behind her, then out the windshield in the direction they were moving. "I had *plans*," he growled, then crushed her right bicep with his left hand. Rose yelped from the pain, let loose of the steering wheel with that arm, but continuing to steer the car away from their former captives.

"We was gonna get *big money*, Rose," Barnaby repeated, increasing the pressure on her arm. "'N *you* screwed it up! Now we'll git nuthin'!"

Still yelling, Barnaby unfastened his seatbelt, obviously preparing to move closer to her and do something else to her. When she saw what he was doing, she instantly jammed down on the brake pedal as hard as she could, bringing the car to a sudden and complete stop. Barnaby, no longer restrained by his seat belt, was thrown forward, his head striking the top of the windshield. He immediately put both hands to his head, holding them there to help ease the pain. Rose then stepped hard on the gas pedal and accelerated the car, throwing Barnaby back against his seat.

He again started to scoot across the seat toward her, his eyes glaring, his mouth forming words she couldn't quite hear but knew were obscene. When he was almost close enough to grab the steering wheel, she again slammed on the brakes and he flew forward, his head again hitting the windshield, but this time his forehead first struck the right end of the rear view mirror. Blood then gushed out from cuts in his forehead, flowing down his face and onto his shirt and the dashboard.

Fighting through his pain, Barnaby struck out with the back of his left hand, catching Rose's cheekbone and nose. Blood spewed from her nostrils onto her blouse and jeans and she screamed out in pain. Unable to drive in such agony, she pulled the car over to the curb, again slamming on the brakes. A third time Barnaby was thrown forward, again hitting his skull against the windshield, but this time his right ribs absorbed some of the blow, adding a different and sharper edge to his suffering. It forced him to stop trying to pummel Rose and hold his chest to ease the pain. When he did, the terrified and bleeding woman opened her door and ran away from him as fast as she could—straight into oncoming traffic.

Chapter 82

You Win

In less than thirty seconds, Lee found himself spread-eagled across the side of Doris's car, arms wide apart and on the roof, and his legs spread so he couldn't move. From inside the police car a second policeman joined the first, standing back about ten feet, his right hand on his holstered pistol, clearly ready to draw and fire if Lee tried to attack the arresting officer. Then he felt the officer's hands and fingers work their way up both legs, pat down his abdomen and chest, and then check his sleeves. When that was complete, he pulled Lee's right hand down behind his back and put one of the handcuffs on his wrist, then did the same for the left.

"You're making a mistake!" Lee said so loudly it was nearly a yell. "I haven't done anything wrong! I'm on my way to get my wife and babies. They were kidnapped, and—"

"Sure, Mister," the first officer said, "and I'm sturgeon fishing." Holding the handcuffs with one hand and Lee's shoulder with the other, he pulled Lee erect and away from Doris's car. He then led Lee over to the white squad car, its lights still strobing in red and blue to alert other vehicles to keep their distance.

"But I'm telling the truth!" Lee insisted.

"Well, sir," the first policeman said, "I wasn't: I'm not sturgeon fishing." He pushed Lee next to the back fender of the police car while his partner opened the back door. Pushing Lee into the vehicle, and holding Lee's head down so it wouldn't strike the doorframe, he said, "Watch your head."

Once Lee sat down, his handcuffed hands behind him, the second officer fastened Lee's seat belt, slammed the door, and took his place in the right front seat, still having said nothing. Then he withdrew a small laminated card from his shirt's left breast pocket and began reading Lee his rights. When finished, the officer asked, "Do you understand these rights as I have explained them to you?"

"Of course," Lee snapped as the car began to pull out into traffic. "And do you understand that my wife and kids are at a service station near here, waiting to be picked up by me and taken to safety after being kidnapped for the last two weeks? You're keeping me from getting to them!"

The two officers exchanged glances, then the second said, "You win, sir. That's the best story either of us has heard in ten years."

CHAPTER 83

Mommy's Hurt

Benji couldn't believe what he'd just seen and heard. His mother helped Verry and the babies escape—something he'd never expected. And his parents had an awful fight! Tear ran down his cheeks and his nose began running, but he was scarcely aware of anything except his mother running out of the car, then the screech of tires on the pavement, followed by a terrible thud.

Two good things about Mommy letting Verry go. Kidnapping is wrong. And Mommy let Verry get away. It fooled everybody, especially Daddy. But he was awful! He shouldn't have kidnapped Verry, but did it anyway. Now he hits Mommy really hard, and her face bleeds a lot, and he hurt her arm. So she screamed and ran away because she didn't want to be hurt any more.

He looked out the window at the crowd gathered in the street, looking down at Rose's motionless body, his own body now shaking from the shock of the last thirty seconds. *Now Mommy's dead!*

Chapter 84

Like Sturgeon Fishing

The Fresno police were thorough and professional, but wouldn't listen to what Lee kept trying to tell them. After he was booked and placed in a holding cell, one of the officers in the booking area checked the national crime database—over an hour after Lee was booked on suspicion of kidnapping. Fortunately, that officer didn't send the report down by office mail, but hand-carried it directly to the desk sergeant. He read it, and then gestured for the arresting officer to come to the desk.

When that officer read the document, his face paled, he looked at the ceiling as if in prayer, then down at the floor. Turning to Lee, still handcuffed, he said, "Mister Kaaler, you are no longer under suspicion. From about 24 hours ago."

Taking his key ring from off its belt loop, he unlocked Lee's handcuffs. When Lee turned around, rubbing his wrists to ease the pain and get the blood circulating properly in his hands, he said, "Tell me, officer, how do you expect me to pick up my wife *formerly kidnapped* wife and kids now that you've held me completely *incommunicado* for the past hour or so? Or do you know where they are?"

"I don't know what to say, sir."

"Well," Lee continued, still angry and not afraid to show it, "perhaps you'd better go back to something you know how to do. Like sturgeon fishing."

CHAPTER 85

Help Me!

Verry was frantic! The kids were screaming and she was getting fish-eyed stares from the cashier who, Verry found out only after an hour of waiting, still hadn't called the police. Worse, Verry knew no one in the Fresno area except the Snoyls, and she wasn't about to contact them.

She was so upset, frustrated, and frightened that she couldn't think straight. *I've got to get out of here! Barnaby may come back, and I don't want to see him ever again, let alone let him get hold of me again. So what can I do?* The more she thought, the more frustrated she became. *I only know two telephone numbers of any use, and they aren't in Fresno. One is ours, and the other Clem Maestre's*

A "hunger cry" from both kids interrupted her thoughts, but the only place she could go to feed them was the women's restroom. Rather than try to get permission to use it for only baby care, Verry simply took one baby in each arm and walked around the outside of the building to the restroom. She entered the door, locked it behind her, and then laid both babies on the diapering shelf. As she changed her babies' diapers, using some she got by begging a young mother in the service station to give her, Verry thought hard about her situation.

Alone in Fresno. Know nobody here. Babies are healthy. Lee is somewhere near—don't know where, only he didn't pick me up when he said he would. Why not?

She felt herself getting depressed, and immediately changed the subject. *If anyone can find Lee, Clem can.*

After feeding and nursing the children, Verry returned to the payphone in the room housing the cashier and made a collect call to Clem's office. From past experience, she knew any calls coming there after working hours were automatically routed to his home.

After four rings, the familiar soft tones came on the line.

"Hello," they began, "this is the phone of Clem Maestre. Ah'm not able to answer the phone right now, but if ya'll'll leave your name and telephone number and a short message, Ah'll get back to you first thing in the mo'ning."

Right after the familiar beep indicating the recording function had started, Verry began her message. "Clem Maestre, I know you screen every call you get, so you can hear me! This is Verry Kaaler, and I need your help right—"

Clem's voice interrupted her in mid-sentence. "Verry? Really? Are y'all OK? Where are y'all?"

"Clem, stop talking and listen! I'm in Fresno and free of the kidnappers, but Lee was supposed to pick me up and never came. How can I contact him?"

Even though Clem was raised to begin all conversations with polite, small talk, he knew this wasn't such a situation. "Ah'll give y'all his cell phone number. Can y'all write it down?"

"No, I can't! I'm juggling two babies and this telephone thing. And even if I had a pencil, I don't have an extra hand to write with. Just give me the number! Believe me, I won't forget it."

As soon as she had the number of Lee's borrowed cell phone, she hung up on Clem and dialed the number. It was answered after two rings. "Hello," said a strange woman's voice.

Verry was totally confused. Clem wouldn't give her a wrong number, and she knew she'd dialed it correctly.

"I'm trying to reach Lee Kaaler," she said. "Isn't this his phone?" It was hard to hide the growing desperation in her voice.

"Yes, ma'am," the woman said, "but he can't answer right now."

"Why not? I'm his wife. He was supposed to pick me up nearly two hours ago. I was kidnapped, but I escaped. Now, where is he?"

"Ma'am, this is the Fresno Police Department. Your husband's downstairs. I've been told he'll be released soon, but I don't know exactly where he is right now."

"'Released'? From what?" A feeling of dread began to grow inside Verry's stomach, feeding off her exhaustion and frustration. "Where *is* he?"

"Well, ma'am, there was a misunderstanding. He was arrested and brought—"

"Arrested?" Now Verry was shouting. "You arrested my husband? Why?"

"Ma'am, there was a bulletin out. Suspicion of Kidnapping."

Tears began streaming uncontrollably down her cheeks, and she could no longer control her voice. "Officer," she said, her words now breaking from the strain she'd been under and her inability to control herself, "can you get someone to pick me up? I need—" she began sobbing, "—help!"

Chapter 86

Mi Casa . . .

"Doris, this is Lee." He was using a wall-mounted telephone installed for prisoners to make personal calls, even though he was no longer under arrest.

"Lee! How're your wife and kids? Where are you staying?"

Before responding, Lee looked around him. All he saw were uniformed police, a few men being taken to Booking before being sent to cells, and the chagrined officers who arrested him. No Verry, no babies, nothing comforting or familiar. "The answers to your questions, Doris, are 'I don't know', and 'I don't know.'"

"How can that be? You were going to pick them up when you left here three hours ago. What can go wrong in three hours?"

It angered Lee to think about all that had happened, but Doris was a good and trusted friend. Not the person to vent his anger toward.

"I was arrested for speeding before I got halfway to where Verry was. Then I was taken to the police station and booked on suspicion of kidnapping. Then, over an hour after I was supposed to pick up my family, I was released. Right now, I'm in the police station, about to pick up your car and drive back to your place. There's something there I need to use, and I want to make certain I can get into your house. I didn't take a key."

"I'll be waiting, Lee. The house is yours."

CHAPTER 87

Consideration

Benji was in shock. He sat beside his father in the waiting room outside the Intensive Care Unit where his mother was being treated. His father had several stitches taken in his forehead and had his broken ribs taped to minimize the pain he suffered with every breath. Barnaby, however, wasn't worrying about Rose or talking to his son. He was watching a professional wrestling match on TV, oblivious to his wife's suffering and Benji's state of mind.

All Benji could think about was his mother's brush with death, how badly his father had hurt her, how hard the ambulance people worked to keep his mommy from dying in the middle of the street where a car hit her, and how little his father seemed to care.

It made Benji think about how Verry's husband her treated with such care. He showed more concern for her from a long distance away than Benji's own father did for his mother. Benji remembered how many times Verry's husband even talked to him, though they'd never met. *Lee wouldn't watch TV if Verry ever got hurt.*

CHAPTER 88

Alone

The police picked up Verry at the service station nine minutes after she hung up the telephone. A social worker got out of the police car, introduced herself, took the babies, and handed Verry a small brown paper bag. Verry didn't understand at first, but the woman nodded for Verry to open it. Inside were the personal supplies Verry so badly needed.

She rushed back to the women's restroom, reappearing shortly looking much relieved, and entered the squad car. It took her directly to a home used by social services for support to families of persons in jail.

It was the first decent bed Verry had seen for two days, complete with two bassinettes and a set of clean clothes for her. Plus a private bathroom!

She was too tired to worry about contacting Lee right then, especially since she didn't yet know where he was. When her children were bathed, fed, and asleep, it was time for her to take care of herself—to be selfish for unselfish reasons. Unless she was healthy and rested, she couldn't take care of her babies.

Her last thought before crashing to sleep was, *Lee, where are you?*

CHAPTER 89

OK As Is

It was one of the longest short drives of Lee's life. He checked and obeyed every traffic sign, stopped on the yellow lights instead of waiting for the light to turn red—angering almost every other driver on the road behind him, and signaled before every turn. He wasn't going to chance an arrest for speeding or any other infraction.

When he finally arrived at Doris's home in Clovis and started to drive into the carport, the door to the house opened and Doris stood there, doing her best to minimize any delay in Lee's efforts to find Verry. He got out of her car and walked purposely up to her, then smiled weakly as he handed her the car keys. "Thanks, Doris. You're a real friend."

"So are you, Lee," she responded. "Now go find your wife—however you do it." It was a clear reference to the Guardian's unknown powers. Lee let it drop.

The golden plate was exactly where he left it in Doris' guest room. Even though it was dark, he couldn't let concern about Verry's sleep—if any, keep him from finding her. He sat on the edge of the bed and looked straight down onto the plate, his mind reeling with thoughts of his wife and children. It took only a few seconds for the plate to find her: she was obviously sleeping and looked good. He pulled the view back a bit and saw a room resembling a motel room rather than a kid's bedroom, as in the Snoyl's house, or any room in a private home. As he moved his view around the room, he saw the bassinettes, and couldn't keep from looking into them: two sleeping babies, both with their left thumbs in their mouths.

I didn't want my kids to be thumb-suckers, but I'll take them as is, no questions asked!

CHAPTER 90

Bad Boys

Doris didn't expect to see Lee appear so soon after he went to the guest room, but only a few minutes after he disappeared into it, he returned. She was in the living room, sipping on a glass of fresh lemonade and eating some spicy tortilla chips.

Her surprise was obvious; he said only, "Sleeping." When he saw what she was drinking, he realized he was intensely thirsty, and the chips reminded his stomach it had forgotten to growl in hunger for several hours. Doris recognized the look on his face, and immediately brought him some food. When he tried to refuse her offer, she silently pointed at the biggest chair in the living room: he was to sit down and shut up.

After downing the lemonade and destroying a large bowl of chips, Lee told her the story of the last three hours of his life. When he finished, she didn't know what to say or do, but he helped her. "Tomorrow morning," he began, "after I find out where Verry is, I'd like you to drive me there."

"You can have the car if you want, Lee. You know that."

He shook his head. "Don't want to chance anything. You drive, then take us to the nicest motel with suites in Fresno, if you don't mind."

"You can have this house, Lee."

He slowly but intensely shook his head. "No, thanks, Doris, you've already done enough. We'll stay there for a while." After a few seconds of thought, he said, "But we've still got some unfinished business to attend to."

"What? What haven't we done?"

"I've got to contact T.K. and Drella. They're supposed to be watching Snoyl's buddies, guys who need to be taught a big lesson—like they were still kids."

Chapter 91

The Feds

Verry woke with the babies about two in the morning, fed and cleaned them, then fell back onto her bed, asleep almost as soon as her head hit the pillow. Four hours later, she performed the same function, with the same result. This time, however, she dreamed. First, she relived the joy of conceiving her babies with the man she loved almost more than life itself. Then the fun they had learning about how babies were growing inside her. Next, a quick repeat of the kidnapping and the terrible trip to the Snoyl's house, followed by the first time Lee contacted her.

She could hear his voice in her mind. Concerned, comforting, loving. *Verry,* he said, *I'm here.* Then it changed to something she'd not heard before. *Are you awake? Can you hear me?*

Her eyes snapped open. She wasn't dreaming those words, she was *hearing* them!

"Lee," she said aloud, "what happened? Why didn't you pick us up? And where are you?"

She could almost hear him take a deep breath to control himself, but the sound of his voice betrayed none of the frustrations she knew he felt. Immediately she regretted her questions, because she knew she'd learn the answers when he had time to give them.

I'm in Clovis, at a Kaaler friend's house. Tell me where you are and I'll be right there.

Those were the most welcome words she'd heard in what seemed like months, but really was only a few weeks.

When he and Doris arrived to pick up Verry and the babies, they were met by three people in business suits; one brunette woman about five foot fours, and

178

two men, each just over six feet tall. Lee didn't like their officious and serious expressions, but decided to ignore them and get his family back.

Just as he started to walk past them, the woman held up a small ID case and flipped it open so Lee could see her badge and ID. "Mister Kaaler," she said, "I'm Special Agent Darlene Schneider from the FBI. We'd like to talk to you." Before he could say anything in return, she added, "Now."

Chapter 92

FBI First

Lee couldn't believe it! *I almost get my wife and kids back, and now the FBI steps in?*

"Agent," Lee said, unable to remember her name with all the stress he'd been under, compounded by the fact he didn't really want to, "I presume you know my wife and kids were kidnapped a couple of weeks ago. I haven't been with them for even *two minutes* since then, and you want me to talk to you first?" He looked the agent straight into her eyes, making no attempt to conceal his anger and frustration.

She didn't back off. "I understand how you feel, Mister Kaaler, but it is vital to our investigation of your wife's kidnapping that we talk *now*."

Lee looked at her, searching for any sign of backing off or flexibility. Seeing none, he looked back at the door separating him from his family, then angrily said, "What do you want?"

"I think it would be better if we talked somewhere less open, Mister Kaaler."

"Well, Agent," Lee responded, clearly angry, "I *don't*! Now tell me what you want to know, so I can meet my wife and the babies I've never seen!"

Agent Schneider glanced at the two men with her to get their opinion of Lee's stance. It was clear they agreed with him.

"Very well, Mister Kaaler, then at least let us move out of the sun."

Can't argue with that. Besides, it looks like I won this little battle.

She led the three men to the shelter of a large maple tree. Once there, she turned to Lee and said, a small threat in her voice, "Now, Mister Kaaler, we need some answers."

"Ask your questions."

"You understand, Mister Kaaler, we'll talk to your wife on these same matters a bit later."

Lee just nodded. *No surprise. She's the better witness.*

"Who kidnapped your wife?"

"Barnaby Snoyl and three of his friends."

All three agents began writing in their note pads.

"Their names?" Agent Schneider asked.

"Doug, Billy and something like Jim. But that's not it. Verry might know—I don't."

"Last names?"

"Don't know. I *do* know, however, that they all often go to a bar west of Fresno. Owned by a friend of mine, as a matter of fact." He let a small smile flicker on and off his face. *Pretty clear they didn't know that.*

"It's name?"

"Don't know. Call Jerrilee Perez—she's the owner, and she can tell you." Lee again turned serious. "That's all I know, agent. Now can I go inside and meet my new son and daughter?"

Before answering, she folded her note pad and put it into her coat pocket. "Thank you, Mister Kaaler. We'll be in touch again, so we can talk to your wife."

Lee turned around and was already walking away from the agents before giving a weak, "You're welcome."

Chapter 93

It had to be done

Once again, something his daddy did shocked Benji. Something bad. After sitting in the ICU waiting room for over five hours, a nurse from the ward came up to Benji and his dad. She was short, a little overweight, with a pretty face and wearing light blue, short-sleeved hospital working pajamas and white sneakers.

"Mister Snoyl?" she asked.

Benji's dad slowly tore his eyes off the wrestling match on TV. Barnaby still hadn't left his seat in front of the TV set, but now looked at the nurse with real interest. "I'm Snoyl," he said. "Wha' d'ya want?"

"I'm Marilou, one of your wife's nurses. She's asked to see her son."

"What?" His temper was already beginning to show. "I'm her *husband!* She's s'posed to see me 'fore her kid."

The nurse looked a little non-plussed, but held her place. "She can only have one visitor at a time, sir, and she asked to speak to her son." Now the nurse turned her attention to the boy and held her hand out to him. "Come on, Benji—isn't it? My name's Marilou. I'll take you in."

Barnaby jumped to his feet and knocked the nurse's hand away from Benji. "You'll take *me* in, lady," he growled. "*I'll* decide if Benji sees Rose."

When Barnaby struck the nurse's hand, a loud slap filled the waiting room. Marilou immediately backed away, holding her hand, already turning red from the force of his blow. She looked back at the entry from the hallway into the waiting room, and yelled, "Security!"

Within seconds, two uniformed Fresno policemen rushed in. They saw the nurse holding and rubbing her hand, and Barnaby standing in front of her and glaring; a big, angry man. Marilou pointed at Barnaby and said, "He struck me when I tried to take the boy to see his mother in the ICU."

The senior man, nearly as tall and strong as Barnaby, stepped directly in front of the clearly angry man. "Sir," he said, "you have two choices. You may stay in here while your son visits his mother, or you'll be arrested for assaulting this nurse. In no case, however, will you be allowed to see your wife, because she's been given a restraining order against you."

Barnaby looked both angry and confused. "A what?"

"Mister Snoyl," the policeman continued calmly, not backing off, "you are forbidden from seeing your wife for the next 30 days, and are to remain no closer than one-half mile from her for that entire period. That's why we're here, sir. If you disobey the court order now that you know about it, you will be taken into custody."

"Jail?" Barnaby's temper erupted. "Fer seein' my own wife?" he yelled. "Who d'ya think yer talkin' to? I see my wife when I want to!" Completing his tirade against the officer, he started walking toward the double swinging doors marking the entry into the ICU itself.

When the second policeman moved directly into the line between Barnaby and the ICU, Barnaby straight-armed the man out of the way. As the policeman recovered his balance, the first policeman moved up behind Barnaby and hit the angry man on the back of his thighs with his nightstick. Yelling out in pain, Barnaby fell to the floor in a near-fetal position, holding his legs. Immediately both policemen leaped on him, quickly pulling his arms behind his back and handcuffing them. Barnaby struggled against the cuffs, shouting obscenities at everyone in the room, including both Rose and Benji.

Marilou immediately sensed what had to be done. Taking Benji's hand again, she gently pulled him out of his chair, putting her body between Benji and the scene on the waiting room floor. "Let's go, Benji. Your mother's anxious to see you."

The last thing Benji heard was one of the policemen say to the other, "Call for backup."

CHAPTER 94

Charles Who?

Finally inside the foyer of the building where Verry and the kids were staying, Lee went directly to the reception desk at the end of the room, in front of a large color photo of El Capitan, the magnificent cliff in Yosemite National Park, only a few hours north of Fresno. The reception area was only ten feet wide and fifteen feet long.

Had Lee the time to think about his surroundings, he'd have liked them. The room was more comfortable than pretty, but still attractive. Medium tan carpet, multicolored drapes over the Venetian blinds protecting everything inside from the hot, bright sun of this part of California. Well-used but comfortable-looking furniture: tan sofas on each side of the room with small coffee tables in front area, and one large frame containing the Rules for the shelter. So much better than the motels he'd camped in on the way here.

To the receptionist, Lee said, "Vera Kaaler, please. I'm her husband."

The receptionist was a small, gray-haired woman with wire-rimmed glasses and a sweet smile "Yes, sir," she said. "I'll need to see some ID, you understand." Her smile faded somewhat, but her expression remained pleasant. "Some of our clients have been abused and we don't want to have anything like that happen here."

Lee was so anxious he could barely control himself, but he knew the woman was right. He quickly retrieved his billfold and flipped it open so she could see his Oregon driver's license.

The expression on her face told him something was wrong.

Deciding to ignore it, he asked, "Now can I see Verry?"

She peered closely at the small document, then back at Lee. "Sir, the picture is correct, but this license was issued to a Charles Cortron, not anyone named Kaaler."

Chapter 95

Nice Car, but Wrong

With Jerrilee driving her old pale yellow Ford pickup down the farm road ahead of their Corvette, T.K. and Drella saw a section of the San Joaquin Valley they'd normally never visit; vineyards, cotton fields, livestock. Some large, ranch-style houses stood well back from the road, reflecting the Spanish influence common in Californian architecture. Large irrigation systems watered some fields; others had their water siphoned from irrigation ditches. Still others used large electric water pumps to draw water from aquifers thousands of feet below the surface. After about a half-hour drive from Jerrilee's bar, almost all on a rough, gravel road, she slowed her truck, and then stopped it on the side of the road. T.K. drove the rented Corvette up beside her.

Jerrilee pointed across the road to a white, doublewide manufactured home with a gray roof, about a hundred feet from the main road. It stood beside a one-lane gravel road apparently leading to the landowner's house, a hundred yards or so beyond. "That's Billy's place," she said. "Doug and Jimbo live in their places about a half mile on down the way. On this side," pointing to the right. "You can't miss 'em, because both have old wrecked cars parked behind."

She smiled at her new-found friends, then put her pickup back into gear. "I've got to open my place," she said. "Call me if you need anything else." Waving good-by, she drove off down the road before either T.K. or Drella could respond.

"You know what I think?" Drella asked. This was her way of telling her husband what she wanted him to do. He'd learned that in less than two weeks into their marriage.

"Tell me?"

"A Corvette is not a very practical car to track someone in. Stands out like a sore thumb."

She was correct and he knew it. When he first rented the Corvette, he knew they'd have to change cars, but he rented it anyway because he wanted to drive a Corvette just once. Now the fun was over.

"Let's do it now, then go back to the motel before lunch." A slightly lewd tone then colored his voice. "Who knows? We might even have time to eat."

Drella just smiled.

CHAPTER 96

The ICU

Benji often watched "ER" and other TV programs that showed emergency and post-operative care, but they weren't something he could really experience. Now he found himself in a genuine Intensive Care Unit, engulfed with beeps and peeps and steady tones, and by smells he couldn't identify. Around him, on both sides of the aisle between small cubicles for beds, he saw all kinds, colors, sizes, and shapes of medical people. He also saw patients with tubes coming out of their arms and mouths and noses. Some even had tubes snaking out from under their bed sheets. Benji decided he didn't want to know anything more about them.

Two things impressed him even though he didn't know the words to describe what he observed: the professionalism of the medical personnel, and the obvious concern they had for their patients. The contrast between the coldly sterile high-tech equipment and the caring people surprised him.

Marilou kept up a steady stream of talk, constantly deflecting Benji's attention from what he was seeing and hearing: the weather, how nicely dressed he was, whether he had thought about what he wanted to be when he grew up, how many good colleges and junior colleges there were in the Fresno area.

Suddenly she stopped beside a blue-gray curtain screening one of the cubicles. Kneeling down so she could look Benji straight in his eyes, she said softly, "This is your mother's place, Benji." She took both his hands in hers, her eyes watering slightly. "Some of what you're going to see is a little frightening, maybe, but don't be afraid. Your mother was badly injured when she ran into the traffic. She has a broken leg and arm—both of them are in splints, but we'll put them into casts in a few days, when the swelling goes down." She squeezed Benji's hands, both to keep his attention on what she was saying and to reassure him. "We don't usually let young men and women in here, Benji, because this place can be scary." Now she smiled. "Actually, it's just the opposite. This is where we can treat badly injured people, and some of the scary stuff is really wonderful. It just *looks* scary. Like the tubes you saw as you walked through the ward, and all the computer screens with their little green lines wiggling across them."

Her face became a bit more serious, but a smile stayed in place.

"When the car hit your mom, it hurt some of the things inside her. We had to operate in order to treat them, so she has a cut in her tummy and some staples holding it closed. That makes it hard for her to move. Also she has a broken cheekbone"—Marilou didn't remind Benji that his daddy hit his mommy there. "That made her face swell and gave her two black eyes."

She released his hands and put both of hers on his shoulders. "I want you to know this, because these are normal results of injuries and operations. Your mommy doesn't look very pretty right now, but in a couple of weeks she'll look fine."

Marilou stood up and pulled the curtain back, so Benji could enter the recovery cubicle. "Your mommy's awake, so go in. Tell her you love her, Benji. She needs that a lot right now."

Chapter 97

Desperate Tears

When Lee realized he'd shown the receptionist a piece of his false ID, he nearly lost his composure. Uninvited, he sat down in the visitor's chair adjacent to her desk, put his head in his hands, and began talking. For over fifteen minutes he talked non-stop, omitting only details which might indicated the existence of his heirloom silver spoon and its powers, and the golden plate with its own set of awesome capabilities. By the time he finished, his eyes were watering and his voice quavering.

"Ma'am," he began, "could you just call Verry and tell her someone claiming to be her husband is here? I'll stay right here and not even watch while you dial her room, so there's no chance I could ever know where my family is." Now he looked at the woman. "I've told you all I can about why I had that piece of false ID. You have no idea how badly I feel about having to use it, let alone have you see it, but I was desperate then, and I'm desperate now!"

The woman said nothing for a few seconds, then spoke. "Mister Kaaler, while you were telling me your story, I called your wife. If you'll look down that hallway there," pointing to her right, "you might see someone you recognize."

At that, Lee stood and looked where she pointed. From out of the security door came a woman carrying two babies, her face streaked with tears of joy and her eyes radiating love.

Neither said anything until after they shared a long and passionate kiss and embrace, greatly complicated by the fact that Verry had each arm full of fidgeting baby and was unable to return her husband's strong, possessive, and joyous hug. Then Verry pulled back a bit, a huge smile on her face "Dannice and Daniel," she said as she looked directly onto their little faces, tears of joy and relief now streaming down her cheeks, "this is your daddy."

CHAPTER 98

Not a Dream

Lee scarcely remembered what happened during the next 24 hours, except for the first incredibly few ones. It began when he helped Verry take their babies back to her room in the social services "hotel." After many kisses and much hugging, he watched his wife nurse their children. It was an incredibly emotional moment: Verry proudly showing how well she could provide them the best food possible; seeing his son and daughter suckle and slurp and push their little faces against her breasts, instinctively doing the very thing needed to stimulate milk production and, simultaneously, stimulate Verry's body to return to normal. Much to his surprise, he even enjoyed changing his children's diapers, although he admitted, to himself only, that he was glad they weren't dirty.

The best part was the hugging and kissing and caressing, even knowing they couldn't enjoy the intimacy possible before the birth of their children. Lee also found he recognized his wife's fragrance, something he'd never thought about before. And the way she kissed him and caressed his cheeks and neck. And the feel of her back, her ribs, her hips. And how good it felt to kiss her eyelids, and cheek, and forehead, and ears. Most of all, Lee felt complete again in spite of being in a strange place, with its uncomfortable bed and odors of industrial strength cleansers and deodorants. But he also knew they'd soon have to stop reacquainting themselves and move to the motel suite he'd reserved.

Most surprising, after the weeks of worry and concern, false identities, and substandard temporary living facilities, Lee woke from a short nap to the sound of a baby whimpering. That, as much as anything to that point, told him this wasn't a dream. Then something else convinced him otherwise. After checking

Dannice and Daniel, Verry returned to the bed she and her husband had just napped on. Sitting beside him, she slowly unbuttoned and removed her blouse, then her nursing bra. "If you'd like to make sure these are what you remember," she said, her voice husky and her face smiling, "it's perfectly OK."

Then Lee knew it *was* a dream. A real-life one.

CHAPTER 99

She *Was* Kidnapped

D
r. Jeremy Snoyl loved his job, in spite of the long hours and innumerable calls at all hours of the day and night. He'd wanted to be a doctor for as long as he could remember—a surgeon or an internist. However, his studies in OB/GYN in medical school convinced him he had found his niche. He saw the things his instructors did, how they helped women who came to them with seemingly unsolvable problems: their lives changed from being nearly unbearable to being joys. Jeremy Snoyl knew he *had* to be part of such a world: his previous "calling" had merely been a "leaning."

His working conditions were state-of-the-art. As an MD associated with the best hospital in the San Joaquin Valley, he had not only a large clientele, he could pick the best people available to be his staff. Never had he so enjoyed himself. As hard as the work was, as demanding as it had become, it was a joy to help women and work with a staff that enjoyed their work and got along well together.

He arrived at his office after his hospital rounds, looking forward to treating some of his patients, and was met by three people—two men and a woman—who were clearly *not* interested in consulting with him on female problems.

After a few moments for introductions and a display of IDs, it was clear to Doctor Jeremy Snoyl that his first appointment was not with Missus Joylene Walker, but with Darlene Schneider, George Williams and William Manser.

Once inside his private office, the meeting became coldly serious. The agents sat directly opposite the doctor. The woman sat in the middle, but was clearly in charge. Although Doctor Snoyl couldn't know it, her blue suit was a drastic change from her usual dark pinstripe outfits. Her partners wore sport coats and slacks. It softened their images, but not their serious purpose.

Doctor Snoyl's story, like so many aspects of the FBI investigation, generated as many questions as it answered. "The whole thing began strangely," he said. "My staff and I had just arrived at work and were going over our schedule. In the midst of this, my Uncle Barnaby barged in, demanding I deliver a baby for a woman he brought with him." He shook his head, a slight smile on his face. "That was peculiar because I hadn't seen him since before I started college. He always belittled my intent to become a doctor, yet here he shows up with the very pregnant woman I'd never seen or heard of, and said he wanted me to deliver her baby—*singular!*"

"You mean he didn't know she was going to have twins?"

"Right. Seemed completely unaware of what she was carrying." A slight pause. "And one other strange thing—he didn't know her first name."

The agents exchanged knowing glances, but said nothing, merely wrote something on their note pads.

"How did you know that?" Agent Williams asked.

"Simple. Before admitting her, one of my nurses asked Uncle Barnaby her name—for the insurance forms and hospital registration. Uncle Barnaby had to ask the patient!" Another quick smile. "Then he wanted to be with her in the birthing suite!" Now a chuckle. "That was such a stupid and ignorant request, I just said, 'No way, Uncle Barnaby.' Then he got really angry."

"What'd he do?" Agent Manser asked.

"Started swearing and making all kids of threats. Finally I just said, 'Uncle Barnaby, you're *not* going in there. You're not her husband and, besides, she hasn't asked for you to be there. Now, you get back into the waiting room and stay there! I'll tell you when she's done.'

"Then I closed the door to the birthing room and got to work. Didn't take much time to discover she was about to deliver twins. So we delivered them." He stopped talking, then his eyes began the random movements almost always associated with deep thought. "But," he said slowly, his eyes intently on the brunette in the tailored blue suit, "one unusual thing happened while she was giving birth."

None of the FBI agents said anything, their attention riveted on what he was describing.

"Just before her first baby arrived—the girl, the mother acted like someone began talking to her."

"Talking to her—who? Your nurse?" Agent Manser asked.

Doctor Snoyl shook his head back and force with obvious certainty. "We were only telling her what to do or that she was doing well—normal delivery talk.

"No," he continued, "she acted like she'd been given some good news. In addition, while she actually delivered one of the babies, she nodded her head and seemed to mouth the words, "Yes, Yes!" A few more seconds, then he added, "Then she held her baby up in the air, like she was showing it to someone—or to a video camera. Then she said the baby's name—aloud."

"Showing it?" Agent Schneider asked. "To whom?"

"There was no camera and no one else in the room," the doctor said. "It was really unusual."

He thought a bit more, then said, "And she insisted we do all the birth certificates before the babies were completely cleaned up."

"Is that unusual?" Agent Williams asked.

"Very. We usually clean the babies before foot printing them on the birth certificates." He shrugged, "But we complied. And it was then that I learned her full name—Vera Willards Kaaler. Moreover, she insisted—absolutely adamant—that the children's family names be shown as Kaaler, not Snoyl. I thought that also odd, because babies usually take their fathers' names anyway.

"Then I became involved in stitching her up and making certain the babies were OK. They were, of course, as was she. She was exhausted—multiple births usually do that to the mothers, especially first-time mothers. But she didn't want to let go of her babies—almost like she was afraid someone was going to take them away."

Agent Manser broke the silence of the moment. "You mean kidnap them from the hospital?"

"Exactly!" Doctor Snoyl said. "That's the exact word she used—kidnap!" His eyes began their rapid blinking and flicking back and forth again. "No!" he said, "that's not what she said." More thought. "Past tense—she said 'kidnapped', not 'kidnap.'"

"Past tense?" Agent Schneider said. "She said 'kidnapped?'"

Several nods. "That's exactly what she said."

"Could she have been talking about herself, do you think?" she asked.

"In all honesty, that never occurred to me. Never would have."

The agents traded glances, and then she added, "What happened then?"

"As soon as we put the babies in their cradles and moved Missus Kaaler to a gurney so we could move her to her bed, Uncle Barnaby barged in and demanded to help prepare the birth certificates. When I told him they were already done, he exploded again." He chuckled once, smiled briefly, and shook his head back and forth. "I didn't understand the man when I was a teenager, and I still don't." A quiet shrug. "And that's what happened. Unremarkable births; remarkable events."

"Doctor Snoyl," Agent Schneider began, "I owe it to you to tell you that Missus Kaaler was, in fact, kidnapped."

"You're not serious!"

"I am, and it seems she was kidnapped by your uncle."

"Judas Priest!"

Chapter 100

Damage, Hope and Promises

The next day Lee moved his family to a motel. Their suite was small but luxurious: king-sized bed with electric massagers and vibrators; large, fluffy bath towels; showers with massagers; television sets in the bedroom and living room; telephones in every room; thick, soft carpets everywhere but the bathroom; water-jet tub; completely soundproofed. The decor reminded Verry of Mexico: bright reds, blues and yellows on the bedspreads and drapes, sofas, easy chairs and dining chairs; a Mexican theme on the ceramic tiles; framed photos and impressionistic paintings of bull-fighters, adobe rancheros, and men and women performing Mexican folk dances. There also was a large bowl of fresh oranges, apples, and bananas on the dining table and a large carafe of sangria in the refrigerator. The only bad thing—and it wasn't the hotel's fault—they had to tell the FBI where they were.

Lee wasn't at all accustomed to being awakened every three or four hours by crying babies, so his night wasn't restful. Verry, of course, had to nurse their babies, but Lee helped change diapers and clean them. He'd even helped bathe them, something wholly outside his experience base—he'd never, ever, baby-sat.

So he was tired, sleepy, but happy, but he found himself loving Verry more than ever, and enjoying the feeling that he had helped produce two healthy children.

Occasionally something would forcibly remind him of how they all got to Fresno in the first place, and that made him resent the circumstances and everything concerned with them. Then he'd slow himself down and think softer and kinder thoughts. They were together again. Everyone was healthy. He'd met other Kaalers—especially Doris and Jerrilee, now good friends. Everyone he'd asked to help had willingly done so.

There were many things to be thank God for, but there were also bad things to be made right.

After feeding the babies and putting them in the crib provided by the motel, he and Verry shared a quiet breakfast: fruity yogurt, toasted bagels slathered with butter and jam, and several cups of hot tea. Neither of them said much; they'd occasionally hold hands, or share a quick kiss—enjoying being together again and feeling safe.

Breakfast over and the kitchen cleaned, Verry thankfully returned to bed to try to regain some strength, while Lee thought about what more he needed to do. He knew he should talk with T.K. and Drella, and Doris, and Clem, but he didn't want to do anything to disturb Verry.

Time to look in on some people. He quietly moved from the small kitchen to the living room, then removed the golden plate from the coat closet. Sitting on the sofa and leaning back, he rested the plate on his abdomen and thought about Benji.

He was sitting next to a hospital bed, holding someone's hand. His eyes were red, his face drawn in sadness. It was the worried, confused, and hurting face of a ten-year-old boy with one parent in the hospital and the other in jail. Very softly, trying not to frighten the boy, Lee aimed his thoughts at Benji.

"Benji," he began, *"can you hear me?"*

First Benji jumped, startled by Lee's words intruding into his consciousness. Quickly realizing what it was and who was speaking, he gave an ashen smile and nodded.

"Verry and I have been worried about you," Lee began. *"We didn't know where you were, but I'm glad I found you."* He saw no need to remind Benji that there was no place on Earth that Lee couldn't find him through his golden plate.

"Is your mother getting better?"

Benji nodded, then his eyes began to blink away tears, and he leaned onto the bed, his shoulders shaking with sobs. After only a few seconds, he sat up again, pulled tissue from the box on the small hospital stand next to his mother's shoulders, and blew his nose. After disposing of that tissue, he wiped his tears away using another, then again weakly smiled.

I'm going to look at your mother now.

Her face was swollen and seemingly painted in ugly shades of black, blue and yellow, eyes swollen almost shut, nose bandaged, hair lying flat against her scalp. From her nose extended a transparent tube, adding to the cadaverous image. Lee realized he really couldn't see enough of her face to recognize her if he ever saw her again. Pulling his view back, Lee saw two tubes snaking out from under the bed sheets. Her left arm had an IV inserted into it, draining transparent fluid from a transparent bag hanging from a stainless steel pole attached to her bed frame.

For one of the few times in his life, Lee really *wanted* to be there, to try to comfort the boy, but he didn't yet know where Benji was. "*Benji*," he thought to the boy bravely trying to play the man's role and comfort his mother, "*is there anything around you that has the hospital's name written on it?*"

Benji looked confused, then gently put his mother's hand down on the bed sheet and carefully rose from the stool he'd been using. He moved toward the wall behind her bed and pointed to something posted on the wall. It was the emergency escape route chart, and on top of it was printed the name of the hospital.

"*Thank you, Benji. That's exactly what I wanted to know. We'll try to visit you soon, if that's OK.*"

Several quick nods, then he held his arms as if holding a baby.

You must be a whiz at Charades, Lee thought. "*The babies and Verry are fine, Benji. We're staying in a motel on Blackstone Avenue, and we'll be here for at least a couple of days.*"

Benji nodded, in both understanding and agreement.

"*I have to leave you now, but I'll try to call you soon—if they'll let you take calls. Will they?*"

At first Benji gave no reaction at all, then merely shrugged.

"*I'll find out and let you know, Benji. Now you stay with your mom and I'll get back to you again later today. OK?*"

A quick nod accompanied by a more sincere smile than the last one.

"*Good, Benji. Now whatever you do, don't think we'll leave you all alone, OK?*"

Another smile—a false, brave one. It almost cut Lee's heart.

"*See you soon.*" With that, Lee cut the contact. It also gave him the chance to blow his nose and wipe the excess moisture from his eyes.

CHAPTER 101

Suspicious Answers

At the meeting in their motel suite, all sat around the small dining table as Verry related to the three FBI agents her story of the kidnapping. Lee and Verry ordered in a large pot of coffee and some shortbread cookies for the meeting, deciding to be hospitable in spite of how much Lee, in particular, resented the FBI's presence. The agents sipped their coffee, ate several of the rich, creamy and buttery cookies, even exchanged some small talk with their hosts, then placed their notepads on the table in front of them.

Except for a few questions on details of how she identified her captors before their unmasking after the babies' birth, the agents listened intently and politely. When Verry finished her story, the agents talked quietly among themselves, seemingly making no effort to conceal what they were saying, yet talking so softly that neither Lee nor Verry could understand what they said. After a few minutes, they stopped huddling and sat up at the table, all looking at Verry. Their expressions gave no hint of what they were thinking.

"Missus Kaaler, we've already confirmed almost everything you've told us except the identities of the men who helped Barnaby Snoyl in your kidnapping. You've given us two details on that: the belt buckle worn by one of your guards, and the name you heard one of the men say shortly after your capture." As Lee expected, Darlene Schneider, the senior agent, gave the summary.

"Billy," Verry said. "His was the only name I heard until I got to Barnaby Snoyl's house. Then, of course, I met Rose and Benji."

"And they were the only other people you met?"

"Until the hospital, Agent Schneider," Verry said. "But I'd guess you've already talked to Doctor Snoyl and his wonderful staff." Her eyes began to water, and she held Lee's hand tightly. "They really helped me, when I felt the lowest and most alone."

There was a short period of absolute silence, then Lee said, "Are there any other questions you'd like to ask?

This time there was no hesitation. "Yes, Mister Kaaler, but for you rather than your wife."

Both Lee and Verry were shocked and surprised, then exchanged confused glances. "I can't think of anything I could add to this, Agent Schneider."

She didn't hesitate even one second. "Sir, you're never really explained what they wanted in ransom."

Two thoughts flashed through Lee's mind: the silver spoon and the golden plate and how he used it to frighten his tormentors and communicate with Verry. *And Benji.* "I told you some time ago. Snoyl said he didn't know what I had that was so valuable that the Gerits wanted it a couple of years earlier, and he wouldn't accept my offer of money. He never contacted me again: that was one of the things which worried me so much." Lee squeezed Verry's hand again, both as a show of affection and to let her know how much he had worried about her. "The whole thing was terrifying—knowing nothing about Verry's condition or location and not knowing what to do to get her released."

"But," Agent Mancer said, "you headed directly toward Central California."

"We'd like to know why," Agent Williams added. "Why did you head down here?"

Verry started to say something, but Lee shook his head and cut her off. "Excuse me, agents," he said. "I don't understand the reasons for your questions. You know I had nothing to do with Verry's kidnapping, you know I informed the FBI as soon as I learned anything about Verry's location, and you know I tried to use my relatives around here to help find the guys who kidnapped her. Now you seem to be attacking *me*. What's going on?"

Leadership of this phase of the investigation had passed from Agent Schneider to George Williams. The other two looked at him when Lee asked his question, and the dark-haired man responded for all. "Mister Kaaler, there are many things about your story that don't make sense to us."

That response confused both Lee and Verry. Verry partly out of ignorance of everything Lee did while they were separated, and partly Lee because he wasn't certain what these FBI agents were seeking. "You'll have to be more specific," Lee said. "Now *I* don't understand what you're saying."

Agent Williams adjusted his position a bit before responding, and then attacked. "Mister Kaaler, we find it very hard to believe you have no idea what Barnaby Snoyl was seeking as ransom, even if he didn't. You were the target of a concerted effort by men paid by Jefferson Gerit to obtain something—as yet unspecified to us—that both Gerits considered of great value. They spent much money over many years to find you and then obtain whatever it was you had, and—"

"Whatever they *thought* I had," Lee said, interrupting the agent's statement. "The fact they were trying to find me doesn't mean I had anything. It only means they *thought* I had something. And it doesn't change the fact that Barnaby Snoyl didn't know what it was." He stopped for just a moment, but before the agent could begin his attack anew, Lee added, "I presume you talked with the Gerits. Did they say what they were after?"

The agent checked with the woman to his left, received a curt nod, and then looked back at Lee.

"They weren't particularly helpful, Mister Kaaler," he said. "In the first place, the elder Gerit died of a heart attack a couple of weeks ago, so we couldn't talk with him. His son was very cooperative, but didn't say much. We have access to all of his records, however."

"You mean he proved he had me and Verry under illegal surveillance, had his men set fire to my parents' home, and caused automobile accidents to scare my father and which injured Verry and killed her good friend? You have all of that documented, yet you're coming after me for something you just *think* may be? Do I have that correct? Or did I leave something out?"

"We've proved what Mister Gerit had his people do against you," the agent responded, "but we've not yet determined that what they sought wasn't obtained illegally by you. That's what concerns us, and why we've enlisted assistance from the IRS and SEC."

CHAPTER 102

Leave This Place

After Jerrilee left, T.K. drove the corvette to the rental agency and traded it in for a minivan. He then drove to the field where Doug, Billy, and Jimbo were working. Watching farm hands work in the fields wasn't what either T.K. or Drella considered fun, but it was the best way to keep an eye on the kidnappers. For this effort, they pretended to be free-lance writers researching an article on one facet of farming in the San Joaquin Valley. They'd gone up to Doug, Billy and Jimbo, introduced themselves, and sold this story idea to them—even had been invited to share a few beers at the end of a day's work. At Jerrilee's bar, of course.

It let T.K. and Drella learn much about their targets, take innumerable photos, spend hours watching the men, and try to learn anything they could about Barnaby and the kidnapping effort. After nearly a week, however, they'd learned little.

They parked their rental car on the dirt and gravel shoulder of the farm road, occasionally sitting on the roof of their mini-van to get a better view. This day, however, there was more traffic than usual, subjecting them to more dust and wind than normal. Just at lunchtime, as they were getting ready to leave, a dark blue late-model sedan stopped behind them. Two men exited, each moving toward them, effectively bracketing both sides of their van. When the driver of the car reached T.K., sitting in the minivan's driver's seat, he retrieved an ID folder from his shirt pocket and flipped it open so T.K. could see the badge and picture ID identifying him as an FBI agent; his partner did the same for Drella. That mandatory act completed, the short, black-haired, and steely-eyed agent next to T.K. said, "You've spent several days watching these men. Why?"

Drella's eyes were dilated, her face suddenly moist with perspiration. T.K., however, seemed unfazed by the sudden appearance of the FBI and an implicit report that he and Drella had been and were still under FBI surveillance. "I don't understand," he began, "what we could possibly have done to warrant FBI attention." Rather than attempt to respond to the agent's question, T.K. simply stopped talking and looked expectantly at the agent.

There was a momentary war of silence, then the agent said, "Mister Pajaro, at the risk of stressing the obvious, we aren't obligated to answer your questions."

"And," T.K. responded, "we aren't required to respond to your questions unless you tell us why we're being questioned. So far, you've only told us you're the FBI. Since we are clearly violating no laws, let alone Federal ones, you owe us some explanation for this interrogation."

The shorter agent looked through the mini-van toward his partner, standing next to Verry's door. That agent was so much taller than the other that he had to lean down in order to see the shorter man across the inside of the vehicle. A few seconds passed, then the shorter agent again spoke.

"We're investigating a kidnapping. Some of the suspects are working in the field you've been watching for three days, and with whom you've been socializing. That makes us wonder exactly what the relationship is between you and them."

Both newlyweds smiled in relief, visually exhaling as some of their nervousness began to evaporate. "It's very simple," T.K. began. "My wife's sister was kidnapped a couple of weeks ago and brought to this area. Through some family contacts, we learned that these three men were talking in a bar about a kidnapping, and we tried to learn something about them. So far we've learned where they work, live and drink, and that they're friends of the guy we think kidnapped my sister-in-law. What we're doing now is gathering information for a make-believe magazine article on farming out here. Those guys think they're going to be in it." He exhaled, smiled at the agent next to him, and then said, "How's that for an answer?"

"Very useful," the agent responded. "I'd like to know the name of the kidnapped woman." With that, he withdrew a small notepad from his right hip pocket and a cheap ballpoint pen from his shirt pocket.

"Vera Kaaler," T.K. said. "Missus Lee Kaaler."

The agent wrote something on his note pad, then closed it and replaced it in his pants pocket. "Thank you, Mister Pajaro. That was most useful and confirms much of what we thought. Now we'd like you to leave this area."

"Leave? But—"

"Mister Pajaro," the agent repeated, "this is an FBI matter. If we need your help, we'll call on you. In the meantime, you need to do as we say, or we could charge you with interfering with our investigation. You don't want that, and neither do we."

Chapter 103

A Foster Home?

"Fine," Lee said after the FBI agents told him the IRS and SEC were investigating him, "They'll find nothing irregular, because I've done nothing irregular." He looked at Verry; received a shrug meaning, *I don't know what they could possibly find, either.*

"Perhaps we could ask *you* some questions," Lee aid. "There are several things that bother us, still."

Having failed in their attempt to elicit any useful reaction from either Lee or Verry after mentioning IRS and SEC audits, Agent Williams just nodded.

"I'm really concerned about Rose Snoyl," Verry began. "She helped me from the minute I arrived, and saved my sanity after the twins were born." She looked at all three agents, but concentrated her next statement on Darlene Schneider. "No matter what anyone says, two babies are more than twice the work of one. So I want to know Rose's chances of not being punished along with her husband. After all, he and his buddies kidnapped me, not Rose."

The time for threats was over, and the woman agent calmly replied, "That's true. Nevertheless, the fact remains that she was an accomplice to kidnapping. That's a very serious crime. Letting her go without punishment is quite a step, something *I* can't decide on. It will take someone a lot higher in the FBI."

"But what if I testify on her behalf?" Verry asked. "Wouldn't that help? After all, her husband was abusive, and she has her son, Benji, to care for. He also helped me a lot." Verry peered at the woman agent, trying to see if there was any reaction to what she'd said. Seeing none, she asked, "He's too young to be punished for something his dad did, isn't he?"

Now Agent Schneider nodded. "Yes, he is. But I think his biggest problem will be if both parents are jailed—he'd have to go to the care of juvenile authorities."

"You mean a foster home?" Verry asked, clearly aghast. "Little Benji? But he helped take care of me and the babies lots of times." Her eyes were tearing up again so intense was her pain. "Can't we do something about that?"

"What do you suggest, Missus Kaaler?" the woman said.

Verry looked at Lee for help, but received only a loving smile, a nod to continue on her line of thought, and a quick hard squeeze of her hand. "Well," Verry continued, a bit unsure of where she was really going, "could he stay with us until his mom was released?"

"I don't know for certain," Agent Schneider said, "but even though the kidnappers were caught in California, and their conspiracy occurred here, kidnapping is a federal crime, so the FBI has jurisdiction. As far as the young man is concerned, I'd expect the California juvenile authorities would have jurisdiction. That being the case, they'd almost certainly not let him be sent to a foster home somewhere out of their jurisdiction—like staying with you in Oregon, for example." She frowned in thought, quickly checked her partners, and received reassuring nods. "But we'd have to have that confirmed."

Now Verry was feeling better and pushed ahead on the matter. "So if we could have some of our relatives here apply to be his foster parents, they might be selected to take care of Benji?"

"I suppose so," Agent Schneider carefully replied, "but why do that? There are probably lots of families who already qualify as foster parents."

Now Lee spoke. "Because, Agent Schneider, there's a better than average chance that one of Benji's birth parents is related to us."

"Related to you? Whatever gave you that idea?"

Verry looked at her husband, having absolutely no idea what he might say, knowing he couldn't disclose and wouldn't tell the FBI anything about Benji's unexpected talent to hear conversations between Lee and Verry when he was using the golden plate. "Verry noticed some characteristics Benji has that we feel are unique to our family. They are so unusual that we believe at least one of his parents was a Kaaler."

"I don't supposed you'd tell us what those traits are," George Williams said.

Lee let a small smile color his expression. "Not really," he said. "They probably wouldn't make much sense to someone outside the Kaaler family. But for that reason we'd really like to keep Benji with people who will love him—members of his real family."

Agent Schneider then spoke. "For what it's worth, Missus Kaaler," she said, letting a smile show, "I agree with all of that. But," she said, clearly setting the stage for something less likable. "I can't guarantee anything, especially since that young man's adoptive records are in the California court system. In the meantime," she added, "we'll be leaving now. You should plan to stay here until you're given official release to leave."

"But," Verry protested, "I'm free now. Why can't we go home?" Her eyes were again teary. "I want to take my babies to their nursery in our home. I don't want to stay here any longer."

All three agents stood and adjusted their clothes so they hung properly. "Nevertheless, sir and madam," Agent Schneider said, "you must stay here. At least until the IRS and SEC give us some idea of what they're learning about your financial dealings."

"Fine," Lee said, his facial expression clearly angry, "then where do I send the bill for this motel?"

Lee's questions clearly confused Agent Schneider, her frown reflecting her inability to understand Lee's logic. "What are you talking about?"

"If you won't let us go home, Agent, then you should pay the costs of our staying here in Fresno. I can't believe the FBI actually expects me to pay the costs of keeping me here against my will." He stood, acknowledging the three agents were leaving. "So all I need is the address where the motel can send the bill for our stay here."

On the way out, Darlene Schneider felt, for the first time since being on the case, that she had lost control of it.

CHAPTER 104

Reunion

The solid and loud knocks on their suite door reminded both Lee and Verry that the only visitors they'd had since moving there had been the FBI. Neither wanted another official visit, but knew they could do nothing to stop it. Since the three FBI agents left the apartment about an hour before lunch, Verry had fed the babies twice; she and Lee now ate a lunch brought up from Room Service. Lee had a fresh fruit salad with sweet and sour poppy seed dressing; Verry ate a cheeseburger with sautéed onions, French fries, and a chocolate milk shake. He said nothing about the sheer volume of Verry's meal, knowing she'd fed both babies every drop of food they'd wanted since their birth, over three weeks earlier. *If that's all it takes,* he thought, *I'm for it!* However, he still had to answer the knock at the door. The only redeeming feature was that the babies had just gone back to sleep. It would take a lot to wake them.

Pushing aside the small curtain covering the window in the entrance door, Lee looked back at Verry and smiled. Before she could ask who was at the door, he opened it, revealing their callers. Both women whooped in delight, then ran into each other's arms. Lee and T.K. simply shook hands and watched their wives hugging and crying. The men knew there was nothing to do until the women regained their composure; Lee closed the door and he and T.K. sat down at the small dining table.

Surprising both of them, the sisters were normal in less than a minute—except for tears of joy. Verry then motioned for T.K. and Drella to follow her into the bedroom, wiping away her tears as she led them. The room was dim but the drapes weren't opaque, so there was sufficient light to let Drella and T.K. see their new niece and nephew. Drella immediately put her hands over her mouth—holding back sounds of wonder and joy. Her husband looked at the babies, and then slowly shook his head back and forth, a slightly silly smile on his face.

Drella stood by the beds, looking and softly touching the little hands and cheeks, murmuring oohs and ahs. T.K. simply turned around, shook Lee's hand again, and then gave Verry a long, slow, loving hug. As the hug ended, he whispered, "I shouldn't be surprised, Verry. A beautiful woman and a handsome man *should* produce beautiful babies."

After moving back into the suite's small living room, Verry sat in one of the easy chairs, Lee in its twin, T.K. and Drella on the sofa. The babies were the first subject of conversation—how beautiful they were, how soft their skin was, how long they slept between feedings—normal subjects consuming about a half hour. The second subject was Verry's kidnapping, captivity, and escape: that took an hour. Lastly, T.K. and Drella recounted their surveillance of Barnaby Snoyl's three co-conspirators. They then told of their recent confrontation with the two FBI agents. On that subject, Lee's attention was total and focused.

When the newlyweds completed their story, they were surprised that neither Lee nor Verry said anything. Finally, T.K. looked at his in-laws, clearly confused by their lack of responses. "What's wrong?" he asked. "We thought you'd be surprised. Or something!"

Lee's expression changed from intense interest to distaste. "They've been here, too. Talked to Verry about what she knew."

"And then," Verry said, her voice shaking with anger, "they told us we can't leave here yet, and said Lee was being investigated by the IRS and SEC."

Both Pajaro's were astonished, and spoke simultaneously. "What?" Both then looked at Lee, and T.K. asked, "What're they talking about?"

For Lee, the answer was best demonstrated, rather than explained. "I'm going to show you something, something that is a Kaaler secret." His mood changed from angry to serious to quickly that both in-laws were already displaying nervousness. "You can't discuss this with anyone, no matter."

He first looked at his brother-in-law. "T.K., do you agree to abide by that condition?"

The brother-in-law's eyes suddenly widened as he realized how serious the situation had suddenly become, but he didn't hesitate to respond. "Yes, of course."

Lee looked at Drella and said nothing. Her eyes were already blinking from the stress of the moment. She, too, responded affirmatively, but only after glancing at Verry and seeing a very surprised and pleased sister, "Yes, I will."

"Fine," he said. "Now you're about to learn why I'm called The Guardian." As he spoke, he casually reached into his left shirt pocket and withdrew the Kaaler silver spoon. "This is what I guard."

He held it in front of him, gently caressing it with his right thumb. "You're not to say anything until I say you can." Concentrating on the face of his best friend, a man he'd never really met, he said, "FarCaller, I need to talk."

Lee's concentration was, to his visitors, astonishing, as was the change in his demeanor. No longer quiet and angry, he showed himself now fully confident in what he was doing, totally ignoring the curious stares of T.K. and Drella.

"FarCaller," he repeated, "come to me."

Another few seconds of silence, then the familiar face appeared in the spoon. "Lee, my friend," the man said, "how can I help you? Many weeks since last we talked has it been. Verry safe is? And your children, healthy are they?"

"Yes to both, FarCaller. Thank you for asking. I have a son, Daniel, and a daughter, Dannice. And they are beautiful."

"Because of their beautiful mother."

"Absolutely! However, I need your help, FarCaller. Things are not going well now, even though Verry is now free and her main kidnapper is jailed."

"For me to look into your future want you?"

"Correct. I find myself in possible danger from someone who thinks I am guilty of illegal acts, and is threatening what you and I can do."

He was clearly upset, his eyes wide and his eyebrows rose in astonishment. "The spoon? Your spoon threaten they?"

"They think our financial success is from cheating, and I can't dispute it without revealing the special gifts you and I share."

"Lee, talking stop will I and to help you try will I." With those words, he reached up, touched the silver plate, and closed his eyes. For over two minutes, his expression remained fixed. Unbeknownst to him, T.K. and Drella were also fixed, amazed by what they were seeing and hearing.

FarCaller's eyes finally opened, but his expression remained unchanged. "Nothing threatening saw I. Of you and Verry in your home, my vision was, and your two children saw I, in white chairs made from woven reeds or grasses, sitting. All of you happy seemed." He stopped talking, his eyes blinking in thought, and then he added, "Does that good to you sound? To me it does."

"Yes. But it means I must do something drastic to reduce the threats to us. However, it also means those actions will be successful."

"What you plan you could tell me wish I, but after home you are, you will?"

"Exactly. Now I must go. Thank you for your help."

Before FarCaller's closing words could be heard, Lee relaxed a bit, exhaled, then leaned back in his easy chair and returned the spoon to his shirt pocket and closed his eyes. For several seconds the room was silent, then Drella, her voice quavering said, "That's unbelievable!"

Verry rose from her chair and moved over to her husband, gently kissing his lips. That unexpected contact startled him enough that his body quivered once, and then he smiled and opened his eyes and looked at Verry. "Thanks. I needed that." Looking back at his best friend and his sister-in-law, he said, "Now you guys understand what's happened. FarCaller told me where to invest my money; I did, and I made millions—literally. How do I explain that to the Treasury Department?" Before either could respond, he added, "We can't take time now to discuss Kaaler secrets. Right now we need to talk about what still has to be done here in Fresno."

Looking at T.K., Lee said, "I agree that you should stop checking on Barnaby Snoyl's buddies. There's nothing you can do there. However, you, T.K., can be our liaison with Doris Mooradian in learning Benji Snoyl's background."

"Drella," looking over at her, "Verry can use some help with the babies. Like giving her time to catch a nap once in a while."

"What about you, Lee?" T.K. asked. "How can we help you?"

"Once I see the Treasury and IRS agents working on this thing, that's about all I need." He stopped talking for a moment, lost in thought about T.K.'s question, then spoke. "Verry, the kids, and I will fly home in a few days, I think. Here to Portland and then down to Redmond. If you could get details on those flights—departure and arrival times—that'll save me from that task. Moreover, if you want, you two could join us on that trip and stay in our place for a while. Look into all of that for me." He leaned toward T.K. to stress what he was about to say. "I know this doesn't sound like much work, or as if it's very important, but it really is."

T.K. smiled, nodded, and merely said, "You got it."

CHAPTER 105

They'll Pay!

The next morning, after Lee and Verry had finished breakfast and feeding and bathing the twins, Drella arrived. She was clearly excited, a mood Lee assumed was related to being with the babies, but he was wrong.

Verry opened the door and ushered Drella in, receiving a warm and loving hug from her sister. Then Drella went to Lee, gave him a quick kiss, and nearly smothered him with the exuberance of her hug. That done, she partially released him, but looked up at his face. "I always liked you, Lee," she began, "but after what you trusted us with yesterday, I'm proud you're my brother-in-law. And I'm thrilled to know someone who can do what you do. Next to Verry, I'm the luckiest woman I know."

Before he could respond, she released him from her clutch and, with Verry, quietly entered the bedroom so she could learn where things were. A few minutes later the women reappeared, talking fast, with animated gestures and bright, excited eyes. "Isn't this neat, Lee? This will be the first time I've had away from the babies since they were born."

"I don't know how to respond to that, Verry. Is that good?"

She moved directly up to him and threw her arms around him in a spontaneous, loving hug, then finished the display of affection with a very satisfactory kiss. Not enough to arouse, but with plenty of promise for times to come. "Of course, silly! I love them, and enjoy nursing and caring for them, but I need time for myself, and this visit to see Rose is it! We won't be gone very long, but it'll be long enough."

With a quick wave to Drella, they left. Twenty minutes later, they were in the hospital parking lot, and in another ten, they entered the ICU ward.

It was Verry's first opportunity to see Rose and Benji since Rose helped her escape from Barnaby. Lee told her some of how Barnaby had beaten Rose, so Verry prepared herself to see her friend with bruises. She hadn't counted on the injuries Rose received when she fled Barnaby's abuse by leaving her car and running into the street. When she saw the blotchy face, the IVs, the splints on Rose's broken arm and leg, she lost her composure.

Verry's instinctive response to Rose's condition went contrary to medical advice, but was probably the best thing for Rose. Fortunately, Benji wasn't there to see both women in tears. Rushing to Rose's bed, Verry gently kissed the bruised face, took Rose's hands in hers, and rubbed them on her tear-washed cheeks. After a few minutes of intensely vicarious suffering, Verry felt Lee's hands gently massaging her shoulders. It was one of those multidimensional acts so often shared by closely bonded couples. It's meaning: *I know you're hurting, but you need to help Rose.*

Verry looked back at him and smiled through her pain, then leaned her head against his left hand, still softly massaging her shoulder. Turning back to face Rose, Verry quietly said, "Rose, it's Verry. Can you hear me?"

A smile slowly worked its way onto the damaged face, then the whispered words, "How are the babies?"

"They're fine, Rose. Wonderful. But how are you doing?"

Rose paused a few seconds, then softly said, "Better. But I don't look like it, do I?"

Verry's first impulse was to lie and say Rose looked fine, but she couldn't insult her friend that way. *Sometimes honesty hurts,* she thought to herself, *but it's still best.* "You look like you've had a pretty bad time, Rose," Verry finally said. "What do the doctors say?" As she spoke, Verry gently massaged Rose's hands, being careful to stay away from the IV needles inserted into the veins at the top of her hands.

Another pause before responding, then Rose whispered, "My arm and legs will heal in six weeks. When my face heals, they'll have to fix it with surgery. But I'll be OK."

"What about Benji, Rose? Who's taking care of him?"

Rose held Verry's hands very tightly, an act Verry felt must have greatly hurt the woman. "I think he's with my sister. But he won't say. He spends most of every day here, even when I sleep." Tears again flowed down her puffy and bruised cheeks, making dark spots on her pillow.

Lee watched the tender exchange between these two women, one once a captive and now free, the other once free and now just as surely a captive. That moment, more than any threats from the FBI, more even than being forcibly separated from the woman he loved, made Lee determined to help Rose and Benji, and make bullies and sadists—civilian or government—pay deeply for the damage they caused their fellow human beings.

CHAPTER 106

Get Out!

After leaving the hospital and treating themselves to a long lunch, Verry was in pain from breasts swollen with milk from the expected feeding. While this was the first time Lee had seen such a thing, he understood exactly what caused it and sped back to their motel. Upon entering their room, an extremely agitated Drella met them, clearly almost in tears.

"They wouldn't leave and come back," she wailed to Lee. "I told them you were out and I'd have you contact them when you returned, but they came on in, sat down, and said they'd wait." Before either Lee or Verry could offer any comfort, Drella added, "And they said they knew you'd be back because the twins were still here."

Both Lee and Verry were so engrossed with Drella's histrionics that they overlooked the obvious: two men calmly sat on the sofa, silently watching the arrival and hysterical greetings. Unlike the relatively nondescript FBI agents, both of these men were memorable because they were so different. It was as if one were an operative and the other some kind of technician, unaccustomed to representing himself and his job to outsiders. In addition, one was tall, well groomed, and wore a pale yellow short-sleeved shirt and tan slacks. The other was in faded blue jeans and a red and white-striped golf shirt, partly bald with curly hair combed across his scalp in a useless effort to hide his shiny scalp. Even though they were "guests" in the room, neither rose when Lee and Verry entered.

Lee felt his anger rising, and knew he couldn't let it overcome his common sense. At the same time, he felt violated by these government people who seemed determined to find something to punish him for, whether there was a real reason for it or not. Turning to his wife, he quietly said, "You'd better feed the kids, before your blouse front explodes."

At first she felt he was being facetious, but when she looked into his face and saw his loving smile, she raised up on her tiptoes and gave him a quick kiss, then headed straight for their bedroom, accompanied by Drella, where she could already hear the twins squalling. As soon as the two women were out of sight, Lee turned towards his uninvited visitors.

"I don't know who you are, yet," he began, moving toward the sofa, "but it seems the very least you could do when I entered *my* temporary home is rise to greet me." His eyes were flashing, his mouth drawn straight, his forehead creased with a deep frown. "Now," he continued, as the "guests" sheepishly rose from their seats, "show me your search warrant and your ID cards."

Sitting on the sofa, both men appeared to be about the same height. Now, standing side by side, that conclusion was proven hopelessly incorrect. The man on the right, in blue jeans, was shorter but heavier than Lee. The other was tall and gangly, with pale skin and blue eyes blinking as if he wore ill-fitting contact lenses.

The shorter man withdrew an ID packet and showed it to Lee. "I'm Harry Lyons, from the IRS." Turning to his left, he said, "This is Gerald Handliman, one of the CPAs in an analytical department of the Securities and Exchange Commission. We'd like to talk to you, Mister Kaaler."

Lee expectantly looked at the men for a few seconds before responding, then said, "And your search warrant?"

It was clear that Harry Lyons was to be the spokesman, for while Gerald Handliman suddenly looked uneasy and blushed slightly, the shorter man began speaking almost immediately. "Well, Mister Kaaler," he began, "we didn't really feel that would be necessary, since you were informed of our mission by Agent Schneider of the FBI team investigating your wife's kidnapping. So—"

"So," Lee interrupted, "you just barged in and told my sister-in-law that you would stay inside my home here." He leaned forward slightly, looking hard at each man's face. "Or did I miss something in translation?"

This time, Harry Lyons swallowed before responding; the CPA remained standing, still uneasy with the situation. "Well, we didn't think you'd mind, and—"

"Well, Mister Lyons, I *do* mind! Both of you get of my home right now! Go somewhere else and call here for an appointment. When you have such an appointment, I'll be glad to talk with you—even without a search warrant. As you probably know, I've been informed that I cannot leave this place without permission from the FBI, so I'd guess I'll be here for the next several days at least. In the meantime, I'm reporting your actions to Agent Schneider." Still facing the two now chastened men, Lee pointed at the door. "Now get out!"

CHAPTER 107

Not Common

"Yes, Mister Kaaler, I understand." A pause as Agent Schneider listened some more, then, "No, Mister Kaaler, you are correct and did nothing wrong: they should not have entered without permission." She held her hand over the microphone and whispered to the two agents in her office with her. "He's really ticked!" She nodded as she listened to more of Lee's words. Finally she said, "Yes, Mister Kaaler, I'll talk to them. I'm very sorry this happened. We know the stress your wife's been in for so long, and it isn't our intention to make things any worse for either of you." Another nod as she listened some more. "Thank you, Mister Kaaler. I'll pass on your complaint."

When she put down the phone, she looked up at the ceiling in a prayerful posture, and then looked back at her compatriots. "Those idiots! All they had to do was wait outside the room, or in the lobby, and then contact him. But, no, they had to play 1940s cops and barge into Kaaler's room without a search warrant. He can have a field day with this if he wants, especially since we haven't a shred of evidence that he's done anything wrong except use fake ID. That's hardly a problem in a matter as serious as kidnapping or illegal stock trading!"

"So what're you going to do, Darlene?" George Williams asked.

"I'm going to call idiot Lyons and tell him to get his stuff into a neat little pile. If he has any chance of finding anything out, he'll mess it all up by treating Kaaler like a common thief. Whatever that man is, he's not 'common'."

CHAPTER 108

No One Needs You

The Fresno County jail attendant reacted to the yells and noise with undisguised disgust. "Acts like a four-year-old!" he said to his partner. "If they'd let me, I'd cool him off with a fire hose."

His partner slowly rose, walked to the cellblock entrance and looked back, nodding. The senior man depressed a switch, followed immediately by a heavy clack, then the door to the cellblock slowly slid aside and the noise level immediately rose. The further into the cellblock he went, the more the jailer could tell the sources: Barnaby Snoyl yelling and pounding on his cell's walls and bed, and the same from the other prisoners—in protest against Snoyl. While Snoyl screamed demands to be released, the others were yelling things like, "Shaddup!" and "Cool it!" sprinkled with a wide variety of filthy expressions.

As soon as the jailer arrived at Snoyl's cell and looked through the small barred window in the cell door, the prisoner stopped his noise making and gave a self-satisfied smile. "So! You're finally letting me out!"

The jailer smiled back, and then shook his head. "Not exactly."

Snoyl glared, holding on to the bars separating him from the blue-uniformed keeper. "Wha' d'ya mean?"

"You're going to talk with a lawyer."

"I ain't got one!" Barnaby yelled. "Got no money f'r a lawyer!"

The jailer stood still, calmly looked at the prisoner. "You've got three choices, Snoyl, and I don't care which one you take. First, you can quietly accompany me to the interview room to meet the *court-appointed* attorney, or you can scream and yell and we'll carry you there anyway, or you can outright refuse to see him." Before Snoyl could respond, the jailer added, "But I should warn you that you're going before a judge soon, and if you don't see a lawyer now, you'll see one in the court room. If there's anything you want him to know so a lawyer can help you, now's the time to see him."

The big farm hand glared at the jailer. "All that lawyer needs to know is that I want outta here NOW!" He yelled that last word, as if volume alone would gain his release.

"Tell *him* that. No good telling me."

Barnaby then realized he had gained nothing with his yelling and noise making. "OK, I'll tell the overpaid wuss what he's gotta do f'r me."

"You going quietly or otherwise?"

They locked eyes, and then Barnaby said, "Quietly."

Three minutes later his were hands in cuffs attached to a chain around his waist, another chain dropped to his cuffed ankles, also connected by shorter length of the same chromed-steel links. He was helpless and knew it. Two jailers, one a big as he, led Barnaby out of the cellblock and down a hall to an elevator. The car moved down several floors, and then stopped and the door opened onto another secured hallway. A short walk from there he was taken into a ten-foot-square room with one light in its high ceiling, one small table, and two chairs. A tall, slender man in a tan business suit stood next to the chair at the end of the table nearest the door. Snoyl's orange coveralls and the man's tan suit and mottled tie provided the only bright colors in the institutional gray room.

After the jailers removed the ankle shackles and left, Snoyl walked up to the stranger and barked out, "When do I get outta here?"

The tall, sun-tanned man responded in a well-cultured voice, clearly not cowed by his client's blustering. "Mister Snoyl, I think you're under a very mistaken impression about what I or any other lawyer can do for you."

"What's that s'posed ta mean?"

"My name is Charleton Heast, by the way," the man said, continuing as if Snoyl had said nothing at all. "I've been appointed by the court to defend you." The tall man sat down in one of the chairs and calmly placed both hands together on top of the table. "First, we have to deal with the charges, Mister Snoyl."

Barnaby looked confused. "What charges? What kinda lies ya been tol'?"

Again, the lawyer appeared to ignore Barnaby's words. "You've been charged with," he began, speaking without notes, "Conspiracy, Kidnapping, Unlawful Movement Across State Lines for Criminal Purposes, Spousal Abuse, Assault—against the two police officers in the hospital, Threatening Harm—to the nurse there, and Resisting Arrest." Looking at the now-calmer man, he added, "Do you seriously believe anyone can get you out of here? Several of the charges are for federal crimes, Mister Snoyl. There's no judge in America who's going to release you, even if you had all the money in the world and could pay any amount of bail he might set."

For the first time since the jailer came into his cell, Barnaby was at a loss for words. After a few seconds, he and sat, facing the lawyer, softly said, "But I got a wife 'n kid who need me."

"The court disagrees, Mister Snoyl. You've been charged with hitting your wife so hard you broke her cheek bone and caused considerable damage to her face and arm."

"But she deserved it! She cost me a buncha money! 'N Benji's sided with her. Hasn't even visited me."

"The court disagrees. As a result of hitting her, your wife obtained a restraining order against you."

"What's that mean? One of them hospital cops mention it, but I don't unnerstand."

"A restraining order is a court order prohibiting you from getting any closer than one thousand feet to either of them, and forbidding you from contacting them by telephone, mail, or any other way. I must tell you that, if and when you are released from jail, and if that order remains in effect, should you break it you'll be right back in jail.

"Mister Snoyl," he continued, "neither your wife nor your son 'need' you. If fact, they don't want to be near you."

Barnaby remained quiet for a few seconds, then, "So whatta I do?"

"You stay here and try to stay out of trouble, Mister Snoyl. That's what you do. For my part, I'm going to try to learn all I can about the evidence against you to see if I can get some of the charges dropped or amended. However, I can only do that on the state charges. The FBI has you dead to rights on the kidnapping and conspiracy charges. If that's true—and I believe it is—you're going to spend many years in a federal penitentiary regardless of what I do and regardless of the state charges—like hitting your wife and fighting with those policemen in the hospital. My advice to you is to change your attitude, because you're not going to bluff anyone into letting you do anything."

CHAPTER 109

With Benji

Lee sat at the dining table, enjoying the quiet in the suite, a quiet that told him Verry and both twins were sleeping. *Lord knows, they need it. She's hardly getting any sleep at night, it seems like. Drella's been a big help with changing diapers and rocking the babies to keep them occupied, but she can't feed them. Moreover, Verry doesn't want to use bottles for some of the feedings.* He took a deep breath and exhaled slowly. *She's a good wife and a wonderful mother. Just like Grandma told me in her letters. It's got to be a God thing.*

That thought took him back to the time he discovered his heirloom spoon's peculiar powers, and how that led to his grandmother's lawyer, Clem Maestre. That led to reading her "puzzle book," and finding out more about being Guardian. Lastly, he remembered the wonderful, loving things his grandmother had written about the Kaaler family, and the powers of the spoon, and how Kaaler women made such wonderful wives for Kaaler men. *She had that right!*

His attention wandered a bit, then returned to the reason he sat at that table in the first place, with the golden plate in front of him. *Don't think Grandma ever heard of this.* He rubbed the heavy, smooth plate, cleaning off any dust while trying to sense anything unusual about it. Try as he could, it felt absolutely normal. *But it's anything but!*

Another deep breath, then Lee visualized Benji's face. The center of the plate clouded, then Benji appeared. He was obviously in the hospital, at his mother's bedside. Lee could see the tubes and familiar surroundings in the background, but Benji's face nearly filled his field of view.

Enlarging the view by imagining he was a camera moving back from a close-up shot, Lee noticed no changes from the scene he and Verry saw two days earlier other than Benji himself. He believed Rose was sleeping, because Benji wasn't saying anything and didn't keep looking up at her, checking on anything.

"*Benji,*' Lee thought at the ten-year-old, "*can you hear me?*"

Benji's eyes widened in shock and he sat upright very quickly, obviously startled. After a few seconds, he smiled sheepishly, looked around the room as if trying to insure no one was watching him, then nodded.

"*Verry and I visited your mom yesterday. She spoke to us a bit.*"

The boy nodded as if he either already knew what Lee said or agreed with Lee's report.

"*Are you OK? Is there anything we can do for you?*"

One nod followed by another. Two questions; two yesses.

"*What?*"

Benji rose from his chair and moved over to the table next to the head of his mother's bed. From the drawer he withdrew a blue ballpoint pen and a small pad of paper, and then returned to his seat. Putting the pad on the bed next to his mother's left hip, he sat down and then slowly printed, WANT TO STAY WITH AUNT RITA.

"*Your mother's sister?*"

One nod.

"*Are the Juvenile Services people talking to you about a foster home?*"

Another nod, accompanied by Benji's eyes watering up.

"*I can't promise any results,*" Lee thought, "*but I'll help you if I can. OK?*"

Many nods and a real smile. Then he quickly looked up and to his right.

"*Did your mom just wake up?*"

Another nod, then he began speaking to her.

"*OK. I'll leave now. If you'll be at the hospital this time tomorrow afternoon, Verry and I'll visit you. Will that be OK?*"

Benji was still talking to Rose, but when he stopped speaking he nodded his head. Then he wrote two more words on the pad: THANK YOU.

Chapter 110

The Audit

At one-thirty, as arranged by their telephone call to Lee, the IRS and SEC men knocked on the door of Lee and Verry's motel suite. When Lee opened the door, he gave no indication of their earlier problems, and escorted the men to the sofa.

"Sit down," he said, and then sat in one of the easy chairs, placed so he could face both of these unwelcome visitors. Coming from the bedroom could be heard the whines, whimpers and cries of one of the twins. Overlaid was Verry's voice softly speaking to them as she nursed the other. Had this been evening, Lee would be holding the "waiting" child. However, they had chosen this time mutually—she'd put the kids to bed and join the interrogation later. Not just out of love, but because both she and Lee wanted a witness to what transpired.

Lee didn't want to waste time on niceties, as this entire matter angered him enough to override any considerations for courtesy. "So tell me what's happening." Before the men could respond, he added, "Understand, I know I haven't intentionally done anything wrong with either my taxes or my investments, so you're not going to find anything there. I think the only thing you can question is my stock investment process. Am I right?"

His visitors exchanged surprised looks, then Harry Lyons, the well dressed and shorter of the two, spoke. "Actually, Mister Kaaler, so far that is accurate."

"Mister Lyons," Lee responded, "it will be so *all* the way. You'll find no evidence of anything illegal—anywhere." He leaned forward, increasing the intimacy and, therefore, the pressure on these men. "Assuming that remains the case—and it will—what do you want to know?"

For the first time in either of their previous meetings, the tall, gangly accountant spoke without being resorting to notes. "How did you select your investments? What was your strategy?"

"I didn't have any."

"I don't understand," the SEC man said.

"I never had any intention of getting into the stock market," Lee said. "I first got into it because a good friend of mine suggested I invest in a small company that makes textiles. I only had a couple of thousand dollars, but I trusted his advice and invested all of it." As he thought about that investment, he couldn't conceal a bit smile. "The company invented a fabric that would almost revolutionize spacesuit manufacture and lower costs. Within a few days after I bought their stock, their value went sky-high, and I made a lot of money." He tried to remember his next investment. "I think my next dip into the stock market was in a drug company—Gerit Pharmaceuticals. Same kind of thing happened: they made an announcement about some kind of wonder drug, and my stocks soared in value." He thought some more before continuing. "I made other investments, but none were as fruitful as the first two. Since then I inherited more money from my grandma's estate, money I didn't know she had—she'd deposited it in my name but with her address. So with the stock doing so well, and with the money I inherited, I pretty much stopped investing—I didn't intend to do any more."

Harry Lyons couldn't stay out of the matter. "Then why did you?"

"That's simple. My grandmother left me a series of personal letters," Lee began. "One of them told me to always trust any advice I got from a guy who turned out to be the grandson of *her* investment advisor. One day he told me to invest money in some company that had an image of a horse and was involved in industrial chemicals. He said it was going to market something that would make me a lot of money. Therefore, that's just what I did. And I made a lot more money."

The only sounds in the room were those from one of the babies in the bedroom, then Harry Lyons again asked the obvious question.

"But where did that guy get his information? And who is he?"

Lee expected both questions, and had worried about how he would answer them. "His name is Johnnie FarCaller. I have absolutely no idea where he got his information. When he first told me I should invest in that textile company, I was about 26 or so, knew nothing about investing money in anything because I was an assistant bank manager and had only a small amount of savings. Therefore, I did as Grandma said: I trusted that man's advice. I found out which company he was talking about,—"

"You mean he didn't know its name?" the IRS agent asked.

"Right. He described the company's logo and its product and said I could make a lot of money if I invested in it—just like I said."

Again the Treasury men exchanged glances, both of them agitated.

"Do you really expect us to believe that?" Harry Lyons asked. "That's the weirdest story I ever heard!"

"I understand," Lee said. "In fact, if it hadn't happened to me, I wouldn't believe it either. But it happens to be true."

The shorter man leaned forward, an aggressive look on his face. "OK, Mister Kaaler, where does this investment guru live? We want to talk to him, too."

Lee nodded, showing his understanding of the question. "I believe you do, Mister Lyons, but I can't help you on that. I have no idea where he lives."

Gerald Handliman jumped in again. "Fine!" he began. "Johnnie FarSeer—or whatever his name it—doesn't know the name of this company, or any others you invested in, I'd guess. So how did he contact you? And how did you know who he was?"

Now, Lee thought, *this is getting tricky.* "He called me," Lee said, having decided to consider the nearly accidental discovery of the powers of the Kaaler silver spoon as a "call."

"From where?" the tall accountant asked. "Where did he call from?"

Lee just shook his head back and forth. "I really don't know," he said. "I didn't know when he first called me, and I still don't."

"But he's called since then, right?" continued the man.'

"Many times, but we never talked about where either of us live. I do know, however, that he lives in the country."

"Wonderful," was Handliman's response. "In America?" His answer was facetious, but Lee's response wasn't.

"I don't really know, but he speaks English, so it has to be either the USA or Canada."

"OK," Agent Lyons said, "you made a lot of money from investments in shares of Gerit Pharmaceuticals. How'd he tell you about that one?"

"The same way. He described the logo—said it looked like a porch or something, with a roof over it, and the letter G under it. And that it involved medicines. The only logo that looked like that was Gerit Pharmaceuticals and, as you know, it produces medical chemicals and products. And he was right on that, too."

Just as Handliman was about to say something else, Lee added, "He did that only twice for those two investments. I think they were about six or eight months apart. Do I correctly understand that all of this is about those first two investments in the stock market?"

Before the accountant could say anything, Harry Lyons turned to him and held his hand up "Let me, Gerald," he said. Then he turned back toward Lee.

"That is correct, Mister Kaaler. However, as you well know, you made well over a million dollars in profits from those two investments. That is decidedly unusual, and is the reason we're here!"

"So what more do you want from me?" Lee asked, now sitting more erect, letting out some of the stresses of this confrontation.

Again, Harry Lyons held up his hand to prevent his partner from speaking. "We want something we can confirm, Mister Kaaler. So far you've told us an absolutely riveting story with not a single fact we can check!" He was angry and made no effort to hide it.

He then stood and gestured for his partner to do the same. "We're leaving, Mister Kaaler. You have two days to come up with something believable."

Verry joined Lee just as he closed the door behind the two angry and frustrated Treasury men. "I heard almost all of it, Lee," she said. "What're we going to do?"

He went to the small coat closet and retrieved the golden plate from the bottom drawer of the chest of drawers. Taking it back to the dining table with him, he sat down and opened the case, carefully taking out the velvet-wrapped weapon. Once he had it in his hands, he looked at his wife. "I'm afraid it's going to have to be drastic."

CHAPTER 111

Nothing's Wrong

Nothing at the hospital had changed except the cars in its parking lot. The same smells, hallways, elevators, uniforms and procedures. Even the nurse on duty in the ICU was the same. In Rose's little cubicle, however, Lee met Benji for the first time.

When Benji saw Verry, he rose from his chair beside his mother's bed and threw his arms around her waist, holding her tightly. She returned the strong hug, and then put her hands on both sides of his face and turned it up toward her own. When she did that, Benji relaxed his hold so he could move slightly back from her. Verry kissed him on both cheeks, unashamedly letting her own tears of joy flow down her cheeks onto his face. "Benji," she said, smiling while still crying at seeing him clean and well, "this is my husband, Lee."

Lee smiled through the whole greeting, and put his hand out to shake Benji's. Benji took it, then also gave Lee a quick hug, completely taking Lee by surprise. "I'm really glad to meet you in person," Lee said. Benji looked momentarily embarrassed. Then Lee knelt down so he could look Benji directly in the eyes. "Thanks for keeping our secret."

That hurdle to communications overcome, Lee stood and looked at Rose, still connected to the IVs, still with splints on her arm and leg, still obviously needing care. "How's your mom doing?"

Benji returned to his seat next to her bed, but spoke aloud instead of in a whisper. "The doctor's say she's OK. I think the medicines keep her sleepy or something, because she can't stay awake very long. But she's getting better." He moved nearer Rose's face. "Mommy, Verry's here. With her husband."

A smile slowly creased her still-bruised face, then Rose opened her eyes. For the first time since she'd been in the hospital, there was a happy glint in them.

226

She lifted her hand toward Verry, and Verry immediately took it in both of hers and began gently rubbing, just as she had done during their previous visit. "The babies?" Rose whispered slowly, her voice raspy, "They're still OK?"

Verry smiled back." They're fine. My sister's taking care of them while we're here. She likes doing it and I love the chance to get out for a while."

Rose closed her eyes again and nodded. "Babies need much love. Twins make mommies work all the time," she seemed to concentrate before each word, but she was smiling even though her eyes were closed. "One of my cousins had twins. Didn't sleep much for six or eight months."

"I believe it," Verry responded. "But tell us about yourself. How do you feel—really?"

A slow smile. Rose recognized Verry's desire to hear a realistic report, not one designed to please the listener. "My arm and leg are pretty good—no real pain," she said, but even then a slight, painful grimace accompanied her words. "My face still hurts and my tummy hurts from the operation. The doctor says I'm healing well and that I should be patient." Now tears started overrunning her eyes. "But we don't have health insurance." Her words were still coming slowly, but now they were almost choked out. "I'm afraid I'll be sent home before I can manage."

Before anyone else could respond, Lee stepped into Rose's view. "Don't worry about it, Rose," he said. "I'll talk to the hospital people about your bill. It'll be paid."

Verry looked back in surprise, then realized what her husband really meant: that he'd pay Rose's bill if it came to that. She, too, began tearing up, and reached out and squeezed his hand.

Turning back to Rose, Verry said, "This is my husband, Rose. You've not met Lee."

Rose opened her eyes, oblivious to Verry gently wiping the tears off her cheeks. Lee was standing behind Benji with both hands on Benji's shoulders. "Hello, Lee. I'm glad you and Verry are back together again."

"Wouldn't have happened so soon without your help, Rose. We'll never forget that."

Rose closed her eyes again and seemed to sink down into her pillow. "Barnaby shouldn't have done all those things." She kept her eyes closed but couldn't hide the tears forcing their way past her eyelids. Tears of shame.

"It's over now," Lee said. "You just think about getting well. We'll make sure you get enough good medical care and will try to help Benji stay with his aunt."

"Thank you so much," Rose said, then turned her head away and began quietly sobbing.

Verry leaned over and kissed Rose, then gave Benji a quick hug.

"We should leave your mommy alone, Benji," she said. "But if you don't mind, we'd like to talk with you a bit."

He looked at his mother, then back. "We could go to the waiting room, I guess." He leaned over Rose and whispered. She nodded her head but didn't turn back to face either him or Lee and Verry.

Once in the waiting room, all three sat in a corner. Lee wasted no time on small talk. "Benji," he began, "we'd like to know everything you remember or know about your adoption."

"Why? Is there something wrong?" He tried, and failed, to hide his sudden concerns.

"No, not at all," Verry said, shaking her head to emphasize her seriousness. "It's just that we may know some of your birth relatives, and would like to know more so we can check it out."

Benji acted as if he wasn't certain how to react, but shrugged once and said, "OK, I guess. But I don't want to leave Mommy."

"Believe me, Benji," Lee said, "we'd never try something like that."

"Well," the boy began, "I don't know very much, and I don't remember anything about my birth parents."

After ten minutes of questions, it was clear he told them everything he knew.

On the way out of the hospital, Lee stopped in the Billing department and arranged for all of Rose's bills to be sent to him. Then he called one of his banks and had $25,000 sent to the hospital to be applied to her account. Throughout all of this, the hospital workers were quietly astonished.

When all the matters had been accomplished, one of the ladies in the office, a slightly chunky, short, middle-aged woman with black hair and a bright smile, said, "Mister Kaaler, this is the first time I've ever seen this done. Usually people try to keep from paying their bill."

He grinned back. "Rose is a very special woman, Missus Zarate. I wouldn't want anything to keep her from getting all the care she needs—certainly not money."

On the way out of the hospital, Verry held Lee's arm very tightly.

"Is something wrong?" he asked, glancing down at his arm, then at her face.

"Nothing," she said, smiling up at him. "Absolutely nothing at all."

Chapter 112

Plain and Simple

Their next stop was the Fresno County Youth Authority. Once Lee and Verry found Benji's caseworker, they explained their interest. "You're friends of the family?" she asked. Marilyn Lamora was a degreed social worker, a native of Visalia, had fifteen years of experience, and was always suspicious of people offering support for a particular child or set of children. This was no different from so many other do-gooders with questionable, but logical, motives.

"We're friends of Rose and Benji, Missus Lamora," Lee said, correcting the generalization.

She chose to ignore the statement. "And you're here to help." Her face smiled, her voice sneered.

"Yes," Verry said. "We're concerned about Benji and want to help him any way we can."

"And what are you recommending?"

"I'm not certain we're recommending anything," Lee responded. "We know Benji's dad is in jail and probably won't ever get out. His mom's in the hospital recovering from surgery and other things, so she can't take care of him. Right now he's staying with his mother's sister, and he says he wants to stay with her. If there is anything we can do to help him stay there, we're willing to do so."

The social worker opened a folder on her desk and read the top two pieces of paper in it. "And how do you know so much about this family? There's nothing in my records to indicate you have any standing with the family, yet you show up today full of smiles and good intentions."

Lee and Verry found them confused by the woman's attitude, exchanged quick glances of understanding on something, then Lee spoke. "Ma'am," he began, "we seem to be in some kind of adversarial situation that I don't understand. We're here because Rose and Benji helped my wife out of a terrible situation, and we don't want them to suffer for the sins of their husband and father. That's our total reason for coming."

How do they know about the boy's father? Missus Lamora asked herself. *That's supposed to be confidential!* She looked directly at Lee, suspicion radiating from her expression. "How do you know anything about this family?"

Lee was getting angry, and having difficulty controlling himself, and his impatience and anger showed in his voice. "Because, Missus Lamora, Barnaby Snoyl and three of his friends kidnapped my wife and brought her here from Bend, Oregon, where we live. Barnaby Snoyl kept Verry in a locked room in his house for over three weeks, she had our twins here in Fresno instead of in Bend, and I've been frantically searching for her for that entire time. When they were returning from a trip Barnaby made, intending to keep Verry and our babies hidden from everyone, Rose helped Verry escape. Barnaby was so angry he hit Rose hard enough to break her face, and when she ran away from him she was hit by oncoming traffic." Now he leaned forward, obviously trying to push this woman's comfort zone. "Benji helped feed Verry while she was in captivity; Rose cooked for her and helped with the babies.

"Now, Missus Lamora, is there anything else you'd like to know about the reasons for our interest in this woman and that boy?" The steely quality of Lee's voice was clear: he was angry with the woman and the treatment he was receiving.

She nodded once, and then rose. "Would you excuse me for a moment? I need to confer with someone."

After the woman left, Verry turned to her husband and said, "Why was she so angry, Lee? What did we do to deserve that?"

"No idea. But she was beginning to get on my nerves."

"Really?" she said, pretending to act surprised while clearly not. "But you hid it so well." She looked him directly in the eyes as she spoke, her message clear: he'd fooled no one.

Before they could say anything more, Missus Lamora returned, accompanied by another woman. Both were about the same age and size, but the second woman seemed to be in charge. "Mister and Missus Kaaler?" she asked.

Lee stood, Verry remained seated, both said, "Yes, ma'am."

"I'm Madeline Farino, Marilyn's supervisor. She just told me of your interest and your reasons for being concerned about Benjamin Snoyl."

"Then I'm certain you understand why we want to help Benji stay with his family, so the pain he's suffered won't be made worse."

"Yes, of course," she said, as if that was a common response. "But we still have to be concerned about him, you understand."

Lee's frustration began to show again, but he tried not to let it be too obvious. "Missus Farino, we're not trying to do anything to impose our wishes on your prerogatives or responsibilities. Verry told Missus Lamora why we want to help Benji. If he can stay with his aunt, then we'll leave. If there is any problem with that—like her financial status or something, we're prepared to provide whatever money may be required to insure Benji is properly cared for by that woman. That, plain and simple, is why we're here.

"Now," he said to both women, "is there some kind of problem with that?"

The two social workers looked at each other, nodded, then they both sat down. "My name's Madeline," Missus Farino said, now smiling.

*   *   *

"Lee," Verry said as they left the Social Services building, "I was beginning to doubt we'd be able to do anything for Benji. That first woman was really awful!"

He squeezed her hand as they continued walking toward their car. "Guess it's like she said: most people go there making demands instead of trying to help. I can understand why both of them doubted us at first. But I also didn't like the way they treated us—at first."

"But now things should go well for Benji," Verry said. "That makes me feel better."

They'd reached their car, and Lee opened the door for her. "Me, too. Now I've got to deal with the FBI and Treasury Departments."

CHAPTER 113

Interrogation

Their meeting was typical of this investigation. The three FBI agents met in a small conference room "borrowed" from the Fresno Police. It consisted of a table large enough for six people, six blue plastic chairs, and a video projector. They sat so their seats made a triangle across the table. Between them and next to their elbows were small piles of documents: reports, analyses, and note pads. At the center was a large shallow bowl containing hundreds of small, colored jelly beans; a touch of comfort and brightness in an otherwise austere setting.

"Let's start with Kaaler himself," she began. "His face keeps popping up under every rock we move."

"Except the kidnapping," George said. "That was planned by Barnaby Snoyl."

Bill Mancer nodded as both his compatriots spoke, then added, "And *that* man was stupid beyond reason! He seemed locked in on something he thought Kaaler had, but he doesn't have any idea what it is—or was."

"Nor," Darlene interjected, "do we. Clearly, the Gerits believed that as well—which is where Barnaby Snoyl got his idea. But Jeff Gerit won't talk about it. It's almost like he's afraid to."

"Afraid of what?" Bill asked.

"I don't know," she responded. "But I do know Gerit's accounting records gave us plenty of reasons to subpoena anything dealing with whatever happened in Bend. If what Kaaler said is true—and it looks more and more like it is, then Gerit and his dad were involved in criminal conspiracy, illegal wiretapping, breaking in, burglary, and I don't know what else." For the first time in many weeks, she started to smile. "If nothing else, this Kaaler kidnapping thing will get us convictions on Jeff Gerit, Barnaby Snoyl and his buddies, and probably several others for a whole series of crimes in addition to kidnapping."

CHAPTER 114

The Twins' Future

FarCaller's face appeared almost immediately after Lee picked up the silver spoon and thought about his friend in Spoonworld.

"For some reason, your call expected is,"

"I have someone I'd like you to meet," Lee responded. As he spoke, he moved across the room to the crib up against the wall at the foot of their bed. Holding the spoon so its bowl faced down, Lee said, "This is my daughter, Dannice. And this," moving to the other end of the crib, "is my son, Daniel." Before FarCaller could respond, Lee turned the spoon so it pointed straight out from him. "And this is their mother, Verry."

With the spoon aimed at her, Verry could see the delight in the other man's eyes and face. "You're way ahead of us, FarCaller," she said. "When I last saw you, you had your own set of twins. Lee tells me you've had three more children since then."

"Yes, Verry, true that is. But at five stopped we. The right number it is. Besides," he added, his eyes twinkling, "about all the children it is that manage can we."

Lee moved away from the crib, through the small kitchen and into the dining area of their hotel suite. He then propped the spoon up against the salt and pepper shakers and sat close to Verry, opposite the spoon, so FarCaller could see them both.

"I wanted to see you before we return home. You have again been much help to both Verry and me, and I wanted to thank you here and now."

"Not necessary. A special friend are you, and many times helped me as well have you. Besides, together well the Guardian and the FarCaller *supposed* to work are. Fortunate are we that we do."

"I agree," Lee said. "And now I must again request a favor."

"Do so, my friend."

"I would like your help in Sensing both our future and that of our children."

The dark, mustachioed man looked uneasy. "Sensing your future no problem is. But with your children's future Sensing, not certain am I. You to do that best, expect would I. Nevertheless, try will I." He started to place his hand against his silver plate, then stopped and looked at Lee. "Once before into your future to look you asked me, and some men saw I with weapons you stalking. What happened never told me did you, or who they were."

"I left the place I was staying right after you told me about that threat. I never saw them and still don't know who they would have been. My best guess is that they were police, still thinking I kidnapped Verry. But I'll never know because I'll never ask anyone about it."

FarCaller looked down at something, shook his head in disbelief, and then returned his attention to Lee. "Part of your world never understand will I," he said. "But now into your future Sense will I."

He placed his hand on the silver plate in his living room effectively blocking off Lee and Verry's view of him in the Kaaler silver spoon. Neither spoke during this period—somehow it seemed appropriate—but after several minutes of silence, both began to become nervous.

Finally, the view in the spoon cleared and FarCaller's face reappeared—expressionless.

"Three things to tell you have I," he began. "First, nothing dangerous in your future Sense I. Second, another opportunity for making money saw I that tell you will I. Third, your children very strong powers have, than either of us probably much stronger."

"What does that mean?" Lee asked.

"My Sensing is that things neither of us can do, they will do. What that might be I know not." He stopped, and then said, "But about the 'investment' as you call it, tell you will I."

CHAPTER 115

You Can't Win

Barnaby sat in his jail cell, thinking about what he had gotten himself into. *'S not fair. 'Til now, I ran myself and the people around me, like Rosa, and Benji, and Doug and Billy and Jimbo, 'n had good times workin' 'n drinkin' beer 'n watchin' football 'n baseball 'n basketball. Now I'm in jail, m' lawyer said I'll prob'ly spend most of the rest of m' life in prison, and there's nothin' I can do to protect myself. And Kaaler still has his stuff 'n we di'n't get a dime!*

At that moment terror struck. Within a minute Barnaby longed for a prison cell and the peace he believed he would find there. He, like others before him, slowly and finally realized something that the Gerits learned a year earlier: no one could attack the Kaalers and win.

Chapter 116

A New Concept

Verry just finished the babies' mid-afternoon feeding and returned to the dining room expecting to see Lee reading the newspaper or talking on the telephone. Instead, he was sitting at the dining table, the golden plate flat on the place mat in front of him, head in his hands, tears sliding down his cheeks.

"Oh, Lee," she said, quickly going to his side and holding his head against her. "What's wrong?"

He didn't look up, but slowly said, "I've got to badly hurt some really nice people."

Verry frowned in confusion. She pulled back from Lee and leaned over to look into his eyes. "Who? Why do you have to hurt them?"

He didn't look at her and continued to stare at the golden plate. "The FBI agents and the men from the IRS and SEC. I don't have any other way to protect us." His voice was husky with grief.

She sat beside him and reached out to place her hand atop his right shoulder. "What have you tried?"

He remained silent, lost in thought, then sat up, his eyes blinking rapidly in thought, looking around the wall opposite him but seeing nothing. Then he slowly turned to look at Verry. "You're right," he said very slowly, his brain obviously still working. "I've only tried the thing I used against the Gerits." Still looking at her but not really seeing her, he said, "I've only tried pain and terror to get the protection we needed from the Gerits, because they were bad people. I've not tried anything else before, let alone against essentially good folks." His words still came slowly, but his voice was regaining its normal timbre. A few more moments of thought, then, speaking slowly and thoughtfully, he said, "Maybe it'll work."

"What, Lee? What are you thinking?"

This time he looked directly at her, into her eyes, and let a small smile escape. "I'm thinking I might be able to 'convince' them to leave us alone without scaring them half to death or hurting them. If it doesn't work I can always revert to scaring them to death whenever they think about us."

He immediately reverted to a pattern of actions Verry had learned to associate with deep concentration. Knowing she was no longer in his mind, she slowly and quietly pushed her chair back and quietly returned to their bedroom. *If this goes like the other times he gets so lost in thought, I'll get a good nap before he thinks about anything else again.*

It took two hours of intense concentration to develop a useful and moral concept of how to implement a new concept of defense for himself, his family, and the Kaaler secrets, then one hour to plan exactly what he wanted to do to each of those targets. Once confident in his plan, he went to the bedroom and kissed Verry, greatly surprising her, since she was dozing while nursing Daniel. The sudden physical contact caused a short but intense body spasm, waking the baby, and causing him to lose his grip on her nipple. Verry quickly guided his mouth back to her breast, and then smiled up at her husband.

"What was that for?"

For the first time in many days, Lee felt happy, and his smile broadcast his joy. "For being such a wonderful wife and mother and having such a great idea about how I could protect us from the government people."

Before she could respond, he gave her another quick kiss and stood. "Now I've got to see what I can really do with your idea."

CHAPTER 117

Glazed & Forgetful

The first indication the others had that Darlene was thinking about something special was when she sat upright, eyes glazed, almost entranced. She remained that way for several seconds—long enough to begin to worry them, then her eyes focused on them and she smiled. "You know what I think?" she asked no one in particular. "I think we're through with Mister Kaaler. At least until the trial for his kidnappers and maybe Jeff Gerit. There's no reason for him to stay in Fresno a minute longer."

"What?" Agent Mancer was obviously confused by her sudden change in approach. However, before he could say anything more, he also sat erect, eyes glazed. He remained that way for several seconds, and then seemed to recover from whatever caused his "time out" and said, "I agree, Darlene. He's not a criminal even if he did use false IDs. Let's forget that and concentrate on the *real* criminals."

George Miller was going to ask both his compatriots what had come over them, but in his mind he surprisingly heard his own voice saying, *They're right! We should close the investigation of Kaaler and get on with the investigation into the kidnapping and the Gerit's conspiracy!*

"Call Kaaler," Darlene said to Agent Mancer. "Tell him he can go home. We can finish the paperwork right now"

CHAPTER 118

No Evidence

Harry Lyons was in his hotel room going over his notes on the interviews with Lee Kaaler, trying to make some sense of them. After reading and re-reading them several times looking for anything to point to any investment improprieties or violations of the law, one thought inserted itself into his consciousness: *Kaaler didn't do anything wrong. It really looks odd, but he didn't break any laws. There's no evidence of any inside trading going on, and his tax documents are clean. I'm going to tell Gerry that I'm not going to pursue this investigation any further, and close the books on Mister Kaaler and his friend FarSeer—or whatever the guy's name is.*

Gerald Harliman had the same experience but with a different flavor. He was in the hotel coffee shop drinking a cup of espresso and devouring a beautiful cream-filled pastry that tasted every bit as good as it looked. Between bites and sips he'd check his own notes on the Kaaler investigation, occasionally checking something in one of the papers comprising the sheaf of documents he'd obtained in the few days since being assigned to the case.

In the middle of raising his cup for another sip of the piping hot coffee, Gerald's arm stopped moving and his eyes began staring at the wall opposite him. He didn't see the mural of the lakes in the Sierra Nevadas, didn't pay any attention to the photo of a hundred-pound catfish taken from one of the small lakes just north of Fresno, didn't see the waitresses and customers moving in and out of his view. In the midst of this sudden interruption to his enjoyment of the espresso, an idea flashed into being: *There's not a shred of evidence that Kaaler did anything illegal. His story sounds odd, but I've not found one iota of data to indicate he's ever done anything illegal or even shady. Besides that, he's not acting like the usual illegal trader: he's not changed his living style, not purchased anything extravagant, not even taken any big trips. In addition, he's investing in such widely diverse stocks that there's no way anyone could be feeding him inside information on a regular basis.*

Gerald's arm resumed its trip to his mouth, and he found the edge of his espresso cup hitting his lower lip. Slowly sipping the beverage, he digested the revelation he just experienced. As he put his cup back onto its saucer, he thought, *I'm going to call Harry, tell him my portion of this thing is over, and that I think he should call Kaaler and release him.*

CHAPTER 119

Minutes Like Hours

Lee thought planning his attack was nerve-wracking, but waiting to see if anything came of his experiment was much harder. The minutes literally seemed like hours but, less than twenty minutes after contacting the FBI agents, his telephone rang. Once the introductions were over, he listened intently, glad the caller couldn't see the smile grow on his face. "Thank you very much," he said to the senior member of the FBI triumvirate. "I appreciate your call." Less than ten minutes later the telephone rang again and he received the same message from Harry Lyons.

That night in bed, his arms around Verry, he finally talked about what he did that day. "It's an awful thing," he said, carefully choosing his words while holding Verry close, "but people place themselves in peril when they try to mess around with the Kaaler secrets. When Barnaby Snoyl and his buddies kidnapped you, and then when Darlene Schneider and Harry Lyons threatened the existence of those secrets, they doubled the threat to us but squared the peril they put themselves in—from me! I don't like the kind of things I had to do, but I know no other way to protect those I hold dear," giving Verry another quick hug, "and do justice to the secrets we've been blessed—or cursed—with. But thanks to you I didn't have to hurt the 'good guys' like I did the Gerits, Barnaby Snoyl and his buddies.

"My real problem," he said, sliding down in the bed so he could nuzzle Verry's neck, "is that I still don't know what powers I really have, and I don't know why they exist. It can't be so we can get rich, and it can't be to hurt and control people, and it can't be to make people leave us alone. There has to be something we haven't seen yet or God hasn't made known to us. Remember,

Grandma's last letter hinted about something that could affect our nation. I just wish I knew what it was, because on days like today the Kaaler secrets are not necessarily something I'm proud of."

THE END

.

.

.

OF THE FIRST CHALLENGE

EPILOG

The two old friends met in their usual place, not recognizable to humans because it was more of an attitude than a position, more of a feeling than a physical setting. They floated in a small room containing no furniture or windows, colored—not painted—a wispy white. The floor, walls, and ceiling weren't solid so much as ethereal—so thin they almost weren't there. In this place, Guardian Ima and Grandfather FarCaller met when it was necessary for them to discuss how their successors dealt with the challenges they faced or were facing.

These reunions usually started with expressions of joy at seeing each other again, followed with a quick review of their existences since they last met. This meeting, however, differed for two reasons. First, they both knew what transpired in the past few weeks, so no discussion of that was necessary. Second, for a long time both had been concerned about having left their own worlds with their work uncompleted, and having passed their responsibilities along without properly training their replacements. Those concerns drove the need for a series of serious meetings. Both looked forward to the time when they could meet without bearing the load of heavy concerns.

Guardian Ima spoke first, only because it felt right. "Speak" is not exactly how she transferred her message to her counterpart, but it is as close as can be described. "It looks, my dear friend, as if things are finally headed toward something useful."

"Agree," he responded, the glow of his smile flooding the ether enclosing both of them. "To think, if the time given is, perhaps this new threat finally discuss together they can. Once that happens, on both the use of and their understanding of the forces they now control, mature should they. Remember, even we, about the golden plate and spoon, nothing knew."

"When should we inform them of the new threats now approaching them?"

He smiled, remembering his own life when he was FarCaller's age. "Perhaps first they should more time with their families have."

The twinkle in her eyes tinged the glow of his smile, and together they shared that communion of thought. Then both essences noticeably paled. "But of those threats we control nothing. What if our successors attacked are, before ready they are?"

A long silence ensured. On some time scales it was weeks, on others hours or less. "Correct are you. To keep them about their responsibilities thinking, without making them like under attack they feel, must we."

"That's not easy," she reminded him. "It didn't work for either of us."

He gave the equivalent of a shrug, a shimmer in the light glowing around both of them. "Even though our foreparents failed, not fail must we, because the next threat faced by the Guardian and the FarCaller will their worlds imperil."

THUS BEGINS THE NEXT CHALLENGE.

Edwards Brothers, Inc.
Thorofare, NJ USA
March 9, 2012